PERFECT PLANT

A MINA KANE NOVEL:
BOOK TWO

AMANDA CARLSON

In 2105, bad guys love gardening.

Mina Kane's next undercover op is of the green thumb variety. Tasked to break into a penthouse at the tip-top of a megascraper and airmeld incriminating data on a hydro-shipping mogul, Mina must first pose as an apt gardener who knows a thing or two about roses. The only problem is the rookie's along for the ride and is a pro at making everything more difficult.

Infiltrating the inner sanctum proves to be time consuming, and Agent Adam has a chance to shine, but that's not all Mina's in for. Her baby brother is in trouble, and Vincent Kramer, the colonel-in-arms of the French Protectorate, is missing. An encrypted locator shows up at Mina's door, but her childhood-pal-turned-international-heartthrob, is still nowhere to be found.

This op is one solar flare away from being the biggest, deadliest one yet.

Other Books by Amanda Carlson

Jessica McClain Series
Urban Fantasy
BLOODED
FULL BLOODED
HOT BLOODED
COLD BLOODED
RED BLOODED
PURE BLOODED
BLUE BLOODED

Sin City Collectors
Paranormal Romance
ACES WILD
ANTE UP
ALL IN

Phoebe Meadows
Contemporary Fantasy
STRUCK
FREED
EXILED

Holly Danger

Futuristic Dystopian

Danger's Halo

Danger's Vice

Danger's Race

Danger's Cure

Danger's Hunt

Danger's Fate

Mina Kane

Futuristic Thriller

Total Enhancement

Perfect Plant

Cupid's Bow

Chapter 1

Horticulture?" Mina's printed spoon hovered above a bowl of crispy rice puffs bobbing in creamy dairy-sub the color of toasted walnuts. "Like a gardener? Someone who digs in the dirt?"

"That's correct," Duncan McAllister, her esteemed, suit-wearing CIU director, responded from his projected position on her wall. "In layperson terms, you'll be a personal gardener—appearing to dig in the dirt, while you're actually digging up incriminating data." He grinned, his sharp features relaxing for a second, his eagle eyes, normally fixed and concentrated, crinkling at the corners. The expression made him look younger than his fifty-odd years, but it wasn't any less weird. Mina's boss did not usually crack jokes.

"I see what you did there." Mina chuckled. She wasn't going to dwell on the fact her director's behavior had changed from just a few weeks ago. "Gardening doesn't sound too hard. I mean, it's just plants and flowers, right? Not a lot there that can go wrong."

It wouldn't be the strangest op Mina had ever been assigned, but it was fairly unusual. Most people in the twenty-second century, particularly in densely packed urban areas, didn't have the space to grow ornamental flowers or vegetation, not to mention having the luxury to do so. And they certainly didn't have enough borrowing power to afford a horticulture specialist, i.e. a personal gardener to dig around in the dirt for them.

That meant whoever Mina was going after on this op was loaded sky-high with currency. On the whole, being flush above borrows wasn't much of a stretch from engaging in illicit activities. Contentment didn't come easy in this tech and byte world. Those who were flush wanted more. Those who had some sought lots. Those who had none had to make do with whatever they could scrounge. It was a never-ending cycle of greed coupled with basic survival.

Mina sat at her meal counter, eating breakfast at four in the afternoon. Her comfortable stool, a smooth white polymer creation with a wide circular base and a form-fitting sink-your-backside-in gel-cush pillow, was one of the many perks that came standard in her new, lux residence. Eggie, her recently cooperative meal printer, had done well, serving her up a nice bowl of mocha-flavored crispy puffs in a dairy derivative that was super creamy and delicious.

She ate another spoonful.

Director McAllister was positioned at forty percent in her living area, which made him look enormous, since her new home came complete with floor-to-ceiling, flawlessly integrated, visual wall comm. In addition to ample screenage in every room, Mina had solar-catch windows with a spec view of the city from three hundred and twenty stories up, a lush sleeping platform with super-soft golden micro-modal sheets, lots of lux chrome and printed marble finishes, and to top it all off...the aforementioned top-of-the-line meal printer that could create a decent mushroom without the need for trace elements.

All in all, Mina was settling in just fine.

As far as hard things went, this ranked somewhere in the negative-particle zone.

"Yes, you're correct. Gardening won't be hard." McAllister leaned over his printed wood-grain desk in his compact office back at headquarters. His astute gaze missed nothing. His eyes narrowed, lips pursed in a steady line, no hint of a smile now. He reminded Mina of a hungry falcon sighting a tasty rabbit. She'd seen that look before. Her boss was a master at spotting the details. "Did you get enough sleep after we concluded our op this morning?" His way of noting the dark circles under her eyes without officially calling them out.

"Some." Mina busied herself, looking anywhere but at her wall, fighting the rush of blood she felt flaring across her cheeks as visions of a snug-comfort-pants-wearing Vince Kramer popped into her brain. They were the very same ones that had kept Mina from acquiring any good-quality REM. "Enough." She wasn't sure if she was talking to herself or McAllister. "Sleep, that is," she clarified. "Yeah, I got enough." Her mouth felt like it was full of elastomer.

To compensate, she shoveled in some puffs. Honestly, it was rude to eat during a meeting, especially an official operative designation. But when McAllister had realized he'd interrupted her afternoon breakfast, he'd insisted she continue.

At the moment, she was happy to have something to do.

Mina freely chomped away, and as she did, she tried to scour the laser-hot images that had been seared into her brain from her last interaction with the colonel-in-arms of the French Protectorate. But comfortably clad Vince was being persistent. He gave her a lopsided grin as he raked his hands through his still-wet hair. The finger tracks were disturbingly sensual.

Mina coughed, covering her mouth with the back of her hand.

She'd slept only a few hours. Maybe one? But could she even really call it *sleep*? It'd been more like restless repositioning.

Her director seemed to be observing her like she was an atom splice under an electroscope. A toddler would be able to tell Mina hadn't slept a wink. A former, decorated FBI-CA agent would have no problem detecting it. And because of that, Mina's scorching-hot blush was in the process of creeping down her neck. The heat seared her like an ozone-free sunburn. She desperately hoped

McAllister wasn't planning on continuing down his path of questioning.

To help things along, she squeaked, "Let's move on, shall we?" *Smooth.*

He raised a single gray-flecked eyebrow. "Indeed."

"Who, or what, am I going after?" Best to get right down to business.

McAllister reclined in his seat, crossing his arms. "The target's name is Franco Tedesco the Third, sixty-three years of age, native city dweller. His primary residence is the top floor of the first megascraper built in the city, aptly named The Mega, of which he owns a majority share. He has numerous hobbies, but his gardens are his pride and joy. They're lavish and encompass the entire roof of the scraper. A team of horticulture specialists tend to them daily."

Unlike Mina, McAllister looked well rested. The man was rarely ruffled.

"Franco makes the majority of his currency shipping goods all over the world in his sleek hydro-fleet, two hundred vessels strong. The Department of Goods and Services has suspected he's been dealing in illegal shipments for years, but they haven't been able to prove it. A recent delivery to a Greek island has been seized, and enough biowaste and chemis were found on board to configure several hive bombs."

Mina whistled. Hives could take out an entire city.

"They believe Franco himself not only ordered this shipment, but might be manufacturing the chemis at one of his facilities, and the records he keeps locked away in his private penthouse will prove it. He's claiming the goods in question were placed on board without his knowledge. That's where you come in."

Mina nodded. "A standard B&E. I go in under the guise of gardener and break into his residence to find the incriminating data. Are we looking for airmelds or confiscating the tech itself?"

"An airmeld is satisfactory. The DGS needs proof, and they can convict using an authenticated airmeld." Authenticated airmelds transferred the data wirelessly to a government-secured satellite. The trick would be hacking into Tedesco's system and setting up the sequence. "We will need complete files pertaining to all illegal activities. We're assuming there will be many."

"It's not going to be a printed treat getting in there," Mina said. "A man swimming in that much currency wouldn't skimp on security, especially if he's been dealing in contraband equating to chemi warfare on such a huge scale. He's going to have surveillance and blocks all over. His tech is likely vault-protected, and he'll have sensicams everywhere. If the blocks are above a Level X, I can't guarantee a break on the first day."

McAllister nodded. "That's why I'm sending you in with Agent Adams."

Mina kept her mouth firmly shut. No elastomer, no puffs. Lee Adams, her former telework partner on the Cullen op, had been an asset recently. Mina couldn't deny it. But he was still a sopping-wet rookie who could ultimately make things harder, even if his presence as a

Level XIII hacker would be valuable. Level XIII was pretty much as high as a hack could go, only thing higher was the term *super.* Level XIII meant Brilliance Level when it came to untangling code.

Mina allowed for a tiny sigh. She wasn't perfect.

"We don't have specific intel on the exact layout of Franco's personal offices," McAllister continued, unfazed by Mina's reaction to his Lee partnering announcement, "but scanners placed in one of the residences below have given us some useful information. According to the readout, Tedesco keeps a concealed superunit behind a north-facing wall in what appears to be a study or a library of some kind."

Only people with currency to light aflame had a library. Physical books were considered collector's items, their borrowing price through the stratosphere, as paper hadn't been manufactured on a large scale in nearly sixty years.

"The barrier wall that protects the tech is made of a top-line composite, likely graphene mixed with chromium hardeners. It's thick enough to prevent an airmeld. You'll have to open it to access the data and set up a sequence, assuming that unit is where he conducts his criminal activities, which is likely, due to the heavy security surrounding it. The superunit is a quantum pico, but there is no bank vault behind the barrier, which is to our advantage."

"I'll say." Mina set down her spoon. Most people with currency like Tedesco usually went the way of old bank vaults to protect their wealth from hackers. Vaults, typically constructed of solid titanium ten centimeters thick, used a rotary handle with an old-fashioned numeric combination and were impenetrable without the aid of a hydro-bomb or barrel laser, which were not sanctioned gardening tools for even the savviest of horticulturists. If Mina entered the penthouse with a barrel laser slung under one arm, things would get messy fast.

McAllister kept going. "Records show that his son, Franco Tedesco the Fourth, identity-chipped Frankie Four, runs a security firm called Four Story Security. The son has been in charge of making sure everything is safe and secure, and it seems the father has put his trust in him."

"That'll either work in our favor or against, depending on how many illegal or unapproved security upgrades Four Story has installed."

It was against the law to add extensions to home security systems, but even so, it happened regularly. Folks with heaps of currency went to great lengths to protect what was theirs, especially if their predilection was to do bad things.

"Up front, Four Story Security is clean. No lawsuits, no criminal activity. But Frankie Four is another *story.*" Maybe a clever McAllister was a better McAllister? Too soon to tell. "Under several layers, we've found a juvenile record. Frankie started out small with petty theft, DNA manipulation, identity misuse. Then he moved on to illicit pharma distribution and had a penchant for co-opting other people's transpo units."

"Let me guess. Each time he came before a judge, his daddy purchased his freedom."

"Correct." McAllister's solemn tone mirrored Mina's own feelings about the rampant corruption in the world. Currency was king. And if you were king, you got what you wanted. Agents for the Corruption Investigation Unit, or CIU, the secret agency Mina worked for, did their best to take lawlessness out at the highest levels, but it was a constant battle. "Frankie Four appeared before a magistrate a total of nine times. Each resulted in max fines, no time spent in a box. The last craft he commandeered belonged to a well-known screencaster, which generated significant media buzz, but no incarceration. Shortly after, this prominent screencaster retired to the Colonies of the Bahamas, void of any debt. Since then, Franco Tedesco the Fourth has kept himself out of trouble."

"Daddy gave him an ultimatum. Stay above the cuff, or I'll laser you off, hot and fast."

"Likely. Then he gave him enough borrows to start his own company."

"And Four Story Security was born." Mina sighed. "I bet they service quite a few prominent individuals with currency-lined pockets in our esteemed community."

"They certainly do. No less than a dozen individuals investigated by various federal agencies use Four Story. That's gleaned from a Level I search. Go deeper, and I'll wager there will be at least a dozen more."

Mina rose off her stool, gathering her dishes. What was left of the toasty walnut-colored dairy-sub sloshed around in the bowl as she carried it to her grinder, where it would be diced up and recycled by weight into the bowels of the megascraper. "This op has the potential to net two crime-ridden extortionists for the low, low borrow of one."

"That's a strong possibility, and if you come across incriminating evidence against the son, so be it. But our prime objective is to take down the father. You're to find and locate any and all data pertaining to the purchase of chemis concurrent with constructing hive bombs with links to *The Blind Fury*, which docked in Santorini, Greece, yesterday at approximately twenty-three hundred."

"Wasn't that the name of a popular vid a couple years ago? Starring Jefferson Manor? *The Blind Fury* and its sequel, *The Blind Terror*? They were released in full holo, too, if I remember correctly. The critics ground them into biomatter and spit them out."

Full holo meant the production could be played in 3-D hologram in the room of your choosing, rather than being consumed strictly on a wall screen or in a pleasure theater—if you were so inclined to spend extra borrows and leave the comfort of your own home. Mina rarely did.

"Yes. It seems the senior Franco is a serious screen buff. He's been known to finance projects. Every one of his fleet of two hundred is named after a major vid production."

Mina sighed again with more oomph. "It takes all kinds." She refrained from engaging her grinder until they were done with the meeting. Instead, she rested her hip against the counter, crossing her arms.

"It does." McAllister cleared his throat, clasping his hands together in a decidedly formal way, which usually meant he was going to say something Mina wouldn't be excited about. "One more thing. You're going into this op with a semiperm alteration." He held up his hand as Mina began to sputter. "I'm giving you a direct order. Your mega rep recognized you this morning. She knows your birth name and has connected you to Vincent Kramer, which means this issue is still at the forefront. We aren't taking any chances that someone else will identify you as the woman who was out dallying with the French Protectorate's colonel-in-arms until this entire spectacle dies down."

Dallying? Mina didn't think she'd dallied. But maybe?

It was her own fault she'd been spotted with Vincent Kramer, so she would take her lumps. So what if she hadn't known at first that her childhood pal Vince was the high-ranking official Vincent Kramer? She should've jettied out when she'd realized who he was.

But she hadn't.

She'd stayed.

It'd turned out to be a Lee-sized mistake.

Because she'd opted to linger with Vince over dinner, her likeness had been captured and circulated through the media, generating a small fervor to uncover her identity. In an effort to quell the masses, McAllister had leaked her full first name, which no one besides family sworn to secrecy and her mega rep knew. The very same rep who had accosted her this morning, fishing for details about Mina's delicious date with the international heartthrob.

"I don't think Suzanne will be a problem," Mina stated. "As I already reported, I convinced her that Vince is interested in purchasing a residence here. She'll back off as long as she thinks there will be a currency commission involved. I can keep that fiber line taut as long as I need to."

"It doesn't matter. She has your name and evidence to associate you with the French Protectorate, and she might not be the only one. Until we get a better handle on this, you will go into your next op as Marilyn Leonard, expert gardener from Milwaukee, Wisconsin, who does not bear any resemblance to Wilhelmina."

Her director politely left out her surname, which was Kandy Kane.

Mina had self-named at the age of three after her parents had left her with no moniker to spare her the burden of accumulating debt, a loophole they'd discovered at the time of her birth. Her chosen name had been cute once upon a time, based on one of her favorite screencast heroes, but she'd identity-chipped herself as Mina Kane at the age of twelve.

"Chance recognition while you're undercover isn't something we take lightly." McAllister didn't exactly huff, but he came close. "Calling attention to yourself can be a career-ender as an agent in this department. An appointment will be scheduled for you at eighteen hundred with an enhancement specialist at headquarters. Then you're to report to Perfect Plants at oh six hundred tomorrow. A craft will be waiting for you at oh five forty-five. All tech needed for this mission will be on board. From there, you'll accompany the other gardeners to Tedesco's. He sends a personal utility craft to retrieve the gardeners. Lee will be joining another group as a transport technician. This entire op has been aligned to coincide with a large delivery of vegetation that, by our intelligence, should take several days to get in order. You'll be on a communication freeze with the outside world while in position. All satellites in that designation are owned by Tedesco and are closely monitored. Once you find the pico, we will assign a government satellite to the area, timing it to arrive and leave again without raising suspicion. Any questions?"

Mina shook her head. "Another short but serious op. I got it." One that came with a semiperm alt. Even though Mina felt like complaining, as living under all that gunk would not be optimal, this fallout was hers, and she'd find a way to manage. "I'll contact Lee tonight and fill him in." Mina had to make sure the rookie kept his cool and his mouth firmly shut. "As well as read the file on Marilyn Leonard and consume enough horticulture techniques to make me competent. I'll be ready by morning."

McAllister nodded. "I'll expect a report tomorrow evening."

"Is there a plan in place if Franco remains at home for the duration?" Sneaking around under the noses of the other gardeners would be tricky, but if Tedesco was present, there would be no getting into his private sanctuary.

"As of last intel, he's booked for meetings at his business holdings for most of the day tomorrow. If that changes, you'll be informed via cuff before you take off from Perfect Plants. You only have two to three days on this, Agent. Make them count."

"That's the plan."

CHAPTER 2

"THAT'S A STELLAR job right there. I can't even tell it's you. And as a solid credit bonus, they didn't make you look like my aunt Phyllis." Kaylee Poston, Mina's best friend and a fellow CIU agent, addressed her from her position on Mina's sleep room wall. "Turn around so I can see the back." Mina did as her friend asked, her new straight blonde hair brushing her collarbones, none of her long, wavy brown hair in sight. "Hard to believe the real stuff is crammed up under there. Damn, enhancement techniques have gotten better over the last couple years. I haven't had a semiperm in a while. How does it feel?"

"Like chewing plexan," Mina groused. "It's stiff like baked clay from the base of my neck all the way to the top of my forehead. They used a new hardening gel on my hair to keep it slicked back, and it's itchy. My cheeks and nose feel tight under the skin cement, but other than that, I'll survive." Mina ran her fingers over her new face. The application was flawless, but that didn't mean it was comfortable.

In order to get this crap off, Mina would have to go through a lengthy process involving purifiers and dissolvers.

On the plus side, Mina could be fully submerged in liquid or be inspected with microchromes, and no one would be the wiser. Kaylee was right that enhancements had come a long way.

"Well, for what it's worth, you look laser-fine," Kaylee said. "They could've gone the other way. A guy once made me look like that bot from zoom tunnel seventeen. The one that looks like she's had one too many hits to the face and her circuits are leaking out."

"You were supposed to look like you'd just been in a fight. So I'd say that was pretty accurate."

"Eh," Kaylee hedged. "But honestly, they don't usually make anyone look that good. You're spec. Totally churning-magma hot. I'd date you."

Mina drew out a few clothing items from her closet, immediately discarding them. She needed something that said she dug in the dirt for a living. "You think I look good because I look like you, but blonde. Blunt cut, upturned nose, scalpel-sharp cheekbones. I think the guy who did it holds a current for you. He brought you up a thousand times, could've been two. Then I walked out, passing as your twin."

"Who was the enhancer?"

"Perry Randle."

"Oh. Yeah. That could be."

Mina glanced over her shoulder, a single eyebrow making its way up. "What did I miss between you and Perry the Enhancer?"

Kaylee swished a hand, then settled it back on her dog. Dag, a big Labrador, shepherd, mastiff mix, was curled up on the lounger next to Kaylee, snoring softly. "It was nothing. A super-quick tryst a couple years ago. It was after all the zoom-tunnel-bot-fight-face stuff."

"And this is the first I'm hearing about it?"

"You were busy with—what was that guy's name again? Harold Hamburger?" Kaylee chortled. One of Dag's ears perked. "The Perry thing lasted three minutes, if that. Hardly worth mentioning."

"Perry thinks it's worth mentioning. And his name was Harold *Hamp*burg, Harri, with an i, for short." Mina tugged a few more items out for inspection. One, a huge, baggy black shirt that two of her could fit inside, had potential. It was from an op where she'd posed as an older, heavyset woman. She should've recycled it, but the oversized look shouted *gardener*, so she was happy she hadn't. "Harri was nice, if not a little awkward. He had a few nervous tics. He blinked twice every time he said the word 'food.' And I wouldn't say I was *busy* with him. Certainly not too consumed to miss out on the quickie Perry stuff."

Mina had met Harri through her younger brother, Quinn. Harri had been a nice distraction, but had been a bit aimless, tics aside. He worked at a Pleasure Emporium, which had been strange, even though he'd been a greeter and not involved with any of the behind-the-scenes stuff. The dalliance had lasted less than a month... That proved it! She *did* dally. Harri Hampburg was proof.

"I wonder how many agents Perry's made in your image over the past few years."

"Now there's a scary thought."

Mina held the shirt she was considering in front of her. "Does this say 'horticulturist' to you? I don't want to have to run out and get something printed tonight if I don't have to."

"I'd say that's fairly spot-on, but I'm not certain. I've never seen an actual gardener at work. Just a few bots, and they always wear boring bot stuff. Bots never have any pizzazz." Kaylee considered. "With a shirt that big, you'll have no problem strapping on all the tech you'll need underneath, so that's a bonus credit right there." Mina's friend leaned in. "Is that from the Greeley op? Where we went in as a pair of sisters trying to burn that debt dealer? He was one weird dude. Stealing borrows from all those poor old ladies. I still remember his hair was tinted that awful chartreuse color, and he had all those loose skin folds." Kaylee shivered, rubbing her arms, which were covered in a scarlet pleated suction shirt with stars embroidered across the neckline. "He actually thought he was sexy. He'll be in a box for another ten years. Good times."

"Your memory's as sharp as ever. It *is* from the Greeley op, which was at least four years ago. Not sure why I still have it, but it might come in handy."

Three chimes sounded, and Kaylee's digital residence manager, a male sim named Kevin with a smooth Southern accent, interrupted. "Darlin', sorry to disturb you.

There's a live chat request coming in from one Pamela Poston. Do you wish to accept?"

"Yes, Kevin. Delay until I say so, screen size same. That's Mom," Kaylee told Mina, "right on time. She wants to tell me all about her trip to the great state of Cuba. I'll connect with you later. Hope this gardening gig goes smoothly and you net this sucker fast. And by the way, I can't wait for Lee to see you like this. That kid won't know what to do with himself." She giggled, giving Mina a short salute.

"You had to mention the rookie when my night was going *so* well. He'd better behave appropriate-*lee*."

Kaylee snorted. Finding ways to add on to Lee's name never got old.

"Have a good talk with your mom."

"Later. Switch it up, Kevin."

Her pal's image popped off the wall, and Mina moved deeper into her closet, continuing to search, coming out with a pair of black linen tuck pants to wear with the oversized shirt. She held up the two items, contemplating. "Veronica," she said, addressing her own residence, "please describe what a horticultural specialist, or gardener, would wear on the job."

"Accessing data," Veronica replied in her proper British accent. "Horticultural specialists wear roomy smocks, wide-brimmed hats, aprons with pockets, and comfortable footwear. They typically don gloves and carry tools such as spades and hand rakes in strategically placed pockets for quick access."

"Damn." Mina glanced at her options. If she was going

to convince anyone she was an expert at anything green, she'd have to have the right clothing and a few tools. "Veronica, contact Dutiful Duds and see if you can swing an appointment tonight. Ask for Jeni Crisfold. Tell her Mina Kane's friend Marilyn Leonard is in need of a quick turnaround."

Jeni was an artisan and could create anything in the time it took to produce a few sketches.

"Once that's done, make an appointment at Print It for an hour later, in their outdoor home section. With an air breather, not a bot." Consulting with the human technician would cost more, but Mina needed all the personal guidance she could get.

"Contacting Dutiful Duds and Print It. One moment, please."

As she waited, Mina walked into her spacious shower room, which held a deluxe sprayer, an air jet dryer built for two, an enormous soaker, a personal health pod, two vanities, a beauty printer, a grinder, and an expansive mirrored wall. "Light at fifty," she ordered. Ultras popped on in a soft hue as she padded toward her reflection, leaning in.

Her resemblance to Kaylee really was uncanny.

It was strange looking into the eyes of her passable twin. The only difference was Kaylee's hair was jet-black, and her bangs were cut straight over perfectly contoured eyebrows the same color. Mina's new hair was blonde, no bangs, eyebrows light brown. Perry had created a subtle swoop over one eye.

Veronica filtered through Mina's top-grade aural system.

"Dutiful Duds appointment secured. Time twenty-one hundred with Jeni Crisfold. She wished to convey she's doing this as a favor, as her shift ends at twenty hundred. Second appointment at Print It scheduled for twenty-two hundred. Consultant's name is Sid Valley, human stylist, located on the fourth floor, second quadrant."

Print It was a massive consumer superstore where individuals could print just about anything they needed in its basic form. For specialty designs, shoppers had to access a licensed design store.

"Excellent," Mina replied. "In the meantime, gather graphics and demo vids about expert gardening techniques. I'll watch those when I arrive home." Mina was resigned to a long night.

One without Vince Kramer haunting her dreams once her head hit the pillow.

Or with?

It was so confusing.

"Hello, my name is Marilyn Leonard."

Mina held out her hand to a disheveled, slightly frantic older gentleman. He was covered in dirt smudges, and his well-worn smock was torn in several places. He had sun-weathered skin, droopy eyelids, a hawkish nose, and tufts of gray sprouting out of his head in every direction.

With relief, Mina noted she'd dressed appropriately. Jeni had aced Mina's order. The artisan had confided to Marilyn that her dear grandmother had been an avid gardener, and she'd been designing smocks for her for years. Mina was thankful she'd had the forethought to smear some dirt onto the clothing this morning so it would appear authentic—or rather, *authentic enough.*

The man darted a glance in one direction, then another, his head tilting distractedly around the room like a bird trying to locate the minute vibrations of a worm.

Mina added smoothly, "I'm here to help out with the Tedesco delivery."

"Yes, yes, yes," he sputtered, reaching out to shake her hand across a battered worktop, the surface covered in generous amounts of plant debris and discarded pots. "You're the one from the Midwest, correct? With a specialty in Magnoliopsida, focusing on Rosaceae?"

Magnoliopsida? Rosaceae? It seemed Veronica hadn't uncovered everything there was to know about horticulture.

Mina replied, without hesitation, "Yes, that's correct."

"Good, good." He abruptly turned and headed back into the bowels of his shop, Perfect Plants, though it was hard to call it a *shop.* It was more like a door that led to a room that led to another room. Over his shoulder, he ordered, "Follow me." His hawk appendage led the way.

The man wore *scatterbrain* like a badge.

Mina followed him into a larger space. This room had high ceilings, bare walls with exposed graphene studs, and crates and supplies stacked everywhere. She counted at least seven other gardeners buzzing around, hefting bags of dirt, assembling tools, digging in barrels, all wearing smocks just like hers. She noted their footwear and was happy Jeni had insisted she print her a pair of what the artisan had called clogs. They were comfortable, if not clunky. It would be hard to make a fast getaway in them, but that wasn't her objective on this mission, thank goodness.

The old man had yet to introduce himself, but Mina knew his background. His name was Cotswold Higgins. He'd been in the business of horticulture for the last fifty years and was considered the best in the city.

Mina took inventory of the place. If this was the premier offering, gardeners weren't overly flush with currency. Or they were too preoccupied with greenery to care about small things, like basic finishes and actual walls.

"Hey, Cots, where are the seed pots?" a man with carrot-orange hair called from a corner where he was rooting around for, Mina assumed, the missing seed pots.

"We won't be needing them for the next few days," Cots all but cackled. "What we need is to get a move on. The delivery is scheduled for less than an hour. If we don't get there first, those heavy-fisted transpo lugs will dump everything all over humanity and beyond. They always make a mess out of things. Let's get a move on, people!" He made his way out a door at the back of the room, plucking things off tables as he went, shoving them into his smock pockets. Almost as an afterthought, he called out, "And this is Marilyn something or other." He gestured a dirt-smudged finger behind him. "She's in charge of the roses."

Roses.

Relief flooded through her. Mina could do roses. Thorny stemmed flowers with lots of silky petals. Veronica had queued up a visual about them last night. They were finicky, if Mina remembered correctly. She'd slip away and figure them out once they landed.

A few people nodded Mina's way. A few more gave quick waves. A short, ruddy-complexioned woman with a curly cloud of yellow hair tottered her way. The woman was as wide as she was tall. Her smock had twice as many pockets as Mina's and looked well loved.

"Hi, my name is Doreen," she said cheerfully. "I'm in charge of the annuals. So many annuals." Both hands, as well as her eyes, lofted toward the beam-exposed ceiling to emphasize her point. "I've never seen a man love impatiens or zinnias as much as Mr. Tedesco. He has us planting them weekly. It's a wonder he finds the space." In addition to hair dyed the exact color of sunshine, her eyes were a diffracted mustard to match. The combination was unsettling, but apt for a gardener. Doreen resembled a walking, talking sunflower. "His rosebushes are his pride and joy, though. He fired poor Katrine last week when some of the leaves started showing black spot. You're supposed to be the best of the best, so I hope you have something in mind for black spot, or it's..." Her tongue shot out the side of her mouth as she slashed her index finger across her neck, followed by a short croaking sound. "Ultras out for you. Cots can't keep enough gardeners on staff to keep Mr. Tedesco happy." She leaned in and whispered like a conspirator,

"At this point, Tedesco is his only customer. It's a requirement to make the big man happy, or it's out of business we all go." She chortled, placing one hand on her belly between a spade and a few packets of seeds. "Come on. We better get going. I can hear the transpo now. They give us a boarding time of about three minutes. Hardly enough, but it is what it is. Mr. Tedesco expects us to be prompt." She turned and headed toward the same door Cots had gone through.

Mina followed, thankful Doreen hadn't wanted an actual answer for how to cure black spot, because Doreen would've received a whole lot of nothing. The craft skimming out of the sky was sleek and glossy, roomy enough to hold at least a dozen passengers. It landed smoothly on a single cushion of air, multiple doors rising in tandem.

Cots windmilled his arms, ushering everyone on board. "Get your behinds inside, no time to waste. Go, go, go!"

Mina joined the fray.

Things were about to get interesting.

AS THE GARDENERS talked quietly among themselves, Mina pulled a mini out of a smock pocket. The clear handheld device made of crystalline fit perfectly into the palm of her hand. It looked like a normal piece of civilian tech, but it contained a microcam monitor embedded in the front, among other sneaky things.

She began a search on black spot, opting for manual operation instead of voice, which would defeat the purpose of being stealthy.

"Whatchu got there?" The man with carrot-orange hair, obviously enhanced, turned in his seat. "By the way, I'm Andy." He stuck his hand out. "Real name is Placido, but I prefer Andy. Don't know what my parents were thinking with that one." He grinned. He was late twenties at most. His smile was genial, and a smattering of freckles were spread across the bridge of his nose. His eyes were diffracted a sensible, but not overpowering, green.

Mina had noticed that most of the gardeners had chosen hair and eye colors to suit their passion. Given that, Mina assumed this man was in charge of veg, carrots in particular.

Mina reached up and shook his hand. "Hi, I'm Marilyn. The name my parents gave me." Mina could give Placido a run for his money on names. She nodded to her mini. "I prefer using a board over a cuff for work. All my notes are here. Easier to access the information."

"Cool. I don't use tech." His voice hummed with pride. "It's all stored up here." He tapped his temple with a fingernail packed with dirt. Mina was beginning to think gardeners never got clean. "I specialize in root veg. Potatoes are a particular passion, but I love all rooties equally." Mina had been right on the currency—vegetables it was. "Tedesco's got impressive raised beds and A-plus irrigation systems for growing. It's completely spec up there. Veg and ornamental everywhere."

Mina nodded along like she was riveted.

"I've only been on the job a couple of months," he said, "but I enjoy it. Been chatting with Cots on vis-media about veg for a while. Just moved from Michigan to work with him." The craft suddenly gained altitude, gliding straight up. "The view from up here is totally insane. Hope you don't have a fear of heights. Even if you don't, it'll take your breath away." He took a quick check out the window. "Honestly, I've never seen anything like it. The gardens are four hundred stories up, literally kissing the sky. We don't have megas in Kalamazoo. In fact, highest anything goes there is maybe two hundred, two-fifty."

He shook his head as if he still couldn't believe what life was like in the big city. "I can't imagine having currency to burn like Tedesco does. But if I did, though, I'd totally have staff. Maybe a few dozen bots, too. Then I'd just mess around with my rooties all day. Eating fresh is way better than printed. I'm not a Nutri Pure, but I come close. Gotta print stuff you can't get in the wild." He winked, giving Mina a big smile full of perfectly straight, micro-enameled teeth.

"I'm not a Nutri Pure either," Mina assured him. "I think a little bit of everything makes the world a better place." Marilyn was practical like that.

A Nutrition Purist, Nutri Pure, or NP, refused to eat printed, insisting that the only way to get proper nutrition and vitamins was to consume freshly grown food. The stance had been refuted by science over and over again, but stubborn people took it nonetheless.

A graphic of a rose leaf dotted with spots blinked on Mina's device. She shielded the board closer to her body so Andy couldn't see.

"We're here," Andy said. "Only takes five."

Mina glanced out the window as the craft began its quick descent, fluttering her stomach. It bounced twice, and the doors opened. Mina, eager to get a look around, pocketed her mini.

A LiveBot with severe features and orderly hair the color of onyx, with precise streaks of gray feathered above both ears, was waiting to greet the craft. His dark, glittering eyes roamed over the crew, missing nothing. He'd been made to look around sixty and was dressed in an elaborate black and white outfit with lots of flounces and ties. *Costume* was a better term.

It seemed Tedesco enjoyed theatrics. Seeing the bot gave Mina some insight into Tedesco's character. *Currency to send up in flames* was an understatement. Tedesco had so much wealth, he could afford to purchase a specialized old-timey butler.

The large, raised platform they'd landed on was twice the size of the one at Perfect Plants. A set of steps led down to another level. Mina followed the other gardeners, activating a microcam hidden in a smock seam to begin recording.

At the base of the stairs, Cots was in an animated conversation with the LiveBot, with lots of gesturing and pointing. Apparently, things weren't to his liking for the big delivery. She ignored him and paused on the steps to look around.

The place was enormous. The roof was terraced four tiers down and appeared to wrap around the entire building. There had to be an acre of greenery up here, maybe more.

"I wasn't kidding, was I?" Andy leaned in, annoyingly invading her personal space. "You can see the entire city and beyond from up here." His arm hovered a millimeter above her shoulder as he pointed out what she could already clearly see.

Mina took in the view, taking a large step forward to distance herself from her persistent new pal.

The vista was breathtaking as well as leg-quaking.

Since there were only a few megascrapers in the

city—the average high-rise was only about two hundred floors—nothing impeded the sights. The city sprawled before her like a sea of multicolored pixels, bodies of water flanking either side in long strides of varying blues. A long patch of greenery ran down the middle, seeming to cut the city in half. "Everything below us is insect-size," she commented. It was a strange feeling. Then she noticed something. "There's no wind up here."

This high up, the wind normally rattled fiercely. In her own mega, even a mere twenty stories up, plexan wind shear blanketed the transpo hub at chest high to protect the riders, and still it felt like a cyclone most days.

Andy gestured upward, and Mina spotted the clear, almost imperceptive shield that flowed like a cylindrical capsule around the entire structure, completely open on top so transpo could come and go.

"Huh. I've never seen anything like that," she murmured as they continued down. Trying to factor in what this all would cost made Mina's brain hurt.

"Me neither." Andy gestured with a broad wave of his arm. "As you can see, Tedesco has terraces for everything. At the top are the grasses and perennials. Maxine and Charlotte are in charge of those. The next tier is food. That's me, Boomer, and Liza. The tier after that is flowering shrubs and bushes. That's you, Cots, and Grigg. Last is ornamentals, annuals, and big bloomers. Tedesco likes to see those up close and personal. That's Doreen and Magpie. Usually, there's one more, but Zeelie found a great job out West aqua-farming in one of those big, flooded domes. They make their own atmosphere and everything. Cool stuff."

Mina nodded while running a critical eye over the tiers. In the middle of everything, massive sky screens stuck out, positioned to let kilotons of light into the interior living space of the residence. But there was no way to see what was down there without climbing right on top of them.

"So, how do you get inside?" Mina asked casually as she and Andy descended to the bottom tier, following the flow of gardeners.

Andy snorted. "Inside? Nobody's ever been inside. What we do is *outside.*" He spread his arms to encompass the vast outside.

"Yes, I'm well aware," Mina stated, placing Andy firmly in the tough-sell category. He was smart and keen-eyed. She was going to have to be careful with him and hoped they weren't assigned to work in the same general vicinity. Having a nosy neighbor would make sneaking away to do undercover spy stuff extremely difficult. "But there have to be waste rooms, a break room, a place to eat meals. What about in inclement weather? If you got caught in an electrical storm up here, it would be very dangerous." Her tone was steady and matter-of-fact.

"I don't know about storms." Andy shot her a questioning look. "I haven't been here that long. I'd assume they'd transpo us out if it came to that. I don't know where you worked as a gardener before, but we eat outside in the sunshine. There's a basic meal printer if you don't want fresh, and there's waste rooms by the delivery area. In fact, here we are now." He nodded for Mina to head around the corner in front of them.

The space was enormous and completely surrounded by a two-meter-high wall of syncrete, a light, super-strong synthetic concrete made of nanofoam balls and mortar. Stacks of pallets and shelving were everywhere, stocked with anything a gardener could possibly need or want. It was a wonder people brought their own tools. Large implements hung on hooks. Buckets were stacked haphazardly on the ground. Water spigots emerged from the walls every few meters. Hoses, most half coiled, lay on the ground like big snakes warming themselves in the sun.

Mina noted two doors, one clearly marked for waste, the other unknown. A few meters away sat a few stools, along with a utilitarian countertop that held a decent-looking meal printer, a small sink, and a grinder.

This was the hub for the gardeners, tucked away from Tedesco's sight so he didn't have to see the riffraff who maintained his palatial gardens.

In the middle, two large X's were decaled on the ground in bright orange.

Props sounded overhead.

Mina glanced up, shielding her eyes from the morning sun. Two delivery drones, clearly marked by their yellow and green stripes, were dropping in fast. Things were about to get busy.

Cots shooed everyone out of the way. "Move back," he ordered. "These pilots can't see their noses in front of their faces!"

Everybody did as ordered, edging close to the nearest wall. The space was big enough for both drones to land, but it would be tight. No room for error. If the props didn't angle straight down and ease up considerably on the throttle, the wash would scatter unsecured items, which could be dangerous.

A few moments later, both touched down without incident. These particular drones didn't have side doors, only one large back end. One puttered open slowly. Mina moved to get a look inside. The entire thing was packed full of green. A moment later, a delivery tech emerged between the leaves.

"Everyone get in there and help!" Cots ordered. "Make room so those poor saps can get out. Who is responsible for the damn planning around here?"

The gardeners rushed in, grabbing various plantings. Mina picked up a medium-size pot with broad leaves, no flowers. Cots began gesturing. "Annuals there. Food here. Perennials across the way. There should be some small trees. Why don't I see any trees?"

A few more delivery personnel squeezed out of the craft. A tall, gangly man with hair the color of green grapes hurried over, a superboard hooked to a ribbon around his neck. He looked haggard, and it was barely seven in the morning.

"Trees are on the last shipment," he informed Cots, tapping his screen.

"They were supposed to arrive first!" Cots ranted, his hands shooting in the air, his hair seemingly more disheveled than it had been a few moments ago. "I made specific orders. They need to be out of here and in place before the rest of the order gets here."

Mina edged around them, hefting her pot, heading toward the food table, where a woman was beginning to arrange things. Mina assumed she was Liza, Andy's cohort in veg. Liza was tall and willowy, her hair as white as an onion bulb, her eyes as green as their stems. She took one look at what Mina was carrying, and her emerald eyes flickered.

Mina recovered before looking overly foolish, and not the garden expert she was supposed to be, as she smoothly inquired, "Where did Cots say to put the perennials again?"

"Oh, over there against the other wall." The woman gestured with a hand that had already found its way into dirt. Before Mina could turn and scoot the other direction, the woman added, "I'm Liza, by the way. It's nice to meet a fellow Magnoliopsida enthusiast."

Mina awkwardly transferred her heavy pot, cradling it in the crook of one arm as she reached out to shake the woman's gritty hand. "I'm Marilyn. It's nice to meet you."

"You better buckle in. It's going be one long day of schlepping plants."

The woman didn't know the half of it. Sliding into Tedesco's private space was going to take more effort than Mina had originally thought. A regular penthouse had a single terrace, maybe two. This place was like a moated castle, the tiers practically blockading what was inside.

"I'm ready," Mina assured her as she backed away,

needing to set this pot down before her arm broke in half.

Mina hurried to the table, making a quick introduction to Maxine as she *thunked* her pot down. Then she immediately made her way back to the drones. Next on her agenda was to find Lee.

It didn't take long. Lee was dressed in a yellow and green delivery uni, and he was helping another technician tug an urn from the depths of the craft. His dirty-blond hair was unkempt, as usual. He looked younger than she remembered, which wasn't hard for the rookie to do since he was still basically a child.

Mina pretended she was busy inspecting something on a shelving unit until he was done. As Lee turned to head toward the craft, she intercepted him, tapping him discreetly on the shoulder.

He turned, his usual hank of hair tumbling into his eyes as he blinked once, zero recognition forming in their depths. "Can I help you with something, ma'am?"

Mina rolled her own eyes while exhaling a breathy hiss. "It's *me.*"

Chapter 4

LEE GAPED AS Mina grabbed his elbow and redirected him back into the drone, where they both approached another large pot. She regretted that she hadn't done a visual briefing last night, opting instead to send him audio.

Once she was near enough to his ear, she whispered, "Getting inside is going to be tricky. This place is covered in terraces, stacked four high, and the residence is hidden somewhere in the middle. I got a glimpse of sky screens and know there's an entrance somewhere, but it looks like Tedesco values his privacy in the extreme."

Lee pulled and Mina pushed the pot out of the craft. Several other delivery personnel and another gardener came on board to help lift things out. Once they'd maneuvered the plant clear, they both grabbed a side and hoisted it up.

"Your alt is spec," Lee whispered, his eyes wider than what Mina thought possible. He just couldn't help himself.

Keeping him on track was like juggling a handful of hot wands. "I never would've guessed it was you. You look so different. I mean, I guess the eyes are kind of the same. But man, your nose and lips—"

"Lee." Mina refrained from growling as they waddled the pot toward what she hoped was the right area. "Focus. How many deliveries are slated to arrive today?"

"Six. I think," he replied.

"You think?" It was his job to know. At the moment, his *only* job.

"Danbury, the tall, lanky guy with the green hair, doesn't seem sure of anything. Before we took off, there was an argument about space and weight restrictions. They were trying to pinpoint how many trips it would take, but never came to a conclusion. This delivery service is not top of the line. If I were in charge, I would've calculated—"

"Not now," Mina ordered as they placed the pot next to the shrub table. It looked like a shrub. It was bristly with a lot of branches, no taller than knee height. No one was at this station, so they could afford to have a private conversation for a moment. "How many technicians are staying behind?" Mina asked. "There's no way the gardeners can get all of these plants to their areas without help."

"Four guys came on each craft. I think four of us are staying. I made sure my name was on the list."

Yay for quick-thinking Lee.

Cots came bustling over. "They never get these deliveries right," he complained, hands in the air. Mina assumed they never came down. "The trees aren't arriving until the end of the day." The vibrato in his voice echoed his disbelief. "We were supposed to get those first. Receiving the trees last is going to complicate matters." He shook his head as he muttered something incoherent about hydroponics and root systems.

Mina knew redirecting a guy like Cots would take time, so she wasn't going to waste hers. People like Cotswold Higgins lived in a perpetual state of agitation and preferred it that way. She took her chances and interrupted, "Is it okay if I go inspect my terrace? Since I'm new, I'd love to take a look around before we start planting." Then, for good measure, she added, "I also want to get a look at that black spot. I'm assuming that's a huge priority for Mr. Tedesco." Mina emphasized his only customer's name to get through to the man who was now rambling about leaf permeation.

As a bonus, sneaking around under this absentminded man's nose was not going to be difficult.

"Yes, yes. Of course. Go, go," Cots replied, his eyes darting toward a delivery person trying to tug an extra-large pot out of the back of a craft. "Hey, you there! Take it easy with that. Japanese yews are very fragile." He turned back to Mina, moaning, "I don't know why Tedesco doesn't employ another service. He certainly can afford top of the line. While I deal with these nitwits, go take a look around. The roses that require your attention face north. Then come back, and we'll start distributing these bushes."

Lee surprised Mina by picking up a plant. Mina had no

idea what it was, but she knew it wasn't a rosebush. "How about I join Ms. Leonard?" Lee wore his eager-to-please expression, which wasn't a stretch from his normal one. "That way, I can start helping with the distribution immediately."

Cots squinted like he'd missed something vital. "Yeah, yeah. That would be fine." His eyes compressed even more. "Are you sure you're with this outfit? I haven't seen any self-starters around here before."

Lee replied easily, "It's my first day, sir. I spent the last two years with Light Speed Deliveries before coming to Rapid Fire. I'm well versed in moving product." He puffed out his chest, proud of his totally made-up backstory.

The old man's face clouded.

Before Cots could get worked up about the obvious downgrade in Lee's professional delivery career, Mina grabbed Lee's shoulders and propelled him away, calling behind her, "We'll be back shortly. I really need to inspect those roses!"

Once they cleared the area, Lee gushed, "That was good, right? I invented a whole story to go along with my alias. My name is Liam Anderson," he began to recite, "born in Tallahassee—"

"*Lee,*" Mina whisper-hissed, continuing to guide him away, scanning the terraces to make sure there were no other gardeners lurking. "You're a *temp*. You have *no* previous experience. You basically told that unhappy, suspicious horticulturist that you *voluntarily* took a crappier job. No one does that."

People who were lucky enough to have actual

employment hung on to it, like a mountain lion grasping on to the edge of a four-hundred-meter drop by its claws. "Most of those companies use bots for this type of work. There are only a few delivery services that still use air breathers. Did you check and see if Light Speed employs bots before you came up with your fancy backstory?" Mina didn't think Cots would check, but he could. That's why their backstories were always boring, containing zero details people could debunk.

The kid's face fell. "Well...I..."

"Never mind. Keep your mouth closed from now on. Agents don't talk any more than necessary. Ever. Let that be your first lesson of the day. Whatever Cots tells you to do, do it, no extra oration about your life necessary." Mina didn't really have time to kindercare the rookie, but clearly she was going to have to make some time.

She headed up a set of steps, Lee following. Once they hit the second tier, Mina wound down a narrow path. Two enormous trenches ran on either side of the skinny, syncrete walkway, packed full of dirt and greenery. An amazing amount of flowering bushes bloomed here, all different colors and sizes, not just roses.

"We're going to inspect the whole area, but we have to do it quickly, before anyone notices we're gone. My guess is once we clear the corner to the west, the view will change dramatically."

Sure enough, once they reached the end, they encountered a small gap where the tier ended for a short spate and the scenery shifted. The interruption was barely visible until you were right on top of it.

Mina peered over the side and spotted a small passageway. "Looks like this could be an entry point into the residence. Doesn't look like the main one. Let's check it out."

"It's not the main entry," Lee said matter-of-factly from his position behind her.

"How do you know?"

"I memorized the schematics."

Mina directed a pointed gaze over her shoulder, more than slightly aggrieved, but managed to keep her eyes from completing a serious roll. Seeing that Lee was still carrying the pot, she ordered, "Set that thing down. What do you mean you memorized the schematics? The Mega keeps them cloaked, and a hack would've set them off. The only info we have is from a scan CIU intelligence did from a single unit below, which was choppy because the floor is insulated with a graphene chromium barrier."

Lee set the plant down, scooting it to one side with his foot, clad in sensible brown work boots. "Well, since Four Story just finished security upgrades, I figured they had access to the building schematics. Any large job like that requires detailed prints." He shrugged, shoving his hands into his pockets. "So I hacked Four Story. It was buried under a lot of blocks, but it cracked. Only took about thirty minutes." Pride leaked out. And rightly so. If McAllister and the intelligence at headquarters hadn't figured out that angle, Mina guessed the kid deserved some kudos.

She just wasn't the one who was going to be doing the kudoing. She was irritated he hadn't brought this up before right now. "Where are they?"

Lee looked baffled. "Where are *what?*"

"The schematics, Lee. I need to see them." She held out her hand so he could hand over his mini or whatever he had put them on.

Lee glanced down at his clothing. He wore a simple pair of beige pants and a starched yellow-and-green-striped shirt with Rapid Fire Deliveries stitched on the lapel. "I didn't bring anything. I couldn't bring my compucase or my handheld. There's no extra room." He held his arms out wide to prove his point.

Except it wasn't proven. "There's always room. Even if you have to secure it to your stomach with skin cement." Mina nodded toward his wrist. He wore an upgraded cuff. McAllister had been true to his word and had given the kid a new, high-tech government toy. "Pop them up on holo."

A soft blush crept over his cheeks, which made him look like he was barely out of puberty. "I didn't link them to my cuff." She shot him a look, and he started to sputter. "I'm sorry! It was late when I figured out Four Story. I should've thought of that."

He read Mina's crossed arms correctly. An agent had to be a dozen steps ahead of everything. He began to babble, trying to recover. "I memorized the whole thing. I know the entire layout. I swear!"

Mina tugged him down the staircase next to the skinny passageway. "Does this lead to Tedesco's inner sanctum or not?" She ducked into the shelter of the small walkway, out of sight of the tiers.

Lee glanced around like they were in outer space and

not right outside the penthouse whose layout he'd memorized. "Um, no. Well, I think."

Mina made the kind of sound a human would make if they'd suddenly fallen on their knees to beg for mercy.

"There are four entrances," he said quickly. "Wait!" He glanced out at the city. "We're standing east. This is a service entrance. We have to go around to get to the main. It faces west."

Mina was already moving. When she spotted another gardener coming toward them, she diverted, taking the next set of stairs up. "We have to stay on my tier," she said. "Make it seem like we're inspecting the roses. We don't want to set off any dar for anyone." Mina began to gesture and point, nodding as the gardener—she thought he might be Grigg, but she hadn't met him yet—passed on the first level below them. He was a tall, burly, heavily bearded man, atypical from the other gardeners in the group. His hair wasn't dyed any shocking color, and he had minimal tools in his pockets. She hadn't been close enough to get a good look at the color of his eyes, and she hadn't heard him speak.

At the moment, he was an enigma, and she didn't want to arouse his suspicion.

Once she and Lee were alone again, Mina took the stairs back down, veering left. She knew the moment they'd found the main entrance to the residence. An expansive entertainment area was set up, decorated with a large, glossy white table containing a rain shield that could be activated at a moment's notice. Ten bronze and blue gel-cush seats were situated around it. Fancy cooking tech included an old-fashioned flame grill, two interesting cone-shaped red brick structures with scorch marks running up the fronts, and three top-of-the-line meal printers sheltered by curved aluminum roofs tinted vibrant shades of orange.

Off to the side sat a full bar contoured out of sleek steel, with knobs and pulls sprouting from below. Mina knew the beverages on tap would be real, not printed, and there was a big cooler for storage.

The backdrop to all of this was an impressive expanse of solar-catch windows soaring straight up to the sky, hitting the peak of the third tier, tinted so dark there was no way to see inside.

They couldn't stand there gaping, so Mina continued on, acting as if she were inspecting the trees framing the area, many of them laden with fruit. Once past, Mina headed back up the steps to her tier and followed it around the next corner.

She squatted by a rosebush, grasping a few spotted leaves between her fingers. Then she pulled out her mini and ran it over the leaves, taking several images. Lee stood awkwardly next to her. He had to work on his blending-in technique.

"Try to look busy," she instructed, barely keeping out of her voice the perpetual hiss she had when dealing with him. Two gardeners came around the corner, holding pots. "Literally do anything but just stand there."

Lee dropped to one knee, pretending to help. They both watched as text popped up on her board.

"Black spot," Lee commented.

"Looks like it's a fungus. I'm supposed to be curing it. I'll crosscheck these on the government database. If there's anything on black spot and how to fix it, it'll be there. In the meantime, talk to me about gaining entrance into this fortress. We can't enter from the main. All those windows make it too risky. Tedesco's not supposed to be home, but we have no idea how many staff or working bots he has in there." She wouldn't get an accurate scan until she was inside. "You said there were four entrances. We saw two. One utility entrance east, the main west. Where are the other two?"

"Um."

Mina sighed. "I'm assuming one is in the interior of the building, which would be too hard for us to breach. Please tell me the fourth is another utility entrance. Is it attached to the delivery area?" Mina asked hopefully, prodding him, knowing Lee was worried about messing up. Things hadn't gotten off to an auspicious start between them. The kid had to start thinking like an agent. It would be nice if he started exactly right now.

Lee closed his eyes, long lashes fluttering. Several pithy comments wanted to bubble out. They were eager to be heard, but Mina stuffed them back.

She needed Lee's brain schematics. They had work to do.

Lee's eyes popped open. A large grin of relief came first, then he rattled off, "You're right, the third entrance is by Tedesco's personal landing pad, and it leads to the main interior door. That will be too conspicuous and is probably heavily secured. The fourth faces south. It's not really a full entrance. It's more of a crawlspace. It's used primarily to service the heating and cooling units."

"Does this crawlspace lead to the interior of the residence?"

"Yes. It connects to a small service door that leads into a laundering area."

Mina stood, slipping her mini back into one of her many pockets, then putting her hands on her hips as she scanned the area. They faced south now. Nothing popped from this angle, but she didn't expect it would if the space was small. "I'm betting a crawlspace entrance won't have many sensicams, if any. That'll be our best way in." She glanced down at Lee, who was still on one knee. "We have to head back to the unloading area. The gardeners will notice if we're missing any longer. With luck, we can find the crawlspace, and we'll be able to infiltrate by noon."

He scrambled up. "Yes, ma'am."

Mina allowed for a tiny eye roll. Lee was an eye-roll magnet. "Stick to Ms. Leonard for now."

"Got it, um, Ms. Leonard."

Chapter 5

Two more deliveries had come and gone. The drones were due back within a matter of moments. The gardeners had already taken their meal break, and Mina was having trouble keeping her mounting frustration in check. The entire south side had been crawling with green-thumb enthusiasts and delivery techs all day. Most of the new planting was being done there. A B&E of any kind would not be happening at that location.

Mina was well aware that her time on this op was limited, and in order to take down Tedesco and his fleet of corruption, she had to make a move soon.

Lee had stuck around after the first delivery, but had been forced to go back with the crew for the last two. He was going to stay here after the next one if she had anything to say about it.

Not for the first time today, Mina wished she'd brought along some kind of head covering. She shielded her forehead with her hand to provide a makeshift visor, surveying the bustle in front of her. Most of the gardeners wore floppy hats with wide brims that they'd magically pulled out of smock pockets. Up this high, the sun was bold, bright, and unforgiving. She'd be smarter tomorrow.

Leaving her current location, where she'd been plucking infected leaves off of a rosebush, Mina headed toward the delivery area. She was anticipating the drones' arrival and contact with Lee momentarily and needed to get some supplies.

Once there, she buzzed straight toward a large shelving unit stocked full of soil nutrient supplements, fertilizer, acids and bases, and just about anything a gardener could need to aerate, feed, and care for a plant. Who knew green things needed to eat more than sunshine and some reliable H2O?

She grabbed a few containers off the shelf and carried them to a long, steel service table.

"Whatchu got there?" Andy poked his head over her shoulder for the fifth time today. Mina had heard him amble up—a step paired with a scuff—so she hadn't been surprised, just annoyed. Andy had been seeking her out regularly. Mina had taken a cool stance with him, brushing him off as nicely and as cordially as she could without arousing hard feelings. She didn't want him pissy. However, being cordial was not a particular specialty of hers. The fact he had her in his sights was going to be a problem. She needed to find a way to dissuade him for good. Point his focus elsewhere. Firmly, yet unequivocally.

"I'm mixing together some chlorothalonil and baking soda," she replied. "Wish I'd brought my special cleanser with me. I stupidly left it at home." McAllister would acquisition her the soap by morning. "If you mix these together, you get an effective cure for black spot." That, according to the US government. Mina was thankful her fake job for this op wasn't overly complicated.

"What kind of cleanser has those kinds of magical capabilities?" Andy cocked a hip into the tabletop, crossing his arms, getting comfortable.

Mina suppressed a growl. "If I divulged my secrets, you could steal my job. Air breather work is hard to come by."

He laughed, his brighter-than-carrot-colored hair bouncing against his forehead. "Black spot is a rarity for veg. Just have to make sure the tomatoes and peppers don't catch it. Too much water is your issue. That kind of rot doesn't travel far on its own."

"Yes, I'm well aware." She added. Playing this right was key. "Watering has been overzealous. Listen, I don't really have time to—"

"Hey, maybe later, you and I can—"

"Andy, can I catch you for a minute?" The low baritone came from behind them. "I need to consult on this."

Andy scowled at the interruption. Mina pivoted to see Grigg standing there, a drooping plant pressed against his expansive chest. He wore a smock, but it was minimalistic. No comfy shoes either. Instead, caramel-colored syn euroboots poked out from a pair of nicely cut tuck pants.

Mina narrowed her eyes, assessing.

She and Grigg were supposed to work the same tier, but she hadn't seen him since early this morning. With his full beard and thick, dark hair, he looked more like a prizefighter than a gardener. Before she could analyze further, props sounded overhead.

Cots instantly appeared, shooing everybody back. The two delivery drones made their landings, their backends opening as people rushed forward to help.

"Look at those trunks," Cots wailed. "You've curved the trunks! That's completely unacceptable." Each craft had been jammed full of saplings.

Danbury, of the green hair, looked like he might take Cots on this time. Either that or quit and take a much-needed nap. But he kept it together, his voice ringing with the kind of exhaustion that plagued people when they dealt with pesky customers. "There was no other way to get them on board. Our craft is only so big and only so tall." He added hand gestures for clarification, his board dangling from the ribbon around his neck, bumping against his chest as he moved.

Cots looked ready to burst, his face as red as the tomatoes up on tier three that were in danger of catching black spot. "The last delivery service secured the soil with carbon fabric and laid them flat. Never mind! Get them out of there. Get them out! No time to waste. I'll have your job if any limbs have snapped, or so much as a twig is out of place."

"Try it, buddy," Danbury muttered as he dutifully followed the agitated gardener onto one of the drones, and they both fought their way between the young, supple branches.

With Cots' attention well taken care of and most of the other gardeners gone to help, including Andy and Grigg, Mina searched for Lee. Now was going to be the only time she'd have to break into the residence. Mina refused to report to McAllister that she hadn't gotten her job done. She was a highly trained agent. She would get into that unit.

"Lee," Mina whisper-yelled after spotting him coming around a craft, helping another delivery tech carry a three-meter-tall tree with bright green leaves and a bunch of whiskery branches. When the rookie didn't turn, Mina changed her tactic. "Excuse me," she intoned. "Yes, you. Could you help me with these?" She gestured behind her at a few pots. "I can't lift these on my own."

"Of course, Ms. Leonard." Lee flashed a toothy grin like he was in on a secret. Oh, great cosmos above, he was greener than the tree he was carrying, and it was ridiculously green. He made his way over, saying something in passing to the other delivery worker. The guy seemed satisfied and walked away.

"Rearrange your face," Mina muttered once Lee got close enough.

"Huh? My face?" The rookie was confused.

"Look like helping me is the most boring task in the entire universe, and you can't wait until you're finally free to meet your pals for a cold froth later. *Not* like you just answered the final question on *Win Big* and are set to receive a huge monetary prize from lugging these pots around."

"Yeah. Okay." Lee's face went slack as he hefted up one of the pots as Mina took the other.

"Better. Read your environment." They slipped out of the delivery area, passing a few gardeners flowing in to help cart trees to their final locations. Lee followed. "Behave exactly like your coworkers, or risk bringing unwanted attention to yourself." Was she actually trying to teach this young shoot something? It seemed she was.

"That's good advice," Lee answered hurriedly. "I'm trying to do better. I'm taking some holo courses—"

"Just follow me. We're taking these plants to the edge of the pathway facing east. Then I'm going in."

"East? I thought you were going to access the unit from the southern—"

"You've been gone for hours. Every gardener here is camped out on the south side. Cots says they're going to uproot plants in that quadrant to fit in the trees. It's a whole thing. I saw the service door. It's masked in the water feature at the bottom of the tier. It's too close to the action. There's no other choice but to enter from the east."

Before arriving at the passageway, Mina stopped, setting down her plant. For the first time, she realized it wasn't a bush, but possibly a vegetable. Hopefully, no one would notice—Andy in particular. She craned her neck around to make sure no curious gardeners were in their vicinity. "Where does this entrance lead?" she asked, gesturing over the edge of the terrace where they'd been this morning. "I need specifics."

This time, Lee was ready. "It leads to an interior hallway that connects to some extra rooms with designations like 'guest powder room' and 'wrap room.' I'm not sure what those are." He hesitated. "I only ever grew up in a three-room unit, with basic stuff like sleep room and waste room. There were too many names to do a full eval last night. I know what evals are. Agents use them to gain information—"

Mina held up a hand. "A powder room is an old term for a bathroom." Which was an old term for a waste room, as baths were only recently making a comeback. "Several centuries ago, people used to powder their faces. Don't ask me why. It's not exactly a high-tech enhancement, but it seemed to work for them. A wrap room must be a place to wrap gifts." Also outdated. "When people have currency to set aflame, they want everything that sounds lux, even if it's ancient lux. How big *is* this place, anyway?" Mina went up on her toes, trying to glimpse the sky screens she knew were above their heads somewhere.

"Nine hundred fifty-seven square meters."

Mina's head snapped around. "You're kidding me. That's enormous."

Most residences were less than one hundred square meters of living space. Over the past fifty years, everything had been streamlined, made compact and efficient. People didn't need that much space to live happily, and it was a good thing, since space was at a premium. Twelve billion people in the world would do that. With a residence large enough to comfortably sustain ten families or more, it was no wonder Tedesco had extra rooms.

"This entire area"—Lee's arm moved in a circle—"gardens included, takes up eight full units below, including hallways and communal space. I believe McAllister only had surveil equipment in one of those units. Any more, and it would've aroused suspicion." Lee looked pleased to have information to contribute.

"Tell me once you hacked the digital schematics from Four Story that you sent the intel to our director." Mina knew the rookie hadn't, or they would've popped up on her cuff or handheld, likely both. Lee's short-lived happiness fell like a ten-ton titanium weight. "Don't worry. I'll take care of it. Hackers aren't used to sharing. I get it. But you're going to learn, even if I have to laser-imprint lessons into your brain." She waggled a finger at him like a NannyBot scolding a tot. She had to admit she didn't hate it. "Anything you gather on or for an op—either on your own or by order—gets relayed to any agent you're working with *after* you send it to the top. No exceptions. Do you understand? No more working alone like a squirrel hoarding nuts."

Lee nodded, if a little confused by the reference. With very little green space left in the city, a squirrel was hard to find. "I understand," he assured her. "I promise I'll break the habit—"

Mina cut him off. "We've wasted too much time. We're risking detection at this point. This is what we're going to do. You're going to stay outside and feed me information, and if I hit a snag, we'll regroup." Mina dipped a hand into a smock pocket, drawing out the tech she'd placed there this morning, courtesy of McAllister and the government craft that had delivered her to Perfect Plants. She unfolded a full-sized superboard, snapping the crystalline together seamlessly, and handed it to Lee.

He stammered, owl eyes fully enlarged. "I...I didn't know they could do that."

The kid really needed his own tech.

But entry-level agents had to work to earn it. Tech was expensive, and there wasn't enough to go around. "It's coded to both our voice signatures and requires a retinal scan to operate," she explained. "It's an X7 2200. No one knows they do that. Let's keep it that way." She reached into another pocket and withdrew a second secret, a top-of-the-line robocam shaped like a skinny noodle. This tech hooked over the eavesdropper's ear with a moldable robotic arm. It received voice commands and could stream live high-def vid and full audio to the superboard she'd just unfolded. She wiggled the robocam over her ear, securing it. Then she pulled out two canal phones and handed one to Lee.

"Stick this in your ear. I'm mic'd through my robocam, you through the board. It's all set up to work together." The microcam on her smock would also be recording, but it would be backup since the tech she'd just activated was far superior.

Mina nodded to the board Lee gripped like it might rupture into ten trillion quarks and float away. "I'm going to need to know if anyone approaches the vicinity, or if there are any other issues out here. If someone walks up, you pretend this board is like the one Danbury uses. If you tap right here"—she showed him—"it will flick over to a delivery schedule. I wish I'd known your boss prefers a ribbon attachment for the neck. I'll try to mock something up tomorrow. Since you know the layout of the interior, you're going to guide me through. I have digireaders, lock disengagers, sensicam detectors, stabilizers, and more. I'll scan for bots once I'm inside. We're lucky the overdressed butler bot stays outside with Cots." She patted her pockets and pulled out one of two sensicam detectors, handing one to Lee. "This will copy the make and model of whatever security I come across. The plan is to get as far as I can. My goal is into his private office. McAllister wants an airmeld, but we'll have to see how much hacking will be involved first. Then the satellite will be sent. Go back up to my tier and pretend you're fiddling with the plants. Stay out of view as best you can." It was lucky no one had come upon them thus far. "Any questions?"

"No. I understand." He nodded emphatically. "I can do this."

"Of course you can." Mina palmed a lock disengager and a cam looper, both no larger than her pinkie finger. "I'll be in contact." She took off down the passageway.

She was hoping for the best, but was willing to settle for good enough.

Chapter 6

IN LESS THAN two meters, Mina stopped before an oversized steel door the color of charred lava rocks tucked into an alcove. The sunlight was eclipsed by the shallow syncrete roof covering.

Inside her smock, the soft beep of the sensicam monitor went off to let her know she was nearing a sensor. The low tone was similar to a meal printer announcing food was ready. If anyone heard it, they shouldn't think much of it.

She muttered, "These cams are going to be all over. Lee, I need location, make, and model." She could get the info herself, but having Lee do it would allow her to focus on other things, like not getting caught.

"Upper right quadrant." Lee's voice was steady in her ear. "It's embedded. No larger than a pinprick. It's a Davis LS, triggered by motion, not heat."

"Lucky us." Mina scanned the wall. "I see it. Good camo, but the shine gives it away. I almost stepped in front of the damn thing. I think our monitors are going to need an upgrade after this. It should've alerted me three steps ago." Getting spotted by Tedesco's monitoring system would place a decided kink in the proceedings. Mina ran a thumb over her cam looper, choosing the right code for a Davis, indicated by a big D. Luckily, there were only five manufacturers of sensor equipment, each with different initials, which made it easier to do the spy thing.

The looper would activate a continuous cycle of clean camera feed, barely registering as a blip on the radar as it happened. Unless, of course, someone was keeping a close eye on it. Mina didn't think there would be. Tedesco was the king of his domain up here, with no one to bother him. No need to check the screens until there was an alert, so she just needed to make sure there was no alert.

Mina aimed the looper at the tiny cam and depressed the button. No chime followed to let her know the gadget had been successful. "Is it looping?"

"Not that I can see. Give it another hit." Mina could tell Lee was hunched over the tiny sensor screen she'd handed him earlier, brain absorbed. "It's showing it's a Davis LS, but the code underneath is indicating it's enhanced."

"Enhanced how?" Mina aimed the looper at the pinhole again.

Steady taps sounded in her ear as Lee did his thing. "According to the code, this Davis has been merged with a Venus."

"A Venus? Those are military grade." She'd never heard of the two being combined, which wasn't surprising since it was illegal to modify tech like that. Going on sixty years ago, some cosmonut had installed a hot laser in a motion cam that had killed an innocent delivery tech and a teenage passerby who'd stopped to help. Incidents like that had prompted a long battle, which had resulted in strict legislation about altering high-tech security and weapons.

In fact, cam manufacturers and makers of other sensor equipment were legally required to install fail-safe alarms that would alert them to such tinkering.

Obviously, that hadn't happened here, which told Mina that Four Story had their fingers in places like the outskirts, where people shunned laws, banks, and borrows, trying their best to survive. There, you could get your tech any way you wanted it—for the right price.

Mina knew this wouldn't be the only issue they'd come up against. If illegally modified tech was their only barrier, this would be the easiest op ever.

She glanced at her looper, wishing she'd brought her chromes so she could see better in the low light. Instead, she went down on one knee, switching the dial to MM for military mode. The device emitted a stark warning in the form of a blinking red light. Federal agents didn't use military mode lightly. Mina had seen loopers that required a thumbprint or DNA to enter MM. She was happy this particular looper didn't. If she truly were in military territory, she would need a warrant before entering.

"If you're wrong about this," she muttered to Lee, "the cam is going to send an alarm to the main security hub, which is the exact opposite of a stealthy break-in."

"I'm not wrong," Lee said. "There's no question it's a Venus. In fact, I'm pretty sure the digital markings of the Davis are just a shell so it doesn't stand out as illegal if anyone bothers to check."

Mina aimed the gadget and pressed the button. With relief, she heard a lone beep from her pocket, this one more like what heralded the arrival of a passenger tube. The beep indicated it was safe for her to proceed without fear of being picked up on the security feed.

"If all the cams are military, the locks might be, too," she commented. Which would make things headachier, but not impossible. Stepping close to the honeycombed entrance, she withdrew a NeuDAR wand no longer than her index finger and scanned the right seam of the door. "I'm picking up three separate locks, each no bigger than five centimeters square." She pocketed the wand and placed a lock disengager where she'd located the first one and fired. Nothing happened. "Regular mode's not working."

Before she could switch to military, Lee said, "Don't hit it yet." His voice held enough caution for her to hold steady.

"These are obviously top-of-the-line digilocks, likely military-enhanced, just like the cams." She kept her voice low. "Military mode is the only option. There might be a sound, but each lock should crack."

"Aim your cam into the seam. I want to see the locks," he ordered.

Mina did as he asked. "Are you getting a clear view?"

"Yeah, and it's what I thought," he concluded. "Those are dummy locks. All that's there is some kind of sensor pad made to look and read like locks. If you'd used your disengager in military mode, an alarm would've tripped."

"Dummy locks?" Mina had never encountered such a thing, but she wasn't going to admit that out loud.

"Wave your wand around the entire door, including the upper and lower quadrants. We're looking for a mechanism as big as your fist. It'll probably require a digital crack. A disengager won't do it. Once you find it, place your signaler up to it, and I can hack it from here."

Mina took out the wand. "A bastion lock? Like, a box lock?" She eyed the door suspiciously. "Are you telling me this place is fortified like a *prison*?"

Federal penitentiaries used bastion locks as standard, usually in the form of a six-centimeter rectangular dead bolt that slid into the floor or ceiling. They couldn't be disengaged by regular means or with high-tech toys and were automated and complicated, with hack-resistant coding. They kept prisoners secured in their boxes.

"It's a hunch, but it makes the most sense," Lee answered. "It would fit with dummy locks and Venus cams. Tedesco isn't taking any chances, and it seems Four Story Security has access to military tech, so this plays."

All completely illegal.

If he had bastion locks, Tedesco was hiding more behind this door than an illegal shipping ring. This op was becoming hotter by the minute.

Mina ran NeuDAR over the door and located an area

of interest at the top. "I'm getting something, but it's partially obscured."

When NeuDAR encountered an area it couldn't read for whatever reason, the result could come up as nothing or, in this case, interference.

"Set your signaler next to it," Lee coached. "Let's see what we pick up."

Mina did as she was told, trying not to be frustrated that it was taking longer than expected to get inside. At this rate, she was going to have very little time to do any real recon. "If this is a box lock, you're not going to crack it that quickly—"

A tiny *shlick* sounded from above.

She stared at the door in wonder.

"It should pop now," Lee said. "Give it a tug."

Mina curled her finger around a groove and pulled. Sure enough, the door swung freely. "How did you do that so fast?" The rookie, however untrained as an agent, had a hack game as serious as a platinum-packed asteroid. He might be the best Mina had ever seen, but she wasn't going to inflate him. She needed him focused.

He chuckled. "It wasn't hard. It's illegal to use these kinds of locks in civilian residences, so the installers weren't allowed to activate its regular encryption parameters. All typical box locks are uploaded to a common system for monitoring. This one couldn't be, so whoever put it in had to settle with bypassing to standard passcodes. I can crack a standard in my sleep."

Mina tugged the door open no more than her body width and slipped inside. The rookie had just saved her hide, and she wasn't going to forget it. "I'm in." She barely spoke above a whisper. It was brighter inside, but not by much. Tedesco's palace relied mostly on sky screens for natural light, and there weren't any in here.

She moved cautiously, giving her sensicam detector time to signal an alert. If there was nothing here that Tedesco considered of value, there probably wouldn't be much added security. Mina assumed Frankie and his dear ol' dad wouldn't think anybody could penetrate the complex outer layer of security, so why bother with the expense of more tech right inside the door?

"Nothing here except for a bunch of sealed doors," Mina relayed, cupping a hand over her mouth to mute her whisper so no house sensors would pick up her voice. "Are you seeing anything I'm not?" Mina swung her head back and forth as she crept forward.

"No, it looks clear," Lee responded.

Multiple voices sounded in her ear.

"Are those gardeners coming close?" she asked.

"No," he replied. "Just a few delivery techs walking by. Nobody's really noticed me. I'm pretending to commune with this bush."

"Commune, huh? Potent visual."

"It seems to be working—" Lee broke off and swore under his breath. "I spoke too soon. Here comes that red-haired guy, and he looks like he's on a mission. He's heading straight toward me."

"That's Andy," Mina muttered. "Switch your board over to the delivery schedule and pocket your canal phone. We don't want to give him anything to chew on.

He's been on me all day. Tell him I'm taking a waste-station break or whatever."

Lee cut out, and Mina tried to oust Andy from her brain as she continued to move forward. Reaching inside her pocket, she activated her LiveBot scanner, which would tell her how many working bots Tedesco had at his disposal and where they were located. This particular device was an enhanced civilian tool, available on the open market. Air breathers had become leery of sharing their physical space with tech that looked and sounded exactly like them. Bot technology had gotten serious over the past few years, and naturally it was freaking people out.

Mina's toy had been majorly upgraded, however, and could perform a temporary shutdown of basic bot functions if need be. But in doing so, a log would be recorded in the bot's data memory. To circumvent that, her altered scanner also included a handy feature that scrambled a LiveBot's reasoning capabilities for short spurts, just enough to make them compliant. The bot became temporarily confused, repeating a request a few times before ultimately following it. Agents referred to this bot hypnosis as the hyppie trick.

Owning altered tech like this was illegal for a civilian, but illegal was Mina's favorite kind.

The scanner indicated five bots inside the residence, two activated. Mina thumbed to a new screen to see locations and enhance the view. The active bots flashed with green circles, one with an S in the middle, for security, and the other an H, for housekeeper. The dormant ones flashed yellow. Another H, one C for chef, and one X. Mina's eyebrows rose. X could mean a number of things, but mainly it meant the bot didn't have a registered broadcast designation. X's were usually sex bots, but some were obscure service bots that specialized in a unique task.

According to the screen, the housekeeper was a few rooms over, and security was on the other side of the residence, likely by the front door. Lucky her.

The hallway Mina had slowly been making her way down opened into a large food-prep area. She eased inside, scanner still in hand. The space was lavish, as expected, with several huge meal printers positioned on sleek, polished-marble surfaces. There was an abundance of storage, all in gleaming white with doors that had elegant silver handles shined to a high sheen. Who needed this much storage? Especially since there were two built-in industrial-sized grinders next to a sink containing six spouts.

Several shiny serving carts were lined up near an oversized door. Nothing was out of order, everything sparkling clean. She moved past a huge center counter space that had no seating around it and sidled up to a massive cooling unit to peek around the corner.

"Honestly, who needs a cooling unit this big?" she said in a bare whisper under her breath.

The cooling unit was taller than her by at least a meter and was the equivalent of three of her wide. She was tempted to open it and see what was inside. People these days didn't have a need to store anything. Print-on-demand was a way of life and had been for the past twenty years.

A buzz sounded in her ear as Lee sputtered back on the line. "Did you say something?"

"No. Did you manage to shake Andy?" Mina's tone was so low she wondered if Lee would pick it up. She had to be very, very careful now. She scanned the hallway next to the cooling unit to make sure there was no movement, then dropped her eyes cautiously back to the bot scanner.

"Yeah, but the guy was persistent." Seems he'd heard her, which made things easier. "He tried to order me back to the drones. I told him I was double-checking orders. He even looked at my screen. I told him you'd be back momentarily, but didn't say where you supposedly went. He finally wandered off."

"He'll be back. Probably sooner than later. I'm almost out of the meal-prep area. Which way to Tedesco's private areas? After this, I'm cutting verbal. Can't take the chance the bots or the house hears me."

"Head left. You have to cross a major living area to get to the other side," Lee told her. "He has several rooms on that side, as well as the one Four Story did recent upgrades on."

"Got it. We need to find something soon, or we're going home empty-handed. I'll be in touch." Mina, scanner in hand, took off to navigate a home ten times bigger than her own.

Chapter 7

THE LIVING SPACE was humongous. Lee hadn't been kidding. Mina hadn't ever experienced a room this size in a private residence. The scope was dizzying. The ceiling soared at least ten meters high and was brilliantly lit by at least a dozen sky screens. This had to be the location she'd spotted from outside up on the tiers, as well as from the front, where the tinted solar-catch windows looked out on the entertainment area.

Dazzling sunshine glinted off of everything, dimpling the plentiful gold-and bronze-colored pillows scattered over large, carved—real, not printed—wooden furniture that had overstuffed cush. Large brass lamps reflected rays off their curvy bases, and beams jutted off their accompanying crisp white shades.

Could you even call it furniture when it was that ostentatious? More like a collection of museum pieces.

Mina had glimpsed items here and there, sometimes in old vids, from a time when humans had felt the need to surround themselves with possessions. Most people today had small, serviceable furnishings, nothing bigger than the person who occupied the space.

These pieces could swallow a lounger whole.

Mina's footsteps were soundless as she tread across gold-and-white-flecked thick-pile floor coverings, making her way quickly through the sprawling arena. She didn't have to side-step anything since the overstuffed pieces were situated meters apart.

Mina guessed that when currency wasn't an issue, neither was taste.

Once on the other side of the room, she took a cautious step into a hallway, and a soft ding sounded from her smock pocket, alerting her to another sensicam. Seemed redundant to have one just outside a common space where guests would linger, but if it was active, that meant the bots weren't programmed to enter this area either, or they would set off the alarms.

Without prompting, because she was on vocal shutdown, Lee said, "Focus above the door on the left. I think I see something."

Mina robocammed in that direction, and as she did, she spotted it herself, another pinhole sensor hidden above a massive, carved-wood door much like the behemoth pieces in the other room. Mina sensed a theme. Tasteless, but a theme nonetheless. This door screamed, *You may not enter if I don't choose to let you.*

We'll see about that, Tedesco.

"I'm getting the same reading as before," Lee continued. "The shell is a Davis, but it's actually a Venus.

Use military mode again. That should do it."

Mina already had the looper in her hand, dial still set to MM. She aimed and fired. Not a second later, a low tone confirmed the camera feed was now looping. She took a moment to check the LiveBot scanner to make sure the bots hadn't moved. The security bot was likely situated by the interior entrance, set to idle unless an alarm sounded or it was summoned. All this worked to Mina's advantage. Neither Tedesco nor Frankie Four thought anyone would get in here.

They were wrong.

"That big door leads to a library, according to the plans," Lee told her. "The door a few meters to the left is the space Four Story worked on."

Mina glanced both ways. She didn't see a second door.

She shook her head to indicate the conundrum and show Lee the long, empty corridor with no visible entrances. That didn't mean a second door wasn't there, it just meant she'd have to hunt for it. Another time suck.

"That's strange," Lee murmured. "There are supposed to be two large rooms in front of you. If you turn and follow the hallway to the right, there are a few smaller rooms, like a game room and a vid screening room."

It didn't take much brainpower to conclude that Tedesco didn't want anybody to see whatever was sitting behind the wooden monster that sported painstakingly tooled animal faces peering back at her. That's why he had an active sensicam above the door. This was the entrance to his lair.

Mina crept closer, wand in hand to scan for locks,

especially around the fussy inset door handle, which was made of iron and shaped like the head of a lion. *Roar.*

There were no reflection issues this time. In fact, no locks registered at all.

She ran the scan again.

Mina waved the wand in front of her cam, indicating to Lee that she was getting nothing. She had to admit it was weird relying on the rookie for anything, but here she was counting on him. McAllister hadn't been wrong in pairing them up. All the high-techs they'd encountered thus far had been illegally upgraded and shiny new. Mina didn't have the brain education Lee had when it came to stuff like this.

But on-the-job training was how an agent honed their skill set. Mina would store all this know-how for next time, so she wouldn't need Lee. At least, that's what she was telling herself.

Finger taps ticked through her canal phone, indicating Lee was doing some research. See? The rookie didn't know everything. "Hmmm," Mina heard him mumble. "Yeah, I get it now." She resisted the temptation to complain and instead pulled out her scanner to check on the bots. They remained idle. She was contemplating breaking her silence to urge Lee on when he said, "It's a dummy door. It doesn't open."

Dummy locks. Now a dummy door?

Mina gazed at the massive entrance with a puzzled expression, one Lee couldn't see because the robocam wasn't aimed at her face. Why in the world would anyone shell out that much currency for a monstrosity that didn't open? Why mount a sensicam above it? Lots of smoke here.

Oh, yes, Tedesco was hiding much, much more than shipping records.

"I don't understand," Lee said. "The schematics say a library is there, with the entrance as marked."

Mina crept down the hallway to the left, knowing time was at an absolute maximum. If they didn't get back outside, her cover would be blown, and she'd be removed from the op, which had never happened to her before in the history of her time at the CIU. It wasn't going to happen today. She had to find a way to access Tedesco's private refuge.

She paced the hallway, dragging her fingertips over blank walls. Since Lee had seen the room on the prints he'd hacked, there had to be an entrance somewhere.

"Wait, wait!" Lee cried in her ear.

Mina cocked her head as she brought a fingertip up and wiggled. Keeping excitement under control with canal inserts was essential.

"I missed it. It *can* open. It's a false front, that's why it doesn't have any hinges. It's automated. Go back. Place your wand on the wall next to it. There has to be a palm plate hidden somewhere."

Automated doors were the norm, but Mina had never seen one this size, or one with a *hidden* palm plate, for that matter. Auto doors were usually made of thin, lightweight metal or sturdy plexan so they could retract into a skinny wall frame, activated by a foot sensor or a hand plate in plain sight.

Mina took her NeuDAR wand and swept it over the right side. After the first brush, she located a square panel. She tapped the wall a single time with the tip of the wand to indicate to Lee it was there.

"Okay. I've got this. A disengage on MM won't work. It's coded. Place your signaler in front." Mina switched out one tool for another and shot the digital reading to Lee. "Ah, I see what he did here," Lee muttered. After a few moments of silence, and Mina trying *not* to be impatient, Lee whined in a wounded-puppy kind of way. "Crap, Andy is on his way back. What should I do?"

Mina cupped her hand in front of her mouth, speaking as low as she could humanly manage. "Move away. Unlock this door. We're not getting another chance."

"I'm moving. I almost have it," Lee insisted. "It's a little more complicated than the box lock." Mina heard Andy shout something. The vegetable gardener was frustrated. Didn't he have work to do? Why did he care where she was?

"*Lee,*" Mina growled in the thinnest of thin tones.

"There."

The door began to retract into the wall, more smoothly than Mina would've thought possible for its size.

Voices erupted in her ear. Two men arguing.

Oddly, one of them wasn't Lee.

Mina slid into the room, eyeing the bot scanner. Neither had moved. That meant the security bot hadn't been triggered to investigate her accessing this room.

Another bonus.

The door slicked shut, and automated lights blinked on. Mina exhaled, leaning her head against the only available area in the entire place. She had never seen so many trinkets. The room was crammed to the absolute max with stuff. There wasn't a nook or cranny without some trophy or a framed doodad, accented by a streaky beam of light coming from embedded ultras.

It seemed Tedesco might be something of a hoarder.

"Another gardener came and intercepted Andy. Tall guy, dark beard." Lee was still moving, breath huffing. "I have to find a new place. I'm pretending to inspect some of these plants as I go."

Mina wasn't going to risk speaking and tripping the residential sim unit or anything in here that might be recording. She glanced around. The ceiling in this room was just as high as the one in the main living area, but it wasn't exposed to the outside. Instead, the faux sky screens contained high-quality vid of wispy clouds and blue sky. The artificial sunlight highlighted rows and rows of books arranged on smooth wood-grained shelves stained a deep red. Hordes of tchotchkes were crammed everywhere.

Some things Mina recognized, like awards from fancy film-recognition ceremonies. Others looked like typical merch from screencasts, such as animated action figures of well-known actors and cups emblazoned with logos and faces.

In addition to the ceiling-height bookshelves, the room contained ad screens for certain vid productions. They took up the skimpy amount of wall space in between the shelving and were paused at particular moments, but Mina knew they could be activated with the right voice command.

This guy had a serious vid addiction. The entire room was basically an homage to the entertainment industry. She wasn't spotting many places where a big vault could be, unless these massive shelving units popped open.

Lee said, "I don't see what we're looking for. There has to be another room. Search for another auto door."

Mina swept her gaze around. The entire room was filled with bookshelves. Wait. She spotted something and moved closer. She nodded so Lee could give her instructions.

"Looks like one of those things clothes used to be stored in a long time ago," Lee said. "They're always in screencasts about the past. Try to open one."

Mina stood in front of two slim doors that were flush with the cabinets. She reached out and grasped a handle. The door opened to reveal a wall of tech. Now they were getting somewhere. She leaned closer, but much to her disappointment, nothing was labeled.

A second later, a sim voice flowed out of the integrated aural system. "What may I help you with, sir?" Mina had inadvertently triggered the sim when she'd opened the doors. It would be voice-printed only for Tedesco. She couldn't risk speaking.

"Wait, don't close the door," Lee whispered in a low voice. Like her, he was worried alarms would sound. "There's video of this guy all over. I can get a voice sample. Just give me a few minutes." They barely had seconds, much less minutes. Thankfully, Lee was quick about it. "Pull out your mini. I'll send a voice-coded message through it."

Mina did as she was told.

Once again, she found it surprising how easy it was to follow orders from the rookie. She guessed what she felt was called trust. She was trusting Lee. Life was strange. She tapped the screen, holding it up in front of her.

A voice that fit the image she'd seen of Tedesco said, "Open doors, please."

Mina cocked an eyebrow. Lee presumed there were doors somewhere around here to access a secret lair. He might not be wrong. After all, he had seen the schematics.

A prim and proper male sim confirmed her suspicions. "Of course, sir. Password required."

Damn.

It was time to abort.

While Mina contemplated her options, her mini vibrated. She glanced down. Another recording from Lee blinked on the surface.

One wrong password, and alarms would sound.

She had no idea how many wrong passwords Tedesco's system would allow before it locked her out. If the man was forgetful, she might get more than one try.

But why risk it? If they tripped something now, there was no getting back in here.

Lee whispered in her ear, "I am eighty-seven-point-three percent certain this is his password. It's based on the hack I did last night. Men like Tedesco tend to use the same password multiple times, making it simple, easy, and redundant. They go with one, maybe two comfortable words. Give it a try."

She swiped the screen.

Tedesco's voice came out. "Pinwheel."

To Mina's utter astonishment, the entire wall began to move.

 Chapter 8

THE HIDDEN ROOM, now completely exposed, was half the size of the one Mina stood in. It was decorated with much less fuss, though ostentatious enough with gilded chairs, shiny surfaces, and a desk the size of a personal craft. The desk, detailed with more of Tedesco's favorite wood carvings, was placed squarely in the middle of the space like a monument to currency.

This man liked animals. And wood. Stealing natural resources from what little environment they had left was apparently not a problem for the filthy-rich man who lived in the sky.

Very few tchotchkes were displayed in here. Mina knew more tech lurked behind the false fronts lining the walls.

Lights hadn't popped on, and there were no sky screens, real or fake, but there was enough light from the library to allow her to get a decent look around. She couldn't risk speaking, but her mind was spinning with the question, *How in the hell did Lee come up with pinwheel?*

Mina moved into the space cautiously.

"This has to be the room Four Story worked on," Lee whispered. "Hold your signaler up. I need a reading. Don't open any of the doors."

Duh. Mina did as she was told. Trust. No sensicam monitors went off. Clearly, Tedesco didn't think anybody could breach his personal space, even though the hack had been simple enough.

"There's a major block coming from the large set of double doors to your right. The ones that stretch all the way to the ceiling. Get your NeuDAR and see what's behind them. If it's the vault, you'll have trouble getting a clear reading." Which was what they wanted.

Mina ran her wand over the space. The bounce back was intense. They were going to need a bigger wand.

She kept at it. Shapes began to coalesce on the tiny monitor that ran the length of the wand. Electronics came back clearer than dense objects, as anything with a charge showed as white. Mina saw what might be books, and then, very faintly, the edges of a supercomputer came into focus in the form of a rectangular object with lots of bright white. This was the vault, all right.

"There's definitely a comp unit behind there," Lee murmured in her ear. "Put your signaler up."

She did.

"The blocks are coming back tighter than military, and the code is all over the place."

What was *tighter than military*?

After a brief pause, Lee concluded, "I can't hack this over the signal amp." Mina heard his disappointment. Apparently, there was a limit to what a Level XIII could do on the spot. "It's just...too complex. But I recorded the code. I'll work it tonight. I'm sure I can break it, given enough time. That will work with coordinating the satellite for tomorrow. It's probably best you come out now. If Andy returns, he's going to wonder what's going on. I can't fob him off again."

Mina nodded, causing the camera to bob. But she wasn't leaving until she got full coverage of the entire place. She began her scan, pacing around the massive desk. She ran her wand over the wood. Images of the inside of the desk were easier to capture here, as the wood was fibrous. She noted office supplies. Then something came across the screen that looked like a key. Actual keys weren't used nowadays since most everything was automated. She positioned her robocam over the NeuDAR screen, making sure she got a good shot in case that key turned out to be something...well, key.

When Mina finished documenting the entire room, she backed into the library. She cocked her head, giving Lee the indication she needed a voice command to shut things up. She stood in front of the doors and waited for her mini to vibrate.

When it did, she held it up. Tedesco's modulated voice ordered, "Close doors. Password, pinwheel."

"I'm sorry, sir," the sim intoned. "That password is incorrect. You have one more guess."

Crap. Crap. Crap.

Lucky for them, Tedesco had allowed for one mistake. But if they were wrong again, there would be trouble. The owner would arrive home to find his secret lair wide open, and she wouldn't be getting back in. Any proof the Department of Goods and Services needed would be gone forever. Tedesco would torch his tech if he discovered a breach.

"Give me a minute," Lee said hurriedly in her ear.

Mina took out the LiveBot scanner. As she watched, the security bot began to move. She held the screen in front of the robocam and hissed in nothing more than a breath, "Lee, look."

"It's probably just doing—"

"Did not compute, please repeat," the sim ordered.

Mina's head jerked up. The fact that alarms weren't sounding was not lost on her. Any system worth its weight in currency would've set off some sort of ping already. In Mina's own residence, if Veronica was ever unable to process a command, she would alert the PPF immediately and lock down all tech.

Tedesco's residence was lax, which probably meant that he gave the wrong commands often enough and didn't want the hassle of dealing with alarms and the arrival of the PPF every time he messed up.

That all worked in their favor, but these chances weren't going to hold out.

Mina eyed the scanner. Thankfully, the security bot stopped moving.

"Do you wish me to enact facial scanning, sir?" the sim asked.

Mina's mini vibrated, followed by a resounding, "No," from an audio-generated Tedesco.

It vibrated again, followed by Lee whispering, "This is the best I've got."

Mina closed her eyes.

Was the hacker really going to get lucky twice?

She had no choice but to use whatever Lee had sent. But she was going to position herself next to the exit across the room. Lee had better remember he had to get her out of here. Mina had to believe that the kid could hack the sliding door open again if Tedesco's security system enabled a lockdown protocol.

Otherwise, she was going to be stuck here to face Tedesco once he arrived home.

She held up her mini, and Tedesco's voice tittered, "Close doors. Password, roses."

A moment later, the structure began to move, shuttering itself.

Mina exhaled, angling the robocam toward the door she was next to, trying to will Lee to speed up the process. She held up the LiveBot scanner so Lee could see the security bot was on the move again.

The door *schicked* open, and she slipped out.

The automated mechanism rumbled louder than it had the first time. She held her breath, glancing at the scanner. The security bot hadn't changed directions and wasn't moving any faster. Good. But it was still moving. Mina couldn't tell if she'd be visible to the bot if she stepped into the main living area. Its location was close, but Mina couldn't remember where all the walls were from her visual surveillance on the way in.

Lee's voice entered her ear in a near-frantic screech, "Tedesco's coming. His private drone is overhead. He's back!"

That boy had to stop shrieking.

Staying calm and collected was a necessary part of agenting. She sighed. The kid had so much to learn. Mina hoped it didn't take a full light-year to get all the needed information crammed into his brain. If it did, they were both in trouble.

Mina had no choice but to risk exposure. She crouched as low as she could possibly go and took off. First through the living space and then through the meal room.

She was almost out. She hazarded a quick glance at the scanner and realized the housekeeping bot was coming straight toward her at a rapid clip. It must've been activated by Tedesco's impending arrival.

Mina opened the first door she saw and ducked inside.

"What are you *doing*?" Lee's hyper-stressed voice was getting to her. "You have to get out of there! The door you came through is still unlocked, but once Tedesco gets inside, he could reset everything. Without your signaler hovering within a meter of the mechanism, I won't be able to hack it to get you out."

Mina glanced around, trying to get her bearings, internally trying to will Lee to calm down. It was dark. She still couldn't risk using her voice. She set her mini on glow and held it aloft so she, and Lee, could see where she was. Then she held the LiveBot scanner in front of her robocam so Lee could see what she was up against.

"Oh," he said. "With Tedesco this close, I guess the staff has been activated. It looks like it's right next to you."

No shit, Lee.

Likely, the housekeeping bot was prepping a meal for its owner on the other side of the wall Mina stood beside. If she tried to exit, one glance down the hallway and the bot would detect her. Even though it wasn't a security bot, the household staff would have to follow protocol when dealing with someone they didn't recognize.

Mina looked around for anything to help rescue her from this situation. It seemed she'd landed in the gift-wrap room, apparent by the rolls and rolls of printed gift coverings in various designs prominently displayed on the shelves. There seemed to be a particular emphasis on Yuletide joy. Strangely, Tedesco was a giver who enjoyed the holidays. Why Tedesco wouldn't print-on-demand like the rest of the world was a mystery. Around any celebratory season, abundant printing kiosks were set up for this kind of stuff. People went wild for it.

All the decorative supplies gave her an idea. She walked over to a shelf containing several large sacks and an extra-long swath of nicely folded fabric. It was bright red, and as she held it up, the jolly face of Saint Nick flowed out.

"His craft just set down," Lee said. "I can see the top of it from where I'm positioned. You have to get out. Once he gets inside, he's likely going to activate an interior security program protocol. We don't know his preferences.

It could be typical for him to do a sweep. If he does, he could enact heat-seeking cams or motion detectors, as well as check all his entry and exit points to see if they've been compromised. That's what paranoid people do. It's what I would do."

I know all this, Lee.

Tedesco could do all that. But Mina didn't think he would. The man felt safe here. This was his garden-moated castle in the sky. He'd been here from the beginning, helping finance the first mega in the city, positioning himself well away from the rest of the universe. He'd set his residence on lax. The only real issue they'd come up against since Mina had broken inside were the blocks surrounding his illegal activities. That's where his paranoia was focused.

It seemed the only thing this man enjoyed more than shipping illegal chemis around the globe was acquiring mammoth furnishings, collecting entertainment baubles, and being ready for absolutely any holiday.

Mina couldn't relay all this to Lee. But she did agree with one thing the rookie was raving about: It was time to get out. Being inside the residence when Tedesco arrived would be ill-advised, especially since she needed access tomorrow to finish her op.

In her ear, Lee whisper-yelled, "He's on the ground! I'm trying to get closer. I can't see anything but the tops of their heads, but I think he's talking to Cots."

Perfect. The frantic gardener would keep Tedesco occupied for a few precious moments while Mina got herself out.

A disguise was necessary. She didn't want a recording of herself on the bot's visual hard drive. That wouldn't help matters. She threw the red fabric over her shoulders, tying it in a big loop in the front, making sure it covered her like a shroud. Then she poked a hole in the bottom of a large sack, which happened to have images of menorahs all over it.

Every bot Mina had ever encountered was required to use a verbal cue before it took any action. That protocol was hardwired into their systems. If the bot spotted her, it would question her. But if it didn't read her as human, seeing no discernible face or limbs, it would be uncertain what she was and subsequently wouldn't know how to respond. Thus, making the hyppie trick even more effective.

That was Mina's thought process, anyway. She'd never used bot hypnosis before. She was looking forward to it.

As the bag went over her head, Lee sputtered, "What are you doing?"

Mina couldn't answer him. Why he kept asking questions was beyond her.

She made two eyehole slits fairly low so she could monitor the scanner in her hand. She'd have to keep her back to the bot. Best-case scenario, it wouldn't see her at all. Second-best was that the hypnosis worked like it was supposed to.

"Tedesco's on the move again," Lee said. "And he doesn't look happy." Nobody was happy after they had a conversation with Cots. "He's heading inside. He just popped out of my sight."

Mina opened the door and slipped into the hallway.

Her back was to the meal-prep area. She crept toward the exterior door, dragging the fabric behind her like a jolly red train. She'd arrived without being detected. With relief, she pressed her shoulder against the metal, easing it open just enough to wiggle out.

As the door moved, it creaked.

From behind, a softly modulated female voice called, "Who's there?"

Mina was ready.

Without turning, she brought the scanner up to her mouth, underneath the damn bag, which made loud crinkling sounds. She swore internally for not being smart enough to make a mouth slot.

She said, "Go back to work. Prepare Tedesco's meal. This is nothing to worry about."

The housekeeping bot replied, almost instantaneously, "Go back to work. Make…make…make meal."

Sounded promising.

"Go back to work," Mina commanded again as she ducked outside. "Tedesco is hungry."

Right before the door completely shut, Mina heard the bot stutter, "Hungry. Hungry."

Chapter 9

MINA DRAGGED HER tired fingers through her faux hair and winced. The action set her sensitive scalp ablaze with new itchy tingles. She kept forgetting not to touch her fake locks. Now all she wanted to do was scratch her head with the force of a craft hitting a graphene wall at Mach 20. Or take a hydro-cannon to it.

But she couldn't do either because she was patiently waiting for her director, whose image was on her wall, to finish analyzing the last bit of the vid footage she'd submitted to headquarters during the ride home in the government craft.

It was almost seven in the evening, and Mina hadn't eaten since her break in the early afternoon. Once she'd snuck out of Tedesco's residence and rejoined the other gardeners, she'd worked double time, diligently digging out plants and bushes to make room for the trees. It'd been backbreaking work.

Nobody had taken much notice of her absence—

except for Andy and Grigg—which had made things easier. The mystery man with the dark beard hadn't introduced himself, but they'd made eye contact several times, and he'd stepped in to redirect Andy at least twice more.

Mina couldn't seem to shake the carrot-top gardener for all she was worth, and it pissed her off.

McAllister finally looked up, clearing his throat. "Good work. I'm sending this to our security department for analysis immediately."

"Like I've stated already," Mina replied, managing to keep most of the exhaustion out of her voice, "I can't take credit for all of this. Most of it lands squarely on the rookie. Modified military tech in a civilian residence isn't something any of us expected. Had Lee not picked up on the Venus disguised as a Davis, we would've exposed ourselves immediately, and Tedesco would've destroyed all evidence. The op would've been a total loss. Lee deserves all the borrow credits for this one." Mina was not above giving the accolades where they were due, even though it pained her on so many levels.

"I'll be gathering Agent Adams' report shortly," McAllister said. "I'm curious, though, once you hypnotized the bot, and Lee reinstated the locks, what did you do with your...camouflage?" His tone held humor, but thankfully he wasn't full-on laughing.

"I buried it."

McAllister's eyebrows rose.

Mina tried to ignore a particularly itchy itch. "I placed it between a nice crab apple tree and one of Tedesco's beloved rosebushes. I'm certain jolly Saint Nick will enjoy his days there."

McAllister actually snorted. "I've never had the opportunity to scatter data in a bot, but it seemed to have worked without incident."

"It was my first time, as well. I wasn't sure if alarms would sound once the bot figured out I was there, or if it would maybe follow me outside. But all stayed quiet. We got extremely lucky. So many things could've gone wrong. Thinking I could've breached that fortress alone was wishful thinking."

She hated to admit it, but there it was.

"It sounds to me like you and Agent Adams worked well together, both of you taking charge of different aspects of the case. All around, it was nice, solid work."

"Thank you."

"What's your take on this Grigg?" McAllister flashed a still image on the screen that Mina had taken of the man.

She walked closer, hands on her hips. "Another agency has a man inside, is my guess. He's most certainly *not* a gardener. From what I saw, he knows a rudimentary amount of gardening to get him through, nothing more. One thing is for sure, he was running interference for me and Lee. He seemed to know who we were—or at least who we weren't. He handled Andy like he anticipated our issues with him. Andy was the only gardener who approached Lee the entire time I was inside, which only turned out to be for twenty-three minutes and forty-seven seconds." Though it'd seemed like an eternity. "I would bet Grigg kept Andy from coming around more often."

There was no question Grigg was an agent of some kind. Whose was the mystery.

"I ran him through facial rec in our internal database. No match. But that doesn't mean much, other than he's likely with a covert unit, or he's wearing an alt. My guess is the DGS has an investigative arm we don't know about. You didn't get any of his DNA, and by the sounds of it, you won't have the chance to get any in the near future. He was careful to stay physically clear of you."

Mina nodded, nibbling on her thumbnail in an effort to keep her hands away from her scalp. It was blissfully clear of dirt after a vigorous scrub when she'd arrived home. "He witnessed me interacting with Lee, but he might be unsure of our connection." She wouldn't blame the agent for being unsure. Lee wore his newbie status like a shining star. If Lee had been working with Grigg, Mina might not have believed it either. "Lee might be able to get closer to him than I can. But if this agent is good at his job, he'll keep his distance. Would you like me to initiate contact?"

"Not at this time," McAllister replied firmly. "I'm going to discreetly pass this up a chain of command I trust to see if I get a hit. I don't want to step on anyone's euroboots. How long did you say he's been with this gardening operation?"

"According to Andy, Grigg has been with Cots and the crew at least six weeks." Keeping Andy off her back was going to be a huge priority.

"This agent may be tasked with keeping eyes and ears on things in general, nothing more. There are very few agencies like ours that have authority to do what we do. And if they do, we don't know about them, and vice versa."

"The authority to break laws." It was an especially fun part of the job. Mina thoroughly enjoyed it.

"We're not breaking a law if the law doesn't apply to us. Article 783, Class triple-A, permits select government agencies under the Corruption Mandate of 2095 'to seek to combat corruption without confines of ordered law.'"

Mina knew that article well, as did all the agents in the CIU. It was literally their get-out-of-a-box-free card. The article went on to state that those "select government agencies" that held such powers would be overseen by a secret arm of the legislative branch.

Since CIU's inception in 2095, it'd stayed that way—secret.

As far as Mina knew, McAllister answered to an unnamed government official who served on a special committee at the highest levels. Names were never mentioned.

"Art 783 saves our backsides," Mina agreed.

"So if Grigg's unit doesn't have the same authority that Article 783 grants us, which is likely, his actions will be limited."

Mina nodded. "I'll hold off on contact unless he approaches me." She glanced down at her cuff. It was past dinnertime. Way past. "Lee is set to give me a report when he figures out the hack. He seemed pretty despondent when he left with the delivery techs. I don't think the rookie has ever come up against something he couldn't hack quickly. If he can't break it, we won't be able to get Tedesco's data tomorrow."

"Lee's been working on it the last few hours," McAllister said. "I had him delay his report to me until I spoke with you. As far as I know, he's not overly discouraged."

"Tedesco was supposed to be gone all day, but he came home and remained inside the residence for the rest of the afternoon. Are we going to run into a similar issue tomorrow?" Mina didn't have to spell out to her director what that would mean.

"We shouldn't. He has morning meetings scheduled, but we're securing his afternoon by setting up a mock introduction with an entertainment company he's been interested in doing business with for years. We've also secured a delivery for tomorrow. There was a dust-up between the head gardener and the head delivery technician. They were going to sever ties until we stepped in today."

"Yeah, Cots is temperamental." Mina had trouble stifling her yawn.

"A government craft will pick you up tomorrow at the same time. Additional tech, based on Lee's parameters and what the team analyst thinks you'll need, will be on board, including the soap you requested to treat the roses. I am arranging a satellite to be well within range by morning and a coded airmeld to be forthcoming. You'll receive the sequence in the morning."

"Got it," Mina replied. "As long as Tedesco doesn't get suspicious and change all his passwords, we should have no problem getting inside again. I can't believe Lee nailed those passwords so perfectly. Not only is he an exceptional hacker, but the rookie has good instincts." There was that credit again. "Though he has to work on his Zen. My ear is still ringing from all his yelling."

"It sounds like the sopping-wet rookie has made an impression on you."

"Possibly," Mina hedged as the guilt welled in her chest that she'd ignored him so thoroughly on their first op together, which had lasted eighteen months. Lee might've been an asset earlier, and they might've gotten Rick the Rat into a box sooner if Mina had spent some time training him. "His tech smarts don't excuse him from the rest. He has a lot to catch up on."

"He's a fast learner and eager to please. Contact me immediately after the breach is completed tomorrow. Send the word 'flower' to Perfect Plants' main line via your mini, and we will intercept. We will monitor the airmeld as it happens. I'll send a craft to pick you up. We'll figure out the reasoning for the early retrieval tomorrow."

Mina nodded. "A craft will be welcome." She hoped they'd be able to breach the interior again right away in the morning so she could get out of there. Another day of lugging bushes and trees and Mina would have to take a spin in her X600 medi-unit to work out all the kinks. But it would be worth it to bring a criminal to justice.

"Nice job, Agent Kane. Now get some rest. I'll make sure Lee reports his progress to you soon."

"Thank you, sir. This is within our reach. I can feel it.

Tedesco is going to spend some quality time in a box. His currency won't buy him out of it this time. Oh, and go easy on Lee. Remember, hackers aren't used to sharing."

McAllister's forehead crinkled. "Sharing?"

"Yes. It's about schematics. I'll leave it at that."

McAllister nodded once, acknowledging that Mina wasn't willing to go so far as to tattle on the rookie. "I'll remember that hackers don't like to share. Screen off."

Mina sighed as she walked to her meal printer, avoiding touching her scalp, scratching the back of her neck instead. "Eggie, make me spaghetti and meatballs with extra Parmesan and a single serving of French bread with lots of garlic butter."

"Processing order. Your meal will be ready in less than two minutes."

Ever since Lee had fixed Eggie so her orders were processed in English instead of a Scandinavian dialect, her meal printer had become the ultimate dream. The food was always delicious, and Mina was happy.

"Veronica, see if there are any live naturecasts streaming. If not, pull one from my archives, display on living-area screen at one hundred percent." Mina padded down her hallway, stripping off her gardening smock as she went, her tools clattering together as she settled the whole thing on the floor of her utility room. She tossed her other clothes into the cleaning pod and shut the drawer, then walked into her sleeping room nude.

In her closet, she pulled out comfort clothing in the form of a loose, silky shirt and soft tie pants, both the color of dark plums.

It was going to be an early night full of pasta and animals frolicking in the wild. Mina couldn't wait. She hadn't really had a nice, quiet evening to herself since she'd moved into her new residence. It was overdue.

As she made her way into the living area, sleek softness caressing her skin with each step, Eggie beeped, announcing her food was ready. The entire wall was covered in a glorious pod of dolphins, jumping and skipping through the waves, chirping and clicking. Mina wasn't surprised to see that dolphins were streaming. You could usually find live ocean coverage anywhere in the world, any hour of the day.

The study of dolphin pitch communication had made leaps and bounds in the last few years, and scientists were beginning to interpret more and more frequencies and their meanings. Dolphins, it turned out, had complex language skills, revolving around eating, social interactions, and safety. The dolphin bots capturing the live footage were completely lifelike and, for the most part, accepted into the pods.

Mina took her food, and the accompanying utensils, to her lounger. She'd just taken a seat, a scoop of pasta on its way into her mouth when Veronica intoned, "Vid chat request coming in from Quinn Kane. Do you wish to accept?"

"Yes. On screen, thirty percent." Mina's brother, looking afraid, popped onto her wall, replacing the frolicking dolphins. Mina leaned forward, setting her meal down, immediately recognizing there was an issue.

"What's wrong, Quinn?"

"You have to come. Right now." His voice shook. Her predominantly good-natured brother was in a state, his eyes darting back and forth, sweat dotting his upper lip, his brown curls disheveled like he'd been raking his hands through them constantly. He didn't even comment on her altered appearance. "I'm at Primal. Something happened. Something's happening to her. You have to get here fast."

Mina held up a hand. "Of course I'll come, but if something's happened to one of your coworkers, or there's an emergency, you have to call PPF immediately."

He hedged. "It's...it's not that. I can't talk about it on screen. This is not something the police can deal with. Please, sis." His eyes closed for a full five seconds before blinking open, wetness leaking down his cheeks at the edges. "You're the only one who can help."

Her brother knew she was an agent, but not what kind or what department she worked for. "Okay. I'll be there in ten." If this was something the PPF needed to handle, Mina would summon them when she arrived.

Quinn's features relaxed by a few degrees. "Staff craft landing is on the roof. Give them my name. I'll be waiting."

The dolphins, still playing, took his place as he ended the vid chat.

Mina stood, gathering her uneaten food, taking a few bites as she walked to the grinder. "Veronica, naturecast off. Summon my personal craft to hub twenty immediately. Destination, Primal bar."

Her wall went dark. "Summoning craft."

Mina hit the grind button and watched her dishes and delicious food disappear, wondering what could possibly have gone wrong at a bar that didn't open for another hour and what her innocent, bordering-on-too-sweet-for-his-own-good brother had gotten himself into.

Chapter 10

Mina arrived on the employee landing pad at Primal. All was quiet as she pushed her way into the establishment through an unlocked door. The entire place was decked out in animal prints, sleek chrome, and black syn-leather. The last time she'd been here, with Kaylee, a holo band had been playing for a packed dance floor. Their drinks had been frothy and delicious, and Quinn had been happy and carefree behind the bar.

Now, an unfamiliar bartender was readying for the evening's customers. He glanced up as she walked in. His hair hung to his shoulders in gold and tawny waves, his eyes were diffused a pale amber, and his leopard-print shirt was cropped above his navel. His eyes crinkled at the corners as he analyzed her, registering that she wasn't an employee. "Sorry, we don't open for another twenty. But be sure to check back. Fidget Galaxy is holoing in from Japan. Should be a wild night."

"I'm not here for the band. I'm looking for my brother, Quinn Kane. Have you seen him?"

Her baby brother had adopted Mina's surname in solidarity. Their parents went by Rose and Damon Leeds. Surnames were no longer needed to keep a family lineage intact. All you needed for that was DNA. Most people, particularly in Mina's generation, had decided during their teen years what they wanted to be called, and as long as they followed the proper channels to officially register their identity, along with matching DNA, the cosmos was the limit.

"Oh, yeah. Quinn. He's in the back somewhere. Feel free to take a look around." The guy gestured with an elbow, as his hands were busy mixing some kind of concoction.

Mina noted the bartender didn't seem the least bit upset or on edge. She headed in the direction of the man's elbow jut, walking into a dimly lit hallway that was darker than the bar, but light enough to see. There were several doors, all shut.

Mina stopped. "Quinn?" she called.

Her brother's curly mop stuck out of a door at the end of the hallway. He gestured for her to hurry. He ushered her inside a small space, then closed the door behind them. A light in the corner gave off a low diffused yellow glow. The interior of the room wasn't much brighter than the hallway.

A woman with long dark hair and wearing a red syn-leather top and matching pants was lying on a lounger, which was covered in a fuzzy zebra print. Primal stayed true to its décor even in the employee spaces.

The woman moaned softly. Her head thrashed back and forth a few times. Her cheeks were flushed pink. Mina watched as her jaw clenched and unclenched, her hands fisted at her sides.

Mina knelt by her side, taking her wrist in hand, trying to register a pulse, searching for the woman's cuff. "What's she on?" When Quinn didn't answer right away, Mina raised her voice. "Tell me what she's on."

"Plush." Quinn stammered, "We're...we're kind of seeing each other. Her name is Daphne. She wanted to try it. I wanted to wait until after our shift, but she thought it would be fun to go on it now, to...uh...to kind of heighten the experience for later." Sheepishness, along with a thick layer of guilt, hung in the air. He glanced away from Mina. "She reacted instantly. She kind of doubled over and clutched her stomach and said she felt weird. Then she passed out. I called you right after that. She's been like this for about fifteen."

Plush was a potent new pharma. The pleasure drug was supposed to enhance the sexual experience, but this girl was in serious distress. Her heart rate was elevated, and she was clearly experiencing severe discomfort.

"She needs a medic. There's nothing I can do for her." Mina stood, beginning to punch buttons on her cuff to summon an emergency medi-unit.

"No, wait!" Quinn stilled her hand. "She...she can't see a medic. She'll lose her job if they find out she's been using while on duty. It's an instant removal. She can't afford that. She's holding on to her borrows by a thin carbon thread. She's close to living in the outskirts.

Both of her parents are dead. She doesn't have anyone else. This job saved her life. I can't be responsible for her losing it. I...I just can't."

"Plush is not illegal—"

"She doesn't have a prescription. And it doesn't matter. Primal is strict on using anything other than an approved energy booster while on duty."

Mina frowned. "She needs medical attention, Quinn."

"She's not the first one to have a reaction like this," her brother stated quickly. "It's becoming more and more common. All she needs is a few hours. If we can just get her somewhere where she can shake the effects in private, I'm sure she'll be fine. I'll make excuses for her here. *Please.* Please help us, sis."

"How do you know this kind of reaction is common?" Mina questioned. "I haven't heard about any adverse reactions to Plush, especially not like what she's exhibiting." Daphne moaned, and Mina glanced down at the poor girl. "If side effects like this are becoming the norm, I'd know. Word gets around."

Daphne's thrashing had abated, but her hands were still balled into fists, her jaw was still clenched, and her body was rigid. She was in no condition to travel.

"Harri," Quinn said hurriedly. "He told me that customers at the emporium have been having these same kind of weird reactions and that they're usually fine after a couple hours."

Harold Hampburg, Mina's former dalliance. It seemed Harri with an i still worked in the pleasure industry.

"Is that where you got the Plush?" It wasn't hard to get

your hands on nonprescription pharma. People with enough resources could get it on the open market.

"No, of course not! Harri would never break the law like that. I'm not sure where Daphne got it, to tell you the truth. She had it when she arrived." He scrubbed both hands over his face as he shook his head. "She was just so excited. I let her do it. I even thought it might be fun."

"We can't risk her life. You know that." Mina brought her wrist up again. "She's in no condition to travel. I have to call a medi-unit."

"Call Harri first," Quinn pleaded, grabbing her hand with both of his. "Please. Just a short vid chat. He can see Daphne for himself. He has experience with this. If he says we have to call a medi-unit, then we will. I don't want to risk her life either. There's a screen right here." He pressed a button inset into the wall, and a panel opened. Before Mina could stop him, Quinn ordered Harri's number and sent the request.

Harri answered immediately. "Hey, Quinn—" He stopped, his eyes widening as he took in the scene, spotting Mina standing next to her brother.

Mina and Harri hadn't seen each other in almost a year. It took him a second to recognize her under the alt. She saw the moment it sparked. Harri knew she was a federal agent and didn't comment.

Truth be told, he looked pretty good. His dark hair was shorter than she remembered.

Quinn stepped forward. "Hey, Harri. Sorry to bother you at work, but I need your help. You've met Daphne a few times. Well, she took some Plush, and she's having one of those reactions you told me about." Quinn knelt next to Daphne, shifting her gently so she would be visible to the cameras.

Harri moved closer. "Is she hot to the touch?"

Quinn placed his hand on her forehead. Mina did the same. They both replied, "No," in unison.

"What's her heart rate?"

"Elevated," Mina replied. "But her cuff is powered off, so I can't get an accurate read."

"How about oxygen intake?" Harri asked. "Is she hyperventilating? Or any pauses in breathing?"

"Not that I've seen," Quinn said.

Daphne moaned again, muttering, "My head hurts."

"She's conscious, that's good," Harri said. "How much did she ingest? A full cap orally? Half? Or did she use an airpen?"

"Orally. I'm not sure how much," Quinn replied. "I didn't see her take it."

Harri moved back. "She should be all right. We're seeing a lot of these kinds of reactions lately. Word on the drone stream is that dealers are doctoring Plush, though the pros I work with don't think that is the case. They think Bliss Corp is doing some sort of experimentation."

"Experimentation? Like what?" Mina was instantly on alert.

"Like testing the effects of an increased dosage or seeing if a new formula works the same way. It's been causing a lot of problems."

"That's against the law." Mina couldn't keep the accusation out of her voice. "You can't test drugs on humans without their consent."

If a company *did* have consent, it could do almost anything. It was an issue, especially for those who were desperate for borrows, because Big Pharma paid very well for experimentation on willing bodies.

"Yes, that's true," Harri agreed, his head bobbing. "But there's no other reason why it would be happening. Plush has been out for over a year now, with no ill effects. The real problem I've seen is, the more people take it, the bigger the doses have to be to achieve the same results the next time. But there's only so much you can take before you experience adverse reactions like this." He gestured at Daphne. "But usually not as bad. Just mild discomfort. Bliss Corp makes ten trillion world currency annually on Plush. It's the company's best-selling drug. If it leaks that its effects weaken the more you use it, they stand to lose a hell of a lot of currency."

"If you're seeing multiple cases like this, how come it hasn't come out in the media?" Mina asked. "This should be all over the newscasts."

Harri shrugged. "The clients are embarrassed. Those who have reactions are mostly clients who come in with their own prescriptions. Nothing we dose here at the emporium has been an issue. Most of them don't want people to know they're using. Some of them have even been fearful when we suggest calling a medi-unit. Just in the last week, some of our clients have asked us to sign waivers that we won't call for any help if something goes wrong. They won't say why."

Mina pondered this new information. She didn't need to be a federal agent to know something was definitely amiss. "So basically, you're telling us that people are intentionally keeping their reactions under wraps—"

"You can investigate this later," Quinn interrupted. "Right now, we need to get Daphne out of here. Primal opens in less than ten, and she has to get somewhere safe so she can shake this off."

"Honestly, as far as I can see, she's going to be okay," Harri agreed. "The more severe cases we've seen involve fever, shakes, and shallow or increased breathing. If it gets bad, we do call for help. Even though the clients usually refuse the medi-unit once they arrive. It's up for discussion whether or not we're going to sign the waivers. If we don't, we're going to lose clients. If we do, and this gets worse, we might lose lives. It's a quandary."

"Not really a quandary," Mina mumbled. But she had no illusions that currency would win. It always did. "Let's get some Jump in her." She turned to Quinn, choosing to believe Harri that Daphne would be okay. "That should get her moving and more alert."

The stimulant Jump came in many forms, but the most common was a mouth spray.

"Don't leave her alone," Harri cautioned. "She could relapse. If she spikes a fever or has trouble breathing, get her help immediately." Someone in the background called Harri's name. "I have to go. I have a client waiting." His eyes flicked to Mina, lids downcast. "It was good to see you. You look really...good, even though it's an alt." He blinked twice and popped off screen, but not before Mina had seen the blush creeping into his cheeks.

Mina's mind whirled with the realization that people

were being affected adversely by a profitable drug, possibly even being used as lab probes without their consent. The fact that no one had reported the issues to any authority stank like a massive sulfur bomb. Mina had to give McAllister a full account as soon as she could.

Quinn called her name.

She startled, looking down at him where he knelt by Daphne. "What?"

"I said you have to take her."

"Take her where?"

"Your residence? You heard Harri. She needs a safe place and a few hours to recuperate. I have some Jump in my locker. I'll get it, and then we'll take her out the back way. You landed on the roof, right?"

"Right." Mina assessed the vulnerable woman on the lounger.

"Mina," Quinn said. "*Please.*"

"Sure. Okay. Go get the Jump. I'll figure out the rest."

"Thanks. I owe you."

"Yes, you do."

Chapter 11

Mina managed to safely escort a slightly more alert Daphne out of Primal and to her residence. She hadn't wanted to put the girl in her platform, mostly because it wasn't freshly cleaned, so she settled for the lounger. It was pretty much the only other place in her home where an adult could stretch out comfortably.

None of this was ideal, but the girl was already fast asleep.

Even with Jump flowing through her system, Daphne had managed to stay awake only a short time. She had thanked Mina profusely on the flight over and had been very sweet. If she and Quinn ever claimed a coupled union, this would certainly be a story to tell.

Mina debated changing back into her comfort clothing once Daphne was settled, but ultimately decided not to. Her guest would be here for a couple of hours, and Mina needed to be able to help her if she needed it.

Instead, Mina padded over to her meal printer, as her

stomach was full-on nasty-growling now. "Eggie, make me a plate of spaghetti and meatballs, extra Parmesan, and add a little spice to it this time."

"Printing your order. Your pasta with a kick will be ready shortly."

Mina chuckled. Eggie was developing a sassy side. Most tech adapted to the personality of its primary user, particularly if the controls were set to Casual, which Mina preferred. Tons of annoying tech stayed stiff and exacting, but for the most part, manufacturers had created decent sim programs that made living with computers and bots more tolerable and sometimes even fun.

Once her plate was done, Mina stood at her counter to eat, her mind wandering to the Plush issue and what to do about it. At this point, she didn't have more than Harri's personal accounting, along with the visibly unstable Daphne. That wasn't much to go on. But the implications of Bliss Corp possibly testing a new formula of a popular drug on the general population were staggering.

Veronica interrupted her just as Mina finished her spiced-up, and delicious, spaghetti. "Vid chat request coming in from Lee Adams. Do you wish to accept?"

"Sure. Screen at thirty." Veronica had Mina's location triangulated within the residence, so Mina didn't have to specify. If Veronica was unsure, she would ask.

Lee popped on her wall.

He began to speak, then abruptly stopped, his mouth snapping shut, his eyes tracking to the lounger behind her.

Shit. Mina had forgotten about Daphne.

It wasn't every day she had to care for her brother's new girlfriend while she recuperated from a mysterious pharma overdose.

The rookie's eyes widened. "Who is that? Is she okay?"

"A friend of my brother's. And yes, she will be. Veronica, switch vid feed to utility room, sixty percent both ways." Mina headed down the hallway toward the place that would afford her the most privacy. The space was soundproof once the door was shut, and although the screen didn't take up the entire wall like in all the other rooms, it was adequate for a meeting of this kind.

Lee was already there when she arrived. He looked to be inspecting her extra printer. "Is that a weapons printer? It's bigger than I thought it would be. I've heard about agents having them, but I've never seen one before. It looks like one of those outdated meal creators from when food printers were first invented."

Mina shut the door, sidestepping her smock on the floor. She grabbed the handle of the printer and tugged it open so her fellow agent could see inside. "It's a model A100. The very first meal creator ever made." They'd been called meal creators first. "The techs who make these into weapons printers requisition the older ones because the interior is enormous. Plus, these printers were insulated with a special fire-retardant foam that came standard. Apparently, people thought the food they were creating might catch fire. Meals don't burn, but weapons with circuitry can. I haven't used this yet, but I've had an operational weapons printer in my residence for two years. It's pretty spec. It took me three years as an agent before I qualified. Don't worry," she told him when she noticed his downcast gaze, "it'll come sooner than you think."

"It's hard to believe you can just order up a weapon like you're ordering a plate of spaghetti."

Mina chuckled. Funny that she'd just eaten a plate of tasty spaghetti. "Yeah, it's pretty cool. But it's a good thing we don't need weapons very often." She shut the door and crossed her arms. Time to get down to business. "Did you crack the code to Tedesco's vault?" Lee's face scrunched into a scowl. Mina took that as a no. The kid was too easy to read, like a puppy about to get a protein chew. "This one has me stumped so far. I've cloned the program, though, and I'm getting closer. But each time I prepare a sequence I think will work, another block slides into place. Whoever designed this is strato-smart. Really up there. Four Story must have access to the best of the best."

"The best of the best...*criminals*," Mina agreed. "But you're better than the best of the best bad guys. I know you can hack this by morning." She couldn't offer to help, certain it was above her knowledge base, particularly if it was military grade.

Lee nodded, not looking entirely convinced. "I'll stay up all night if I have to. But..."

"No buts. And make sure when you show up tomorrow morning that you look bored. Like you can't wait to get out of there. No more eager energy."

"I was thinking more about my backstory. What if I—"

"No backstory, Lee. Like I told you today, we keep it short and simple for a reason. Unless the job calls for it, a detailed backstory doesn't factor in—"

Veronica interrupted, "Vid chat request coming in from Vincent Kramer. Do you wish to accept?"

Mina dropped her arms. "*Now?*" Her voice came out ragged as her hands jumped to her hair, which wasn't her actual hair. She had to quit doing that. She glanced at Lee, knowing she was a little wild-eyed. "I should take this." She glanced around the small space. "But I can't have him pop in here. He'd see the printer. Then again, I can't have Daphne overhearing us. That means I have to take it in my sleep room. But he can't see me, because of my alt." She turned in a half circle, trying to decide what to do.

Veronica answered her first question. "It appears to be now. What shall I do?"

Lee was grinning. So much so, his teeth were on full display. The kid was practically giggling. "Vincent Kramer is calling you back already? The colonel-in-arms of the French Protectorate can't seem to stay away." The rookie shook his head in open wonder. "I think he likes you."

Mina shot Lee a look. "Quiet, you. He sent me a message last night that he was on some sort of secret mission. He's probably just letting me know he's okay..." She trailed off. "Or something like that. Veronica, hold until I say so. Send a message that I'll be right there. Block vid on my side." She'd have to take it in her sleep room. Her lux platform sleeper with its super-silky, soft, skin-kissing sheets wasn't made, but that wouldn't matter, because Vince wouldn't see it. The hair on Mina's arms rose. She hastily tucked them behind her back, clasping one wrist.

Lee made a noise, a cross between a laugh and a gurgle. "If I don't get Tedesco's vault hacked, I'll let you know. Good luck with your vid chat. Give Vincent my best." He signed off with a huge chortle before Mina could add something clever.

Mina hurried into her personal space, throwing her sheets together in some semblance of order, slamming her closet doors shut—not because she had to, but because it felt like the right thing to do.

Then she perched at the edge of her platform. Mina ordered, "Screen on. Forty percent."

A very close camera shot of Vincent Kramer blinked onto her wall. None of the background details were clear, and the video itself was very dark.

She leaned forward.

"Hi," Vince said with a note of wariness. "You blocked your vid."

"Yeah, sorry about that. I just got out of the sprayer, and I didn't want to miss your call," she lied.

Vince looked ruffled. His hair was tousled, and the neck of his shirt was crinkled to one side, like he'd slept in it. There was a slight hint of darkness under his left eye. It could be from fatigue or violence. Mina couldn't tell, though fatigue wouldn't result in a dark circle under only one eye. If he'd taken even one trip into a medi-pod, it would be almost impossible to know without asking outright if he'd been in a fight.

"Where are you?" she asked.

Vince glanced around, agitated, one hand coming up to rub the back of his neck. "I can't say."

This wasn't the time to let him know Mina had a high-level government tracer, mandatory for every agent, on all incoming and outgoing signals. She'd find out his whereabouts later. "Um...okay." She didn't want to ask why he'd called or why he was apparently distressed.

They both spoke at the same time. "Why did—"

"I just—"

They both laughed. Vince relaxed by a few degrees, exhaling. "Listen, I called because I wanted to let you know I'm safe. You know, after I left that message last night. I don't want you to worry."

Mina hadn't been worried.

Vincent Kramer was a high-ranking geopolitical government official who specialized in combat and protection for the French government. Mina figured he was adequately skilled for his line of work and therefore could handle any trouble. Now she wasn't so sure.

She replied cautiously, "Thanks for letting me know." She leaned forward again, trying to get a closer look. "Are you sure you're okay? You look a little...worn out."

"I'm fine. It's just been a long day of travel. Hey, can I ask you for a favor?"

"Of course," Mina replied easily.

"As you know, I'm on a covert mission, and because of that, no one knows my location. But if something were to happen to me..." He appeared uncomfortable, shifting in his seat. "I'm actually not sure I'd be found." Interesting. "Normally, I'd ask someone else to do what I'm going to ask you to do. But that someone is no longer in my life."

Was he talking about a previous significant other? Mina didn't know anything about his personal life, other than what he'd told her.

"Anyway…" He rubbed the back of his neck with a little more vigor. "If it's okay, I'd like to send you something by courier drone. It's an encoded locator. You won't be able to see what's on it."

Not entirely true. Mina had ways. One of them was named Lee.

"It's an insurance policy of sorts," he went on. "If you don't hear from me for an extended period of time, I'd like you to take it to Chaz Burquist. He'll know what to do with it. I'd really appreciate it."

"Chaz Burquist? Isn't he the grand dom of the International Judicial Committee?" Mina pretended that pulling that information out of her brain was a lucky break, as many civilians wouldn't know who Burquist was.

"He is."

So, in essence, Vince was letting Mina know that if something happened to him, he didn't want her to approach the French Protectorate about it. He wanted her to go to the International Judicial Committee, where an inquest would be taken up.

That spoke volumes about what he was involved in.

"Okay, you can courier the locator to me. But I don't know that I'd be able to get anything to Chaz Burquist on my own." Of course she could, but Mina needed more information, so she was going fishing. "He's pretty high up.

But I can take it to my city representative, Casey Bellows, and explain what's going on. I'm sure he could help get it to the right people."

Vince countered, his jaw set, "No, it needs to go directly to Chaz. I'll see that your name and pertinent information get to him. So, if the need arises, you can call the International Judicial Committee reception line, and you'll be on an approved-caller list."

Mina raised an inquiring eyebrow that Vince couldn't see.

She'd been studying Vince's body language the entire time, and he hadn't given much away other than agitation and fatigue. His eyes hadn't compressed at the corners, and the telltale tic in his beautifully crafted cheek hadn't begun to pulse.

But he had to know that his request was highly unusual for someone like her. Nobody asked a civilian to do what Vince was asking her to do. Vincent Kramer had high-level friends outside of the French Protectorate. People he could trust with this kind of information. Hell, he'd been in the banking industry before becoming the colonel-in-arms. Anyone with capital currency had the power to get to Chaz on their own.

This could mean only a few things. The primary being that Vince knew exactly what Mina did for a living. The second was that what he was involved with was so hot, he couldn't trust anyone inside his own world.

It was unsettling to think that Vince might have been playing Mina since the moment they'd met for dinner and might have known that she was a covert agent for the US government. But she couldn't really be all that surprised either. The French had secret intel of their own. Even though the CIU was cloaked, that didn't mean other nations didn't know about its existence. Humans made mistakes. They broke confidences. The CIU was ten years old, and that was a long time for a secret agency to stay secret.

Mina quietly appraised the man on her screen who looked disheveled and uncertain for the first time since their acquaintance had been rekindled. He was the opposite of the confident guy who'd entered the restaurant a few short nights ago.

Instead, he perpetually shifted in his seat, aware of her perusal, saying nothing.

"If you send it to me," she countered, "I'm going to require something in return."

"Anything."

She caught the hint of desperation. "Check in with me once daily around this time. It doesn't have to be a vid. Just send a quick audio or something with a time stamp to let me know you're okay. I'll give you a six-hour window. If I don't hear from you, I go to Chaz."

"I can't guarantee I can—"

"You can't expect me to sit here and worry about you." She stated it firmly. "I'm not asking you to divulge secrets, Vince. I know what you do for a living. Your job is risky. But you can't ask me to wait for days, unsure if I should deliver your encoded message to Chaz or not. It can be a one-word message. Safe. Or alive. Set it to auto and punch a button. I don't care what you do, but make it happen."

He bowed his head. "Okay. I'll make it work." He looked straight at the camera and therefore straight at her. He appeared relieved, his eyes sincere. "Thank you."

Mina's heart gave a staccato beat. "You're welcome."

"I'll be in touch tomorrow at this time. I have to go."

Before she could respond, he was gone.

Chapter 12

To say Mina was distracted was an understatement. She'd boarded the transpo craft at Perfect Plants and snagged a seat in the back, avoiding the other gardeners, especially Andy, who had tried to engage her repeatedly once she'd arrived on-site.

She seemed to be his only target, which was irritating.

Her head was bowed, nose buried in her handheld, trying to make it look like she was engrossed in her research, which wasn't entirely untrue. Her research just wasn't of the gardening variety.

She scanned location points. Her government tracer had pinpointed Vince's whereabouts last night, placing him in the middle of the Pacific Ocean. It was becoming obvious that his location had been cloaked, but she hoped to find an island or a boat or something she'd missed earlier.

Lee hadn't contacted her, so Mina assumed he'd completed the hack and was ready to go.

She shut off her mini and closed her eyes, reclining back, trying to get her brain sorted and back on the job in front of her.

Instead, images of a distressed Vince flickered into her mind like pesky flies buzzing around a smelly prize. It was proving to be a challenge to shake thoughts of the colonel.

Last night, after sending a very thankful Daphne home, Mina had consulted with McAllister a second time to inform him of everything that had transpired with Quinn and Vince. They'd discussed the possible implications of the adverse effects of Plush, along with what to do about the colonel-in-arms.

McAllister planned to contact confidants in France to see if he could gather any details about what the Protectorate was up to. Then he was going to have researchers gather everything they could about recent medical episodes involving Plush.

That had to be enough. For now.

These issues would be ongoing since neither could be solved easily.

Reluctantly, Mina's brain settled back on Vince and his mystery location. His transmission had likely been pinged from one place to another, which was a common form of high-level government location cloaking, but she wouldn't know until Lee took a look. Following the pings wouldn't be complicated, but would take time, especially if there were lots of triangulations. Mina wasn't sure when she would receive the encrypted location device that Vince was having couriered to her, but she assumed it would be soon.

Waiting wasn't her specialty.

Mina's mind was packed like densely woven carbon fiber, so when the irritating Andy ambled up, forcing her to scoot over so he could take the seat next to her, she had to forcibly relax her fist so it wouldn't shoot out into his jaw like it wanted to.

Her gaze fell across the aisle, meeting Grigg's. The bearded man rolled his eyes, and Mina suppressed a smile.

"So, did you bring that soap you were talking about yesterday? The magic concoction that will cure all black spot?" Andy asked jovially, a large-toothed grin on full display, giving him an air of not having a care in the world.

"I did," Mina answered, glancing out her window. She'd never been more grateful for such a short ride. They were already descending into Tedesco's gardens. As the craft lowered, she caught sight of Tedesco's personal landing pad. It held two drones. She swore under her breath. Tedesco had visitors.

"What was that? Did I hear a bad word come out of that beautiful mouth?" Andy playfully grabbed her hand, giving it a tug when Mina didn't respond.

It was the third time he'd found a reason to touch her today. Mina turned a stony gaze on him, pulling her hand decisively out of his grasp. Not only did she not have time for this, but the harassment was going to end. Right now.

"I swore because I just remembered I forgot my hat for the second day in a row. Can I ask you something?" She leaned closer, whispering, "Why are you bothering me?"

When Andy returned a blank stare, she continued, "If you're looking for a date, you're not going to get one. Honestly, I pity any woman who would fall victim to your unrelenting and unwelcome persistence. You need to leave me the hell alone. I mean it. If you don't, there will be consequences that you'll find highly unpleasant." In-your-face tactics were all this guy was going to get through his carrot-topped head.

Mina thought she heard Grigg cover a laugh with a cough, but she couldn't be sure.

Andy arched back, raising both hands in mock surrender, a slick smile on his lips as the craft bounced on an air cushion, the doors rising. "Whoa there. No need to get your panties all wrapped in a double helix. I'm just trying to get to know you. I'm a friendly guy by nature. I like to meet new people. No harm done." Instead of getting up to exit the drone, he pressed in, aggressively rubbing his chest against her arm. This guy was manic. "If you ease up on that titanium rod that's stiffening your backside, I think you'd see we'd be great together. I'm prime at soothing aches and pains and everything in between." He winked at her. The asshole winked.

Mina now knew why two women could've recently left Cots' employ.

Andy wasn't done there. He reached over and stroked her thigh, allowing his hand to linger. His intent was as clear as a solar flare, his fingers grasping her firmly, letting her know he wasn't even close to giving up.

Gardeners filed off the craft in front of them.

Mina changed her expression to cloyingly sweet, complete with a bright, sunny smile. "You know, you might be right." She walked two fingers up the chest that was all up in her personal space. "You actually do seem like a nice guy." She sprayed it on like a thick coat of polyresin. "I tend to be too hasty when I make decisions of the heart. I have trouble knowing what's good for me." Mina pressed herself against him, batting her long lashes, sliding her palm over to his bicep, then up to his shoulder, her fingertips dipping under his collar.

He moved closer, a triumphant expression on his face. What a simpleton. This was too easy.

Mina dug her nails in, surprising him, dragging his head down with strength he hadn't been expecting. He stiffened as she whispered in his ear, "If you don't leave me the *hell* alone, you're going to find yourself buried in the dirt like your beloved rooties. Tell me, *Placido*," she said, using the birth name he'd mentioned yesterday, "if I do some digging, what will I find? I mean, Kalamazoo? Did you actually think I bought that homegrown story?" She emphasized her hold by giving his neck a hard squeeze. "It will be ridiculously easy for me to do that digging, too, since I'm fingernails-deep in your DNA right now. What shit pile did you originate from, I wonder?" He flinched like she'd shocked him. "Glad to see we're on the same comet trail." She gave his chest a few pats with her free hand. "From now on, keep away from me and all the other women here. If you do, I might decide to forget that I can file a harassment declaration and have your scrawny ass thrown in a box before the sun sets."

She released him suddenly, the quickness of it causing him to tumble ass-first into the aisle.

Grigg gave her a nod from the head of the craft as she stood.

Andy tripped over himself trying to get out.

Mina grinned a little more than was reasonable. Teaching Andy a lesson had been thoroughly satisfying, even if it'd been risky. If Andy decided to complain or throw a tantrum, there could be an inquisition, causing a delay or shutdown of the op.

But Mina didn't think so. She'd seen something in Andy's eyes that she'd seen in countless others like him. He was a predator masquerading as a gardener. His hair was bright and fun. He wore a perpetual genial smile. His outward appearance was gracious and giving, while under it all lurked darkness.

This time, he'd picked the wrong woman to mess with.

Mina withdrew a handy vial from one of her smock pockets and scraped Andy the Asshole's skin cells off her nails. She'd analyze it once she got home. His DNA would show any outstanding warrants or past shitty behavior on record. She didn't doubt she'd find something.

This certainly wasn't Placido's first offense.

Mina exited the craft to a familiar sight. Cots and the costumed butler bot were in a heated conversation. Well, heated from Cots' side. The butler bot had not changed his expression since she'd first seen him. She passed by, making her way toward the delivery area.

Andy was nowhere to be seen. Good. The other gardeners were busy doing plant-related things. Mina walked over to the large shelving unit and gathered what she needed to mix with the soap she'd been provided for the anti-black spot concoction. It would keep her focused on the here and now until the delivery drones arrived.

She'd just gotten everything mixed when she heard props. The delivery drones were arriving. Finding out who was here visiting Tedesco was first on her to-do list. She hadn't seen any markings on the two transpo units she'd spied on the private landing, but they might be tagged on the sides. She needed to get a closer look, but she needed Lee first.

Mina didn't have to wait long. Cots materialized, waving his arms around, shooing everybody away. She spotted Lee immediately once the drones landed, noting the dark circles under his eyes. The kid had clearly been up all night.

She grabbed a shrub out of one of the drones. Lee stood in front of her, looking a little forlorn. She muttered, "Are you ready?"

Lee nodded, his face bland. Either he'd taken Mina's advice to keep his emotions in check, or he was too tired to muster up any of his usual excitement.

Maybe a tired Lee was a better Lee?

The rookie picked up a pot and followed Mina. "I'm sure you saw the private drones on your way in," Mina whispered. "They're going to be a problem."

"They're with Four Story," Lee answered.

"Are you sure? I didn't see any markings." Mina set down her plant. Some sort of flowering vine. Honestly, where were all these plants going to go? This place was already covered in greenery. She sidled away from the other gardeners, trying to look as casual as she could. She needed a few minutes with Lee without the threat of anyone eavesdropping.

"I saw the company logo on the doors. We must have come in from different angles," he said. "It's fairly small, a red rectangle with a yellow line through it."

"Do you think Frankie and company are just visiting? Or is this a security check because of something they found after I was inside yesterday?" Mina speculated out loud.

Clearly, McAllister didn't have this intel, or she would've been notified this morning, like she had with the satellite info. Everything was ready to go. But really, if Tedesco suspected his inner sanctum had been infiltrated, the place would be crawling with security. One would think, anyway.

"Maybe it's just a routine check for Four Story?" More out loud speculation. It was possible Mina had triggered something that hadn't sounded an external alarm, but had alerted the system in some other way.

Whatever the reason, having Frankie and company here meant Mina couldn't enter the residence. Therefore, no breach and airmeld of data would happen.

"No work order was on the schedule from what I saw when I hacked in two days ago," Lee said, bordering on lethargic. So un-Lee-like.

Mina raised her brows. "Am I going to have to pump you with a dose of Jump today?"

"Sorry." Lee rubbed his hands over his face. "I haven't

slept. But I did manage to break the code. About twenty minutes ago. And then, when I saw the drones here, I figured it was all time wasted. The minimum on a security visit would be to reset all the basic codes and passwords. For me to break them again, we'd have to get in like we did yesterday, close enough to pull up a direct signal. I can admit we got lucky yesterday. I don't see me coming up with any more correct passwords. And after today, I'm not scheduled to come back here as a delivery tech. We're basically out of time."

Lee was correct on all counts.

Mina shifted in a circle, fisting her hands. In her frustration, she glanced up and met Grigg's gaze across the delivery area. He was openly assessing her. There was no question he knew she was an agent of some kind and that she was working with Lee. He'd probably realized they'd hit the proverbial graphene wall when he'd seen the private drones himself.

Mina's director had given her an order not to engage, but McAllister also hadn't known that Four Story would be here. It was either act—and find out what this possible agent knew—or stand back and let the op fail. Even if she was granted extended time here as a gardener, doing it without Lee was not an option. As much as Mina hated to admit it, she needed the rookie. With Four Story's security prowess and its access to military upgrades, she wouldn't be able to do this on her own.

Mina made up her mind.

She nodded to Grigg, giving him a decisive head bob

toward the exit as she leaned over to whisper to Lee, "Stay here and cover for me. If anybody asks, I went to check on the black spot." Mina took the soap mixture she'd prepared out of her smock pocket, then headed briskly out of the delivery area like she was on a mission.

Which she was.

There was no question Grigg would rendezvous with her. She just had to pick a place for them to talk privately. Since they shared the same gardening tier, in front of the spotted roses was her best bet. After all, fellow gardeners should be able to chat about black spot without arousing too much suspicion.

Mina made her way around to the other side of the residence, near the passageway she'd entered yesterday. She wanted to get a look around to see if security people were lingering outside. She settled in front of the rosebushes she'd been working on yesterday, fingering the leaves, dabbing some of her solution on them, using her fingers to rub it in. She almost felt like a real gardener. Almost.

She'd been at it for less than two minutes when Grigg squatted beside her.

"Busy day today." His voice was low.

"Seems like it."

"Nice soap you have there."

"Hope it works."

"There's been some talk."

Mina quirked an eyebrow, but kept her gaze firmly on the plant in front of her. Grigg was letting her know he had ears on the inside. "A short visit with Dad?"

"Not exactly." Grigg picked up the bottle Mina had set next to her and placed it in her hand, along with a tiny sensor node. Mina had never seen one so tiny. It was smaller than a grain of rice and made of some kind of flexi crystalline.

Grigg stood and walked away.

Mina glanced around. When she was satisfied nobody was watching, she inserted the device into her ear. It was small, but it was sticky and stayed put. Immediately, she heard murmuring that sounded far away and somewhat tinny. She could just make out what was being said.

"...the delivery was compromised," a gruff male voice said. It verged on angry, definitely frustrated.

"It wasn't compromised. It arrived on time, right where it was supposed to." This voice had an older, wiser cadence and sounded poised, like the audio Lee had used yesterday, but she couldn't be sure. She needed more.

An echoing sound followed, like something had been kicked. "It doesn't matter if it arrived! The feds found it. They had a heads-up. They were practically waiting for us at the docks. That kind of stuff can get us locked in a box for a long time. This entire operation is churning down the damn grinder, and there's nothing we can do to stop it."

"Calm down, Frankie," the poised voice advised. Definitely the same voice Lee had copied onto her mini. So the angry guy was Frankie, and the older guy was Tedesco. "I'm purging the system tonight, and once I do, all traces and digiprints will be wiped clean. But along with that, we lose everything. It can't be helped. Jordan is coming to facilitate. A purge of this size needs a professional and a guarantee that nothing can be traced back to us once it's gone."

The name Jordan didn't chime any thought clouds. Mina made a mental note of it. If she and Lee didn't get that data today, it was looking like there would be no evidence left. Damn.

"What are you waiting for? Why don't you do it right now?" Frankie was playing the part of petulant child like a pro. That fit.

A heavy sigh came first, then, "I have a meeting this afternoon I can't miss. It's with a screen company I've been trying to partner with for years. I have Jordan scheduled for this evening. Don't worry about it. Just look at the sim system. Like I told you, it's glitching again. It welcomed me this morning and announced it was time to reconfigure, but I haven't been inside in two days. I want it checked and cleared." Tedesco's voice held an edge. Maybe a warning. Maybe a caution. Hard to tell, since she'd never met the man. But it seemed Frankie had gotten his hard edge from someone.

"It glitches because you refuse to use the settings the way they were designed," Frankie snapped. "It's military grade, and you treat it like a tot fiddling with a basic program. If it says you need to reconfigure, then you need to reconfigure. You must've gone in and forgot."

"I was not in my inner office."

"It's an easy thing to solve." Shuffling sounded. "All you have to do is ask the system for a replay. It'll tell you everything you need to know."

"I did. Nothing came up."

Whew. That meant Mina wasn't on vid, and the system hadn't caught her voice signature.

"Then do it again."

Footsteps sounded. Their voices faded as they presumably moved to another room. Whatever mic Grigg had planted was probably located outside the residence with a limited range.

Mina stood, soap in hand.

It was time to come up with a new plan.

Chapter 13

THE DELIVERY AREA buzzed with gardeners. Lee glanced at Mina as she walked in, his eyes still baggy and rimmed dark. Mina headed over to a table and picked up a pot, indicating with a slight nod that he should join her. She made her way to another table, and just as she arrived, Cots intercepted her.

"I want you to focus on the black spot today," the head gardener lectured. "Then I want you in charge of the bush decoration around the new trees. That should happen sometime this afternoon—"

"Got it!" Mina shrilled, with the sole purpose of cutting him off. "I'm on it. I just have to go drop this off first." She held the greenery in her arms.

He glanced at it and gave her a quizzical expression. "What are you doing with a pepper plant?"

"Um." Mina tried to think of what she was doing with a pepper plant. "Andy said he needed this, so I told him I'd drop it off."

"We're not planting vegetables until later this week. I'll have a talk with Andy." He glanced around. "Where is he, by the way? I haven't seen him since we arrived." Mina knew Andy was tucked away somewhere, licking his wounds. She hoped he stayed gone. Cots nodded. "Set that on the table and come with me." He took off.

Mina made a garbled sound in the back of her throat. Frankie and Tedesco had come back into range of the mic, and she could barely hear what they were saying. She took a few deliberate steps in the opposite direction the manic gardener had gone and set the plant down, straining to hear what was going on inside the residence.

Lee set his pot next to hers, looking like he might speak.

She held up a finger.

"See?" Tedesco was saying. "That proves I wasn't in here."

"That's your voice," Frankie argued. "You asked the doors to open, then you asked them to shut."

"No. I didn't." The older man's tone was resolute. Mina had no idea who was going to win this argument, but she was determined to hear the outcome. This next part would be crucial. Either Frankie believed his dad, or he didn't. If he believed him, there was no getting back in there. They would ramp up security, assuming it'd been tampered with. If Frankie didn't believe his dad, maybe they would just reset the passwords, and she would overhear what choices they decided on.

Lee looked lost.

She gestured to the left side of her head. He didn't get

it. Mina glanced over, relieved to see that Cots had been sucked into an animated conversation with another gardener. That would buy her some time.

Frankie said, "That was your voice using the correct passwords."

"I'm telling you I wasn't in there. I've had engagements all week. Since the shipping incident"—a nice way to sum up being caught with enough chemis to create several hive bombs—"I've been making arrangements to wipe our association. It's taken all of my time."

Cots looked about done with his conversation, his hawkish nose turning toward Mina. She grabbed on to Lee's shirt and leaned forward, murmuring, "Tell him I went to the waste room." Without explanation, she darted in that direction.

Tedesco said something, but she missed it as she ducked inside the small space that held a simple composting toilet and a small basin.

Mina leaned against the door, exhaling, trying to focus.

"Your program is faulty, then," Tedesco accused his son. "This proves it. I should've gone with Bower & Majors."

Their argument ratcheted up. This kind of interaction seemed standard for them. They were communicating the way a spoiled child and a too-rich-for-his-own-good father would.

"If you'd used Bower, the PPF would be here weekly," Frankie shouted. "You forget passwords more often than a bot with circuit failure!"

"I may forget passwords, but I don't forget where I was and where I wasn't. And I wasn't in there."

After a decent pause, Frankie grudgingly admitted, "There's a possibility there's some bad wiring. Kenny is checking now. We'll do a standard changeup, including passwords and commands. What do you want this time?" The sound of a cuff beeping cut in, followed by Frankie saying, "That's—"

Loud pounding—enough to place a dent in titanium—came from outside the waste room door. "Is someone in there?" Doreen called. "My bladder is about to burst!"

Mina held her breath.

Frankie was saying, "I need to get back to him. He might have…"

The rest was drowned out as Doreen pounded and shouted some more. "Is anyone in there?"

Good *grief.* "It's Marilyn," Mina called. "I'll be out in a sec." For good measure, she turned on the faucet.

Doreen called, "Sorry, sweetie! Take your time. But not too long, because, you know, teeny bladder out here. I have no idea why the currency king doesn't have more than two waste rooms. Sheesh! He really should install more, as there are so many of us…" she droned on.

Mina was only able to pick up a few words Tedesco was saying over Doreen's prattle. "Yes…Jordan…here… data…shipment."

Damn.

Mina shut the faucet off and yanked the door open.

Doreen barreled into the tiny space, thanking Mina for finishing quickly as Mina eased herself out and headed back to Lee. It appeared that Cots had departed the area, which was a huge relief.

"What's going on?" Lee leaned in, his expression full of confusion. "I feel like I'm missing something."

Mina grabbed his elbow, steering him. "You are. Come with me."

"But Cots said we needed to check in with him—"

Mina ignored the rookie, trying to hear Frankie and Tedesco, but their voices began to ebb again.

Once they were out of the delivery area, Mina whispered, "I met with Grigg. He mic'd a small area, likely outside the front windows, and lent me an ear node. Tedesco called Frankie over today because his residence said he needed a reconfig. He insisted he hasn't been in his inner office in a while, so he shouldn't need one. They're going to change passwords." Mina was distracted. She ran a hand through her hair and cursed. Crappy faux hair. "He mentioned someone named Jordan, who is coming over to help wipe the system tonight. Time is running out, and we're not getting inside with everyone there. We need another plan."

"Jordan Maybach?"

That name seemed familiar, but Mina couldn't place it. "They didn't specify a surname, only that he's coming to purge the system." She kept them moving, starting up the tiers.

Lee's brow crinkled. "Jordan Maybach is a superhacker. If anyone can purge a complicated system in a single evening, he can. People hire him when they want nothing but a dust trail left behind. They call him The Specter. He's in and out. The cleanest of clean." The awe was clear. Lee held this Jordan guy in the highest esteem.

"Have you met this infamous hacker in person?"

"Once," Lee admitted. "By accident. I thought he was just another gamer at this competition we were at. But he said something that gave him away. A particular phrase he always uses on the boards. I'm pretty sure I was the only one who figured it out. He noticed me checking him out and gave me a sign. You know." Lee flicked his head to the side and jutted his chin out, ending with a wink.

Got it. Subtle. Nonverbal geek-speak for *I see you see me.*

"Can you make this guy in a lineup?"

"Of course." Lee was offended. "He had a very distinct look then. Bright violet hair and a goatee dyed the same color. If Jordan's going on-site, Tedesco must be paying him a crazy amount of currency. There are rumors Jordan clears millions every year. He's been above borrows since he was twelve. He's the epitome of success to hackers everywhere."

"*Hmm.*" Mina pondered this new information. Some of the gardeners were beginning to stream out of the delivery area. She and Lee hadn't gone far enough. They stood on the top tier, but they were too close to where the planting was taking place. As she was trying to decide what to do, Mina spotted movement over Lee's shoulder in the distance. She stilled, then grabbed Lee and pivoted him around. "Do you see that?"

"See what?"

"Crap."

"Is that...Andy?" Lee shifted over a few steps to get a better view. "What's he doing? He has a compucase. Why is he hiding between the private transpo units?"

"Come on." Mina was already moving. "We have to stop him."

"Stop him?" A confused Lee hurried after her.

"Andy isn't a gardener."

"He's not?"

"No. He's a plant." Something Mina should've figured out a long time ago.

Damn. This was going to cost her.

Chapter 14

"Are you sure?" Lee asked as he scrambled behind her. "Maybe he's researching vegetables and, you know, how to grow rooties better."

Mina didn't comment as she made her way down the tiers. They had to be careful not to move too quickly. She didn't want to arouse suspicion in the other gardeners as they exited the area, and they were going to have to be particularly covert when they passed in front of the main residence windows. There was no other way to gain access to the private landing pad than to go past the windows, as far as she knew.

If Andy the Super Asshole rendezvoused with Frankie, it would be bad. Everything could come crashing down.

"Trust me, I know. We had a thing," Mina finally muttered when they were well away from the other gardeners. Though it hadn't been the kind of *thing* Andy had been hoping for. *Dickwad.* "I also heard a call come in to Frankie's cuff while I was listening in. He told his father he had to talk to someone. I'm guessing it's Andy. Or Placido. Whatever the hell his name is." It was probably something more like Monty or Pete. Why? Because that sounded appropriate for a weasel. And what other reason was there for a gardener to be crouched between two drones with a compucase on his lap, head down, trying not to be seen? "We're just lucky Frankie is taking time to argue with his father instead of meet up with his plant."

It was going to be tricky to slip Andy out of the penthouse of a four-hundred-story lux mega undetected. Mina would tackle that when the time came. She couldn't afford to focus on her huge tactical error of overlooking a possible hired henchman.

She would have to eat that crap sandwich later.

For now, she had to set her brain to fixing all the broken pieces that her op had become before they were jettisoned into space, ensuring that the man responsible for delivering and possibly manufacturing chemi weapons and selling them to bad guys would go free instead of being locked in a box where he belonged.

"He seems a little dense to be a hired thug." Lee wasn't wrong. "He could still be doing some research," Lee offered. "Or he's hiding from Cots. That seems more plausible."

"The only research he's doing is trying to figure out who the hell Marilyn Leonard is and how many problems she will cause him." Luckily, he wasn't going to find anything. Mina stopped right before the windows and crouched down. She uprooted a leafy plant, root tendrils and all, in one pull. Lee sputtered his objections beside her. "Haul that one up," she ordered, gesturing to the one next to it. "We're going to walk by these windows like a pair of gardeners with a place to be. Gardeners need plants. If anyone asks, we're rehoming these." Or replanting. Whatever.

"We can't just yank them out of the ground—"

"Lee," Mina growled, "you're wasting valuable time. Tedesco is keeping his son engaged at the moment, but Frankie could be on his way to rendezvous with Andy right now, so uproot the greenery already."

Lee reached down and grasped the leafy base. It took him a few tugs to pull it out. The root bulb was enormous. He wrapped it in his arms as best he could while glaring at Mina.

"Stop whining and let's go. The plants will be fine. The other plant, not so much." Mina pretended to engage Lee in animated conversation, ignoring the plethora of dirt chunks dropping like bombs as they trotted across the open expanse. "Once we clear the windows, ditch the green. Cots will find them at some point and give them a new home. I remember seeing a winding path midway up the west-facing side. I believe that's how we access the private pad. Tedesco likes things tucked out of sight, so it makes the most sense."

They placed the uprooted plants under a small lemon tree heavily laden with yellow fruit, brushing themselves off, dirt flying everywhere.

"What are you planning to do with him once we get there?" Lee asked as he followed Mina.

A valid question. One Mina didn't have an answer for. Yet.

"I'm still brainstorming. Original ideas are welcome." Mina went through options as they moved up the tiers once again. "We could tie him up and leave him until the op is over. But if he gets free, he wrecks everything. We can knock him out, but when he comes to, it'll be an issue. It sucks not having a craft when you need one."

"We could stick him on one of the delivery drones," Lee suggested.

"That would work if they weren't wide open. There's no place to hide a body on one of those things." Mina held up her hand as they approached a break in the foliage. A short path opened up in front of them. "You said yesterday that this landing pad leads to a main entrance downstairs."

"Yes. The front entrance."

Mina eased along the path, crouching low, thankful there weren't any other gardeners around. They were lucky Tedesco indulged in overabundance. The kiloton of trees and shrubs planted around the pad cloaked it well.

She tugged a small stunner out of one of her smock pockets. It was no bigger than her pinkie finger and could knock someone out for a minute or two with a short burst to the nervous system. Unlike the maxi Lee had used during their last op, which could kill somebody if the stream was concentrated for a prolonged amount of time. This stunner had only enough charge to bring Andy down for a few minutes at a time until Mina figured out what to do with him.

At the moment, the plant was hidden between the drones. Not very smart for a criminal.

Or maybe just smart enough.

A shout sounded behind her as Lee lost his balance and tumbled into the shrubbery. Mina didn't waste any time, darting toward the closest drone, staying well out of sight.

Andy sprang from his hiding spot a millisecond later, his compucase still in his hands, his back to Mina. As he went in one direction to investigate what had happened to the oh-so-green rookie, who was now tangled in branches, Mina moved in the opposite.

Maybe Lee was a genius.

Probably not.

"What are you doing here?" Andy sneered. He already thought Lee was an incompetent delivery tech, so this fit his narrative.

So maybe genius after all?

Closing her eyes, Mina willed some encouraging words into the ether for Lee. The rookie needed to come up with something that would keep Andy occupied for the next thirty seconds.

All she needed was thirty. Maybe less.

"Cots sent me to check on the hydros," Lee replied smoothly as Mina heard him clap the dirt off his clothing.

Hydros? Mina took a quick glance around. There were aquatic plants up here? It was the first she was hearing about it.

"Cots wouldn't know his way around a hydro-garden if he'd been born underwater." Andy's tone was caustic and very ungardenerlike. Where was the laid-back guy who loved his rooties? It seemed Andy wasn't a Nutri Pure at all. He was probably a DP—a Devout Printee—and eating all those carrots day after day was a torment to his black, nutri-free soul. Mina hoped so. "Tedesco hires aquaners for that." Aquatic gardeners.

Lee was taking his time and being loud about it. *Sweet, Lee.* Mina slipped closer.

"Yeah. Those guys put some items on the list for delivery." Lee's tone was confident. *Keep going, Lee.* "I came up to see if there was room for them."

"Of course there's room, it's *water*." Apparently, Andy was a sneerer. "Just get the hell out of here. And if Cots asks, I'm gone. Tell him I hitched a ride out with these guys." He shot a thumb at one of the drones. "They're friends of mine, and I'm quitting this lame-ass gig as of right now."

He wasn't quitting. He was being forcibly ousted. *Big difference.*

Mina eased up behind the hired plant, stunner in hand. Andy was so busy with Lee, he didn't hear her approach. She tapped him on the shoulder, wanting to see his face before he went down. As he turned, she stuck the device into a smooth groove on his neck and took moderate pleasure watching him go down, mouth gaping in shock.

As he fell, she caught his compucase one-handed and thrust it at Lee as the rookie moved forward. Mina grabbed e-restraints out of another pocket and rolled Andy over with her foot.

"We have to get him secure and out of here immediately. Where's the hydro-garden?"

"Behind those venting units." Lee gestured. "It's camouflaged with a green sunshade to filter out the sunlight. Too many direct rays and everything fries."

"It's good you know the schematics." The sunshade was why Mina hadn't detected it from the sky. "Good thinking, by the way. Perfect reason to be up here." The only reason.

"Sorry, I fell," Lee started. "I didn't see—"

Mina waved a hand. It was becoming a thing with him. "You turned the situation around. That's all that matters. It worked. Our focus now is getting Andy away from here. I'm assuming you can hack into his computer and see what he was working on?" There was no doubt in Mina's mind that Andy was a criminal. He'd already harassed her, and on those grounds alone, she could haul him into headquarters. It would be nice to have solid evidence of his villainous behavior regarding the op before she did, however. If the man was actually innocent of being Frankie's plant, then this had the potential to circle back on her. Agents couldn't take a civilian out for no reason, much less stun him into unconsciousness. Especially more than once, which was her plan. But if he was standing in her way of saving innocents from chemi warfare, she was well within her duties to take him out for the time being.

Lee made a *pfft* sound, not bothering to answer if he could hack into the compucase.

They each grabbed one end of Andy and half dragged,

half carried him toward the only place that would give them cover up here.

"A few windows on the residence face the hydro-garden. At least it was spec'd for windows," Lee said. "Stay to the east. We should be out of sight there."

"Got it." The water feature was fairly large and had ample space to allow them to keep out of the way on the far side. An assortment of water lilies and large grasses dotted the water's surface. Speckled fish glided through edible freshwater seaweed and bushy cottontail reeds.

Mina stopped between two medium-sized trees and unceremoniously dropped her grip on Andy. The presumed criminal began to moan. The only thing to do was keep stunning him until she could figure out a workable solution. But Mina could use the stunner only about five times before possibly damaging his internal organs.

Inasmuch as she disliked the guy, she wouldn't put his organs at risk.

She needed time to think, so she stuck the stunner against his neck and depressed the button. He quieted. His cuff gave off a low humming tone in small, quiet bursts.

Mina picked up his wrist. One word blinked across the display.

Boss.

That had to be Frankie. They had to figure out a way to get Andy out of here quickly. Or at least down and out for the rest of the day. Not only that, McAllister had to be informed of what was happening as soon as humanly possible. This op had changed considerably. Mina didn't want to think about how badly she'd bungled it. Communication while they were still up here was risky. If she used Tedesco's signal, it could be tracked or even intercepted.

Mina eyed Andy's compucase, now settled on Lee's lap. "Can you configure a cloaked signal boost out of that thing? We need to report to headquarters. McAllister needs to know what's going on."

Lee glanced up, his eyes already glazed over, like they got when he was concentrating. "That's a possibility, but not a strong probability. This comp is probably linked into Tedesco's network already. I'll know for sure momentarily." He began to peck at the keyboard, his head back down.

Mina needed a solution.

She turned in a circle. Too bad Andy wasn't a bot. She could just use the hyppie trick on him. That had worked well on this op once already.

Voices erupted near the landing pad. Mina immediately crouched down. One of the voices belonged to Frankie, and he was agitated.

"I don't care. Just find him," Frankie ordered. "He's only supposed to contact me if something is going down. Tell him to get in touch immediately. And it better not be about the job being boring again. Once you're finished, head back inside and complete the reconfig. Something is starting to reek. I don't like it. Double the layers. I don't care if my father wants things lax. Time to fortify. I'm not spending the rest of my life in a box."

The rest of his life? Interesting.

Participating in the illegal shipping of hazardous materials across the planet would absolutely garner him time in a box. But not for *the rest of his life*. For that, he would have to commit murder in cold blood. And people who did bad deeds tended to know how long they'd be boxed if they got caught.

Something else was happening here.

That aside, with a full reconfig like he'd mentioned, there was no way Mina and Lee were getting into the residence again.

Mina shut her eyes, refraining from rubbing her temples. She wasn't ready to let this op fail. She had to act.

"Once you're in," she whispered, edging closer to Lee, "send a message to Frankie and let him know Andy was trying to get a hold of him because he quit. He's fed up with playing around in the dirt. That should stop any searching." And piss Frankie off. An angry Frankie would be more likely to make mistakes.

Surprisingly, one of the drones fired up, props spinning, sending lots of wind through the area. Since Frankie had ordered his crony to find Andy, Frankie was likely the one leaving. Maybe he had some errands to run or criminals to rendezvous with.

Mina grabbed Andy's ankles, tugging while hissing, "Put that down and help me move him under the screen, closer to the pond. We can't risk Frankie spotting us from the air."

They got Andy tucked away just as the drone ascended.

Andy began to moan. Mina had no choice but to stun him again.

Only two more left.

Mina spoke at the same time Lee did. "We're going to have to use Tedesco's signal—"

"Message sent to Frankie—"

A third voice chimed, "Looks like you two could use a lift out of here."

Chapter 15

GRIGG STOOD ON the other side of the pond, having accessed the area from a different direction. "Don't worry, he didn't see me." The big, bearded man gestured to the sky, where the props were already fading. Mina stood. Grigg nodded toward Andy, who was still out. "I figured that might be his fate today."

Mina glanced down and shrugged. "He's working for Frankie," she told Grigg. "Although I'd like to think I would've taken him down the same way if he'd tried to grope me again, I actually had to drop him so he couldn't contact his boss and expose the operation. Not just because he's an asshole. Well, he's both. But primary was to preserve the op and save lives."

Grigg nodded as he moved forward, his expression neutral. "I swiped some DNA off him a few weeks ago. He's done time for petty crime. Nothing major. But I wouldn't be surprised if there's a level or two more I couldn't access. My clearance doesn't reach that high.

Since he's been here, he hasn't done much more than screw around with his veg and scare a few women off the job with his shady moves. I made sure nothing happened while I was around, but I couldn't do more without blowing my cover."

Mina understood. She reached out to shake his hand as he came within range. "I'm Agent Kane. This is Agent Adams." She didn't specify their department, nor did he ask.

"Grigg Ivers," he said. "I'm a civilian consultant for a large government firm."

"Civilian?" That didn't fit with the narrative swirling around them at the moment.

"Officially, I'm a civilian," he answered carefully. "My department doesn't employ agents. They hire reps and consultants." He crossed his arms over his barrel of a chest.

Tricky.

Today, Grigg hadn't even bothered to don any gardening tools or gardening clothing. It was a wonder Cots hadn't had something to say about that or hadn't suspected that this huge, unsmocked guy might not be a gardener after all.

People saw what they wanted to see.

"So, by all official accounts," Grigg continued, "I'm a civilian who specializes in investigating sensitive matters."

"A privateer." Mina raised her eyebrows. "Licensed?" *Please let him be licensed.* If he wasn't, things could get sticky. Mina would have to include him in her official report, and a private citizen in possession of specialized sensor equipment she'd never seen before would be a red alert.

"Yes. Fully."

"Good." Andy began to moan. Mina glanced down. "I only have two stuns left. I'm going to have to use them wisely. You mentioned a way out?"

"I can summon a craft," he replied.

"How fast?" Mina asked.

"A tap of my cuff. Less than three minutes arrival time."

That meant he likely had a partner standing by within close range.

Even though they were on the same side, Mina couldn't share any sensitive intel with Grigg, especially because he'd designated himself a civilian.

"If you call in a drone, it'll be spotted, and questions will have to be answered. Agent Adams just used Andy's tech to alert Frankie that he quit and is no longer in the vicinity. But I'm uncertain if Frankie has relayed that to the guy who's searching for him." There was a lot to consider.

This op was officially compromised. All Mina could do was move forward. She wasn't getting into the residence, so there was no use playing gardener any longer. An idea began to form. She had to talk to McAllister first to get it all worked out. If she hadn't had time to spare before, she had zero now. Tedesco and Frankie were hurtling toward crisis mode faster than a mag-lev rocketing fric-free toward its station.

"We're going to play sick gardener," she announced.

"What's sick gardener?" Lee asked.

Grigg nodded. "Works for me."

"Can you get him over your shoulder?" Mina asked Grigg as she unclipped Andy's e-restraints. "Once we arrive in the delivery area, I'll do the talking." For Lee's benefit, she added, "We're basically going to commandeer one of the delivery drones. I'll direct Green Hair to fly us out. That's all we'll need."

"Are you sure—"

Mina silenced Lee with a single look.

Lee got the message, clamped his mouth shut, and busied himself helping Grigg lift Andy off the ground. The imperfect plant started to moan, so Mina stunned him again. The next one had to count.

"The biggest obstacle we're up against is Frankie's sidekick," Mina murmured. "If he's still looking for Andy, it might be a problem." The former vegetable gardener was limp as he went over Grigg's shoulder. "Frankie should call him off immediately, but the corrupt son might have other things on his mind."

Lee picked up Andy's compucase. "Wait. A message from Frankie just came in." He read, "'You can't quit, you little halfwit. The stuff I have on you means you stay in my employ until I say so. Get your ass to the meeting place. I want to talk to you. Forty-five minutes.'"

Mina quipped, "Well, somebody's going to be sadly disappointed that Andy has a previous engagement with a couple of federal agents."

"Frankie will be suspicious when he doesn't show up," Lee said.

Mina took the lead, followed by Grigg with Andy, then Lee. "Yes. But not more than he already is. Unless Tedesco stays home and decides to wipe everything right this moment, we still have a few hours to make this mission a success. I'm going to do everything in my power to ensure that happens." She asked Grigg, "Do you know how Tedesco enters and exits this place?"

"He usually has a craft pick him up and drop him on the landing pad up here. But sometimes he takes the tube down to a private hub on the fiftieth floor."

"Okay, then we'll assume he's still inside. That means we can't take Andy by the windows, so we're going to have to take the long way around." It was risky to carry Andy that far, but parading him where Tedesco could see them would be riskier.

Thankfully, it didn't take them long to make it around. Grigg was barely huffing with the effort. It paid to have a strongman around.

They turned the last corner before the delivery area and encountered a bunch of gardeners buzzing around doing their jobs of planting things. Mina slowed. Cots wasn't among them. Mina didn't see Frankie's henchman anywhere either. Good luck all around.

Grigg grunted as he rearranged Andy. "We go in full of purpose, no stopping."

"Agreed," Mina said.

They started moving toward the delivery area with intent and were just about to turn inside when an audible gasp sounded loudly in front of them.

Doreen ran forward, waving her arms, a frantic

expression on her face. "What happened? Oh, my goodness! Poor, poor Andy. Did he fall? What's wrong with him?" Her voice carried. People stopped what they were doing and moved closer. Not what the plan needed at the moment.

"He collapsed," Mina answered. "Grigg found him. We've got to get him to a medi-unit quickly."

"Collapsed from what?" Doreen asked, following close on their heels.

"Did he have an allergic reaction?" another gardener intoned.

"Is he bleeding?" someone else inquired.

As if that wasn't bad enough, Mina almost slammed into Cots as he hurriedly left what looked to have been a heated argument with Danbury of the green hair, judging by both their expressions.

Mina ignored the horticulturist altogether and purposefully addressed Danbury, the person in charge of their transpo out of here. "We need a craft immediately. This man requires medical attention. You can either pilot or let us do it. Either way, we're taking him out."

Danbury appeared relieved at the interruption. "Of course. Put him inside." He gestured to the closest drone.

A lot of people began talking at once, the eruption of voices rivaling a hot crowd at a sports arena. Cots' voice rose to the top. Naturally. "What's going on here? What's happened to him?"

Mina rounded on the tufted gardener, her face set. "He collapsed. We're working to ensure he gets medical attention as soon as possible."

Andy began to moan. Mina, with her stunner palmed, made as if she were checking his vitals as Grigg dutifully waited for her assessment. Andy quieted immediately. "We're not sure what happened. It could be heatstroke, an allergic reaction, or a heart condition." She turned so she could address the concerned crowd. "We'll give you a full report as soon as we have one. But right now, we need to get him out of here, or he could die." Her voice was authoritative, daring any of them to contradict her.

Not one of them uttered a word, including Cots, which was something.

They loaded Andy in, and Danbury lowered the door.

A second later, they were in the air.

"That was a total shitshow," Mina groaned as she ran tired hands over her face. Her fingers bumped over a nose and cheeks that weren't hers. She was beyond glad her ops didn't break down on a regular basis, because it was fairly depressing.

But she wasn't ready to admit defeat yet. She, Lee, Grigg, and a still-out-cold Andy were in the air. There was a chance they could still salvage this if they acted swiftly.

She made her way to the front where Danbury was piloting and placed a hand on his shoulder. "I need you to set down at Government One. Red X on the roof. They'll hold you there for a short time, ask you some questions, then you'll be free to go."

Danbury was utterly unfazed. "Okay. Cool."

Once they were out of range of The Mega's satellites, Mina engaged her cuff. "Op aborted. A single perpetrator and extras in tow. Landing home in five."

Less than ten seconds later, McAllister responded, "A recovery team will be waiting."

He didn't need to say more. His tone had said it all.

This excrement extravaganza was going to demand a reckoning.

Chapter 16

LEE'S PANIC, CLEARLY pronounced in his eyes and pursed lips, bounced between Mina and Director McAllister.

"You can do this," Mina assured the rookie. "As I've been explaining, this will work. And you're the perfect person to execute the new plan." The only one, in fact. "We pick up Jordan, bring him in, and you take his place. You and your new purple hair will then get to bust a big-time criminal, and Tedesco and his fecal stain of a son get put in boxes for a very long time. It's your chance to shine, Lee. It's what every agent dreams of." Mostly.

"What if you can't find Jordan?" Though he was still panicky, his eyes were a little less wild.

"I'm not going to find Jordan, you are," Mina said. "We have faith in your abilities to coax him out of his superhacker hole and to our side. You said you communicate with him regularly on the boards. He'll be readying for his big night. And I promise you, he'll want to cooperate once he hears his only other option is to sit in a box." Mina shrugged. "If he doesn't, he'll spend the next forty-eight in quiet seclusion—and that's only if we don't pin him with something else. Interfering with a criminal investigation is minimum five years. As for the op itself, we'll be in the residence below the penthouse with a full set of eyes and ears. You won't be alone. If there's any issue, we can send a team up in seconds. This is not a stretch job for you." Mina reminded him gently, "You'll be a hacker pretending to be a hacker. As far as ops go, this is about as on laser point as you can get."

Mina, Lee, and McAllister had been shut up in a conference room for almost an hour, going over specifics. This play was all they had left to net Tedesco.

Andy was in holding. Grigg had slipped out without giving them much information beyond what he'd told Mina. Danbury had been sent home with a gag order, and another agent was sent in his place as a new delivery tech with a story about Andy's miraculous recovery. Everything was moving along. They just had to secure this next piece before they ran out of time. Bringing Jordan in was key.

McAllister pushed his chair back and rose. "It's clear Tedesco is involved in something bigger than just an illegal shipping ring. With the presence of altered military tech and his own son worrying aloud about spending the rest of his life in a box, we have to assume bloodshed is involved. What is your trepidation on this, Agent Adams? As Agent Kane has pointed out, this is our last— and only—viable option to get inside the residence and procure what we need before all evidence is destroyed."

Lee's face flushed a deep red while he fiddled with his new cuff, running it in circles around his wrist. "It's not trepidation. Well, I guess maybe it is. It's just that..." He hesitated. "If I take over Jordan's job on this, I'll be labeled a zartlet...or worse."

"A zartlet?" Mina had never heard that word before. And what could be worse than a zartlet? "That sounds like something Eggie would make me for a bedtime snack. It can't be that bad."

"Yeah. It's not a bedtime treat." The rookie absently scratched the side of his face. "A zartlet is a hacker who breaks an oath. It's a big no-no. It's an acronym for zim-altered, rot-tasting, Linux-emulating tool. It's a nonsense saying for the most part, but every hacker knows what it means. If Jordan objects and lets anyone know I did this, I lose any and all standing in the hacking world. I become persona non grata. Hackers don't mess around. There are no second chances. They take their oath seriously, and they take it to the grave."

McAllister made a sound resembling a grunt, but didn't comment otherwise.

"Then we make sure Jordan doesn't know it's you who's impersonating him," Mina persisted.

Lee looked skeptical, but nodded. "That should be okay, then. Maybe."

Mina refrained from launching into the diatribe on the tip of her tongue about agent duties and how spies operated and that they could be pretty damn stealthy when they needed to be.

Before she could formulate her response, McAllister

said, "He's right to be worried. Agent Adams' connections within the hacking world are a valuable resource that warrants protecting. Not only are those contacts necessary for future ops, but safeguarding his standing and reputation was a stipulation of his joining this agency. In good faith, we cannot put Lee in a precarious position within the hacking community."

Mina refrained from tossing both eyebrows up, even though they were itching to get to astral heights. Instead, she glanced at Lee, impressed, nodding along.

The rookie had negotiated his place in the CIU. That took confidence. Not very many agents would be successful in that endeavor. Lee had been facing time in a box after being caught performing illegal activity to get a relative out of a hard borrow restriction, and his only real option had been to join the CIU. Under that kind of pressure, most people would agree to anything.

But it seemed, even though Lee had been on precarious footing, he'd managed to sway things in his favor.

Mina suggested, "Okay, then. How about we do it like this? Lee gives me the access codes to the sites Jordan frequents, and I inform the infamous hacker what's up. Jordan either agrees to cooperate on his own, or we go get him. I haven't participated in a good raid in a while, and with Art 783, we have the authority to hold him until at least tomorrow, which would keep him from compromising the op. To make the grab, we need a partial warrant, which should be easy enough to obtain. Once Jordan is safe and muted, you go in and do the job."

Mina nodded toward Lee, hopeful he would see solid reason soon.

"That won't work." Lee's expression was pained, his cuff on number eighty-three of the nervous turn cycles. "The sites are hyper voice-encrypted. They don't let just *anyone* in. We're hackers, not factory bots." He gave Mina a look like she should know better. Maybe she should.

"Okay, then I'll pretend I took you hostage. This isn't a hacking job anymore, Lee. It's a federal investigation. No one is going to think you're taking over a job meant for Jordan, including Jordan." Once the superhacker saw reason. Mina refrained from huffing. "There are literally a hundred ways we can navigate this to achieve the result we need, but we have to move forward, and getting Jordan to cooperate is imperative. We either convince him to cooperate, or we take him in. We'll work out the details as we go. Meet me at my residence, and we'll go from there." She glanced toward McAllister. "If that's okay with you. I have a plan brewing that would involve Agent Poston. I think my home works better than here. The environment needs to seem nonthreatening if we're going to convince Jordan to come to our side, which is my preference."

McAllister nodded. "That's fine. As long as Lee's credibility is protected, you have permission to proceed as you see fit, including using Agent Poston. Once you're finished negotiating with this hacker, dissolve your semiperm."

A holo band began to play full blast in Mina's head. *Hallelujah.*

"I don't want Jordan or any of the gardeners recognizing Marilyn Leonard for the foreseeable future. But I expect you to make yourself unrecognizable as Wilhelmina once you're done."

Mina refrained from actually lofting herself in the air. "Yes, *sir.*"

McAllister glanced at his cuff. "It's ten twenty-three. As far as I know, Tedesco has not canceled his meeting with our production crew, scheduled to go until eighteen hundred. Once we get Jordan Maybach here—*willingly*, if possible—we will secure a time for Lee to get his alteration to look like the superhacker. I'll have a team set up in the unit below Tedesco's by seventeen hundred." Their director settled his gaze on Lee. "The success of this mission rests firmly on you, Agent Adams. It's not optimal to have an op go into a free fall, but it happens. Operation parameters can and do change."

He was being generous. If Mina had suspected that Andy was a plant like she should've, things would not have slipped so far off course. They *could* have, but not as likely.

"If you can convince Franco Tedesco the Third that you are the renowned hacker Jordan Maybach," McAllister went on, "and subsequently airmeld any and all data to a government-secured satellite, I will see that you receive a commendation."

A commendation would fast-track the rookie's rank within the agency and would mean he would have access to more tech and receive more complex ops. It was a very generous offer.

"I have faith in you, Agent Adams," McAllister said. "This is not outside your knowledge base. It rests securely within your abilities. Remember that."

Lee looked queasy. Mina took pity on him. They all had to remember that this would be his first solo op, where the outcome was totally in his hands. She patted him on the back as they made their way to the door. "We'll be surveilling your every move. You'll be wearing an ear node, and either I or the director will be in full contact with you throughout the entire mission. You won't really be alone."

Lee nodded, resigned, the queasiness leaking out of him like helium seeping from a personal airfloat. "I can do this." His voice was determined. "Most civilians don't understand layered hacking anyway, so if I have a problem, Tedesco shouldn't pick up on it."

"That's the spirit." Mina gave him a clap on the shoulder. Then she turned to McAllister. "I'd like to do a quick one-on-one with Placido Delray before I leave, if that works." A DNA check had revealed the carrot-topped faux gardener's not-so-pretty past. Grigg had uncovered only the petty crimes, but Mina's access had gone deeper. The genial-looking man-child with a smattering of freckles across a slightly pointy nose had a background filled with illegal activity, including gross misdemeanors involving explosives, banned weapons, and transportation of stolen goods. Even her sanctioned high-ranking governmental search had come up against a few blocks that had yet to be eliminated. Someone with clout didn't want Placido's full history getting out to the masses, which was interesting.

McAllister nodded. "He's been with an agent for the last hour, but hasn't been forthcoming. I have little doubt you'll be able to get him to spill a few more necessary details."

Mina didn't doubt it either. The man loathed her now.

Placido Delray had been taken down by the very woman he'd tried to assault. Guys like that were nothing if not predictable.

"After I'm finished, I'll make a quick trip down to enhancements to pick up what I need to dissolve my alt. I'll let you know how it goes with Jordan." She told Lee, "Give me until noon. Come to my residence ready with whatever you need to access the hacker sites. We'll plan to have Jordan voluntarily in custody by thirteen hundred. That should give us enough time to finalize everything and get into our places. If Jordan fails to cooperate, I'll contact headquarters to have him picked up."

Lee nodded, his head in the game.

McAllister said, "Good work, Agent Kane. I'll have a team ready to apprehend the hacker if need be. Either way, we will proceed with the op as planned tonight. The DGS will be ecstatic to bring this criminal to justice. They've been trying to get something on Tedesco for nearly a dozen years. It'll certainly be a *story*."

Mina chuckled. "He's not in a box yet. I'm just glad we came up with an alternate plan. That doesn't always happen. And it's thanks to the rookie here." She tipped her fingers against her forehead and gave them both a quick salute as she walked out.

Placido Delray sat at a skinny metal table in a small white room, e-restrained hands clasped in front of him, a petulant look on his face. With a nod, Mina excused the agent who'd been interviewing him, taking a seat across from the criminal faux gardener.

She sat back, waiting for him to speak. She didn't have to wait long.

"I knew you were a tricky bitch the first time I saw you," he declared. "Prissy, rod-up-her-ass, reeking of biowaste."

Mina leaned forward. She wanted him riled, so she was going to speak his language. "I knew you were a sucker from the first moment I saw you, with your comically dyed hair and sappy-ass comments. You screamed 'shitty lay' with a heaping side of stupid."

His eyes hardened, a smirk lengthening on thin, pursed lips. "Oh, lady, you couldn't be more wrong." He pretended comfort, even though she could see he was tense as hell. "I'm the smartest person you've ever met, bar none. And an excellent lay. I'm a gymnast in the bedsheets. Women *sing* my praises." He shoved back in his chair with a thump, drumming his restrained hands on the table.

Mina sat back, crossing her legs, looking bored. "Doubt it. What you mistook for singing was probably laughter. And as far as smarts go, yours are somewhere at atomic level, residing in the bowels of the building waiting to be made into something useful. Honestly, intelligent people don't suck so bad at life. Intelligent people have fulfilling, meaningful existences. They achieve things." She tilted her head toward the ceiling, before bringing it back down and raising her hand. She ticked off fingers. "Unlike you, who got caught altering weapons." She touched her index finger. "Making bombs." Middle finger. "Distributing illegal pharma." Ring finger. "Concealing a deadly on your person." Pinkie. "And taking joy rides in other people's crafts." Back to index. "All before the age of thirteen. It goes downhill swiftly from there. Honestly, if I listed all your indiscretions, my hands would get tired." She leveled her gaze back on him, dropping her arms. "We opened your sealeds, because that's what government agents get to do. I have all the dirt, and it has absolutely nothing to do with gardening. Smart people *elude* the law. But here we are." She gave him a syrupy smile. "Brought in by a girl who knows exactly the kind of lay you'd be—*premature.*"

He sputtered for a moment, his expression shifting to rage before it abruptly changed to smug. He was following her leads nicely, proving his idiocy. "I haven't been in a box since I was seventeen. You've got nothing on me. You can't keep me here or hold me. What I did as a kid doesn't count. Juvie sealeds can't be used against me." He'd been studying up, but apparently not thoroughly enough.

"I've got your cuff. I've got your compucase. And I've got access to investigate them both. Do you know why?"

Placido pretended indifference, but he couldn't hide his creeping confusion. The dickweed really thought he was going to go free.

"You laid hands on my body. Sexual harassment is a very serious offense, thanks to the Assault Protection Act of 2099. Too bad for you, I'm a federal agent. With a sex-assault charge, I'm allowed to search, seize, and access records—"

Andy aka Placido shot up in his seat. "You can't prove I did anything! It's your word against mine." He jabbed his e-restrained hands into his chest. "I'm *innocent.*"

Mina reached into her pants pocket—she'd discarded her gardening outfit earlier—and pulled out the minicam she'd had pinned to her smock. She laid it on the table, settling a single finger on top of it. "Would you like me to play it back for you? There's a screen right behind me."

He sneered. Because they'd already established he was a sneerer.

"There's a lovely image of you groping my leg."

"I didn't touch bare skin."

"It doesn't need to be bare." She bent forward, pounding her fist onto the table. "It just needs to be *uninvited.* And it was. Because of that, you lose. You're already halfway into a box, and we get to search whatever we want. I think we're going to find lots of interesting stuff on your comp to accompany the groping charge, don't you think? Several years' worth? I don't know, you tell me." She sat back, crossing her arms.

"You don't have shit." Andy had paled considerably. "I...I don't have to tell you anything."

"No, you don't. But if you do, I might decide to make things a little easier on you. Even if that leaves a bad printed aftertaste in my mouth." Mina uncrossed her arms and leaned forward. "Boxes are zero fun. I'm sure you remember. Sterile white walls, no adornments, no screen time, nothing but a stripped-down place to sleep and a serviceable place to relieve yourself. Even your meals will be bland. Ultras on all the time, no sunlight, no exercise, no outside contacts." Boxes were like that to dissuade criminal behavior. Confined isolation coupled with sensory deprivation, or CISD. It had worked in the beginning, nearly twenty years ago, but crime had been on a steady incline over the past five years.

They sat in silence for a few moments.

Placido didn't offer up anything. Mina shrugged. Maybe he didn't have information she could use. There was a chance Frankie hadn't clued him in on any details. And if Andy, the carrot-topped gardener, didn't have anything to add to the Tedesco case, Mina was wasting her time.

"I don't have to grant you any favors," she told him. "We have everything we need to box you up." She indicated the minicam, scooting it around on the table. "My real reason for stopping by was to give you a big cosmic bon voyage. Honestly, it's too bad our blossoming relationship got off to such a gropy start. If you would've behaved yourself, I'm sure we could've shared a few blissful seconds together, that is, before I hurled my breakfast all over your moronic platoboots."

"Bullshit." Andy lunged out of his seat. He was quivering.

Maybe he had something of interest to share after all.

"I'm not bullshitting you." Some words from the past

were funny. Mina happened to like the word *bullshit.* What did bulls shit, anyway? Wasn't it just grass?

"You can't wait to cut a deal. You're practically salivating for it."

"I don't need a deal." Mina cocked her head.

"Haven't you been listening? I have you. I have access to all your tech. You'll pay for what you did, and we'll add time in the box for whatever bullshitty things we find on your comp. It doesn't even have to go to trial. No dealing is necessary."

He sneered yet again. "What I know isn't on my tech, you douche drone. It's all up here." He tapped a dirty fingernail against his temple. "You're a federal agent. You pretended to be a gardener so you could snoop around Tedesco's house. But I *know* what he did. I know all about the shipments. I know about the dead people. I know *lots* of stuff."

Dead people?

The reason why Frankie thought he'd spend the rest of his life in a box.

Andy stuck out his chin as he sat back in his seat like a cocky bastard with a secret. Mina guessed he was.

"That's not what I heard." Mina let that hang between them, knowing he wouldn't be able to resist the bait. Guppies were starving like that, always hunting for a filling morsel as they swam in circles.

"You heard nothing."

"I heard Frankie tell his pal that they never should've trusted you. That you were—what were his words again? Oh, yeah." She braced herself forward. "A loser who didn't know his carrot-orange ass from a crop of potatoes." Not exactly true, but sounded like something Frankie would say. "They're ready to cut you loose. You're disposable to them." Mina shifted her features to concern. "By your reaction, I take it you didn't know that. I thought you said you were *smart.*" She paused to allow Andy's brain to tick through the possible scenarios. "Big-time criminals need box guys. And guess what? You're it this time. Frankie can't *wait* to be rid of you. I wonder—as we speak—if they're loading up your comp with evidence of crimes you didn't even commit." She shrugged. "Whatever we find, we'll use. You'll be stuck in here long enough for them to gather all the evidence they need so they look perfectly innocent and you look guilty as hell—"

Andy didn't bother to conceal his fear or his anger. He sputtered for a good ten seconds before shouting, "I'm nobody's asshelmet! I know plenty. Nobody's going to lock me in a box for shit I didn't do!"

Mina arched a brow. *Okay, asshelmet, let's talk about dead people.* "Tell me what you know, and I'll make sure you only do your own time."

 Chapter 17

"YOU NEED TO project," Mina ordered. "Do it again, Lee. If I'm not convinced, Jordan won't be either. Right now, you sound like a child pleading with a NannyBot to release a treat. I promise you're not going to turn into a zartlet. Give me more decibels and add some quake to your voice so it sounds authentic, like you're really panicked."

"You don't *turn into* a zartlet," Lee grumbled. "You carry the name." He gave her a look. "Never mind."

"She's right," Kaylee agreed. "You have to sell it, rookie, or nobody's going to believe we two badasses took you hostage." She gestured between herself and Mina.

They'd settled on the hostage scenario since Lee needed to be physically present. Jordan would run his voice sig before answering, so there wasn't a better way on short notice.

"Twin agents on the warpath." Mina grinned. "I guess we have Perry to thank for this." Both Mina and Kaylee wore jet-black, skin-suctioning, high-sheen, syn-leather from head to toe. Mina had her gem laser hooked to her waist to add a little extra danger.

"Damn straight. Perry and Dutiful Duds," Kaylee said. "Jeni Crisfold is an artistic maven. I can't believe she pulled this off so fast. These syn suits are to die for. I'm so using mine again. Honestly, I'm scared of us."

"It's hilarious that civilians think government agents walk around looking like this on a daily basis. It's hardly a subtle vibe."

"Not exactly their fault," Kaylee said, adjusting the freshly added neon-orange hair streaks. Her eyes were rimmed in kohl, lips creamed a deep blood red. To finish off the look, her eyes were diffracted a clear, haunting ice blue. She played the role of kickass agent with aplomb. "I haven't seen a screencast or a viral vid in the last ten years that depicts agents as anything other than this." She flashed her hands down her front, hyperglo scarlet nails blinking. "Works in our favor. This is going to be fun. Almost makes me wish we could dress like this every day."

"Kind of hard to catch criminals when they see us coming from a hundred kilometers away," Mina said. "Last time I wore syn, I had a gritty op in the outskirts." In the outskirts, wearing clothing like this was necessary. It told everybody to back the hell off.

Lee's outfit was the exact opposite. He wore a pale, nondescript pair of comfort pants and a crumpled dull-colored shirt. His hair was even messier, and enhancements had been added under his eyes to make him look exhausted, along with a few black-and-blue marks dotted along his jawline.

Mina patted his shoulder. "Give it all you've got, Lee. Make us believe you're trying to help this guy. Veronica, start recording."

Lee cleared his throat and laid on the act. "This is a voice-print authentication request. Karmaseeker243 is asking for entrance onto holo45, board name Hot Hack 'n' Sack, code X372. Level XIII's or higher only. Message to admin is as follows: Hey, Jordan...I...I need you to contact me, stat. Something's going down tonight you don't want to be caught up in. I can't say more, but vid request back to Karmaseeker243 as soon as you can."

"Veronica, pause. Better," Mina told Lee, "but you need more intensity. There's not enough angst in your voice for Jordan to hit you back immediately. Sprinkle in more panic."

The rookie shook his head. "That's not how we do it. It's more chill than that. If I act panicked or give away too much, it won't sell. He'll be suspicious and think it's a dupe. This way, it's more believable. I'm sure he'll be curious enough to reach out."

Kaylee crossed her arms and tapped her foot, which was clad in a scissor-heel tangboot in shiny black. The perfect accompaniment to a syn bodysuit. "Yeah, hackers are suspicious by nature. I get that. Coming from Karmaseeker243, though, it's chill already, right?" She nipped at her bottom lip to keep from laughing. "He'll probably hit us back in no time."

Lee scowled. "I came up with that tag when I was ten. When you're a successful hacker, you keep your handle. It commands respect."

Kaylee stifled a snort. "So does that mean there's thousands more karmaseekers out there now? Instead of, like, just two hundred and forty-three?"

Mina ignored them both. "Veronica, play back the message, amp up the low tones, add vibrato."

Lee's voice came through the speakers, slightly enhanced. Once the recording was finished, Mina concluded, "Okay, that'll do. Once this is out in the ether, how long do you think it'll take the superhacker to respond?" Mina refrained from glancing at her cuff. They were running a bit late, but still had time to pull this off.

After Andy had finished spilling his guts, Mina had, in fact, arranged a deal for him. The gropy, criminal, faux gardener would get one to five tops in a box for his role in what might be one of the biggest ops Mina had ever been involved in.

They had a lot riding on this. Getting to Jordan was the first step.

"If I were him, I'd be nervous about tonight," Lee said. "I'm sure he did a deep dive on Franco Tedesco the Third, and that would've brought him to Frankie Four. Jordon knows what he's getting into, and if he gets caught, he knows he would land in a box for a long time. If I were him, I'd be on the boards with my eyes and ears out for anything that told me to abort. Not only do hackers keep our oaths, we protect each other. He'll get my message and follow up quickly."

"When he hits us back, we'll sell it. No worries," Kaylee assured them. "Agents are excellent actors. It's our job to pretend all day, every day. That and bring perps to their knees, cryin' like liddle tots." She shot a fisted hand into her palm, nails blinking. The act was pretty convincing. Along with the huge blaster knocking against her hip.

"Veronica, send recorded message as is to the board already stated," Mina ordered. "High priority on response, accept immediately, block outgoing vid until I say so." She leaned over and pulled a carbon-padded wrap over Lee's eyes. "The pinhole slits will allow you to see. Remember, we don't pull this down unless he insists. He might not remember what you look like. He only knows you as Karmaseeker243 on the boards. Hold your hands behind your back so it looks like we have you secured. You said he doesn't vid chat with anyone. Let's count on him being shy."

"He's not shy. He's extremely cautious," Lee mumbled. "That's how he's gotten so far without getting caught. There's only a handful of hacks on that board. He knows my voice sig. Even with the enhancements, it'll ring as me. He'll run it through a few times to make sure, but it won't take long for him—"

Veronica intoned, "Incoming chat request, audio only. Accepting now."

Mina's wall remained blank as a high voice, obviously altered, floated through her aural system. "Why'd you use my real name, dude? What's going down tonight?"

"Sorry to break proto, but it was necessary," Lee said. "The feds are going to be all over your job tonight. I needed to warn you."

"How do you know about my job?" A spark of anger reverberated through the room in a raspy sim-echoed falsetto.

"Jordan, man, you have to listen to what they say. If you do, things'll work in your favor. I swear on the same oath I swore as a hacker. If you don't, you're going to spend time in a box. Don't jump off." Lee added a nice bit of pleading. "Hear them out."

"Them *who?*" Jordan sounded ready to pop out. Someone had gotten into his space, knew about his job, and was threatening his way of life. Mina gave a silent prayer this would work. Without the hacker's cooperation, and absolute silence on his part, this op would fail, and Tedesco would go free.

Kaylee gave Mina a nod as she spoke. "This is Agent Sunny Ford," Kaylee all but growled. "I'm here with Agent Daisy Ford. We have Karmaseeker243 in our custody. He was forced to work with us through no fault of his own. I apologize, Mr. Maybach. It was the only way to do this. You're a hard man to track down."

"Talk." The word had been barely uttered.

"This is Agent Daisy Ford," Mina said. Aliases were a must with this hacker. Not that Jordan couldn't figure out who they were eventually. But for now, appearances mattered. If he agreed to vid chat and captured still images of Mina and Kaylee, he could do whatever he wanted with them. "First of all, I want to assure you there will be no action taken against you if you cooperate. I can send that immediately in digital capture to any address of your choice. Second, we know you've done your research. You're no dummy, Jordan. Just the opposite. Franco Tedesco the Third is involved in high crimes." Very high. "He's hired you to dispose of links to criminal activities by wiping his comps clean. If you were to expunge evidence like that, it would lead to a conviction that carries a sentence of five to ten under the Crimes and Deadlies Act of 2067."

"I don't know any Franco Tedesco the First or the Third. A guy named Keith Brown hired me to help him erase some old files. That's it. I'm not breaking any laws."

Mina grunted. "How much did Keith Brown agree to pay you?"

"I don't talk about my rate. That's private."

"I bet you don't." Kaylee snorted. "Especially not when that rate is in the million-world-currency-per-hour zone. Drop the front, Maybach. If you're stupid, you can show up at your extremely well-paid job of erasing some old files and get box time with the rest of them. Or you can opt out and save your skinny little ass and have a little fun while you're at it." Kaylee excelled at playing the pissy agent.

Mina went for smooth dealmaker. "How about we agree on something that's lucrative for all of us?"

Kaylee shot Mina a look, her precisely drawn brows arching into two high vees. They hadn't talked about making a deal with the hacker. After all, thanks to Lee, they would lock on to Jordan's physical location if he stayed on the line for more than six minutes.

They had the authority to pick him up, already stamped by a magistrate twenty minutes prior to the call. McAllister had a team waiting.

But Mina was excellent at reading people, even by their voices alone. The department didn't have the resources to get to this hacker fast enough, even if they had his location.

He had the ability to damage this op the moment he blinked off. They needed him happy. They needed him not only on board, but feeling like he was steering the spacecraft.

Mina was determined to make that happen.

"What can a couple government agents offer me that I can't get myself?" He snickered, which sounded funny coming through the voice alt he was using, like a sim cartoon character for four-year-olds.

Mina shook her head to cut Kaylee off before she began to speak. "We can't offer you as much currency as a crook like Tedesco," Mina told him, voice steady. "But we can offer you half your hourly rate, along with a few incentives. But those goodies only apply if you come in willingly. We have private transpo waiting. It's decked out in spec fashion and will fly you to a secure location, where you'll be treated like old-fashioned royalty until you're cleared to leave. The stipulation is you'll have no contact with the outside world, human or digi, and give no warnings once this meeting is over."

"What goodies?" Curiosity rang through, and she might've even heard his lips smack, though that could've been the voice alt.

"Passcoded access to select government sites for the term of one year. I don't have to spell it out for you, but that means the information you hack illegally will be legally yours for three hundred and sixty-five days."

Kaylee squeaked. Lee took in a quick breath.

Both knew Mina didn't have prior authorization to grant this hacker anything. And if he agreed, and those things fell through, he would seek retribution.

"As I told you before," Jordan squeaked, sounding like TinFoot Tooty, the friendly recycled drone from Mars. "I was hired by Keith Brown to delete some files. Why you're contacting me is a mystery. I have no idea who this Tedesco is. I haven't broken any laws."

"This isn't a sting," Kaylee said, her irritation clear. "Our offer stands, but it'll be gone in two. If you want a veri, flip to vid, and we'll give it to you." Kaylee fingered the blaster on her hip and triggered her holo badge from her cuff. Her name was altered to read Sunny Ford.

"You first," he dared.

He wasn't getting the first physical look. "We do it together," Mina ordered. "Full facial, Jordan. No hiding behind a screen. We'll know if it's you or not."

"Fine," he grumbled. "On three. One, two..."

Mina finished, "Three. Engage vid."

A pale young man, with limp purple hair brushed away from his face and a sparse goatee with barely enough whiskers to qualify as facial hair, stared back. He looked no more than seventeen or eighteen.

Key information Lee had omitted.

Mina and Kaylee stood front and center, arms crossed, holo badges out, twin bored expressions on their faces. Mina stood purposely in front of Lee, shifting back and forth a bit so the rookie could catch a glimpse of the hacker. Lee curled an index finger against his rumpled pant leg. It was Jordan.

Mina recognized excitement as it jumped into the superhacker's gaze. Badass female agents dressed in hip-hugging syn had achieved its goal. Jordan was more than interested—he was awed. Just what they were going for.

"I need to see badges. Come closer." He had eliminated the voice alt, though his own voice was close enough to a cartoon sim. How unfortunate for him.

Both Mina and Kaylee stepped forward. Mina commanded, "Enhance camera, middle quadrant, eighty percent."

Jordan exhaled in a rush.

Mina knew he'd seen their badges, as well as an up close and personal of their midsections. Out of camera view, Kaylee rolled her eyes. It seemed the superhacker didn't get out much.

"Got it," Jordan said with a quiver, followed by a quick cough.

"I have to ask, and this is standard procedure," Mina said. "How old are you?"

Jordan stiffened. "Shouldn't you have that intel, Agent Ford?"

Mina made a show of cocking her head. "Hackers can hack anything, including their official birth records. And you're supposed to be the best. If you're a minor, we have to do this a different way." Which would be hard.

Lee groaned.

The superhacker's face went dark, purple whiskers twitching. "I just passed my thirty-second year. I assure you that I make my own decisions and have for a very long time. I want everything you've offered me in writing in five, or there's no deal. Send it to quark1717 dot iamtheultimatehack1."

Jordan popped off the screen before Mina could come up with a soothing rebuttal.

"How was I supposed to know he's thirty-two?" she cried. "He looks like a child!"

Lee tugged down his blindfold. "He has a rare disease that inhibits growth and keeps him looking young. Or at least that's the gossip. He gets irate when asked about his age."

"And you didn't think that was necessary to share that piece of information ahead of time?" Mina pierced Lee with a look. "I offered him half a million world currency and access to official sites. That would not have worked if he was a minor. In fact, making deals like that with a minor could grant *me* time in a box." Mina growled. "Lee, you have to start thinking like an agent. We need every detail. All the time. You can't hold anything back."

Kaylee tapped her cuff. "Yeah, about that deal. I'm thinking the underage thing is the least of your problems here. The countdown is on. One hundred twenty-two seconds left. You better have your slickest sell-this-to-the-boss face on if you're going to pull this off. And can I just say? If you do, you're my heroine. That was some ballsy-ass workaround. It went nicely with your outfit." Kaylee gave Mina a saucy wink.

Mina placed her hands on her hips. "I'm ready. Veronica, contact Duncan McAllister, label it urgent."

Kaylee rubbed her hands together. "Oh, it's on."

Chapter 10

"Pickup is confirmed." Kaylee glanced up from her cuff. "To the sun, the stars, and the great cosmos above, how in the hell do you do it? You had McAllister agreeing to everything you wanted in under two minutes. You had it signed, sealed, and delivered in the next thirty seconds. Now this superhacker is on his way to a safe house, and this sting can roll. What in the *holy hellfire* is your secret?"

"There's no secret." Mina chuckled as she poured the rest of the purifiers and dissolvers into her soaker, which was already churning with piping-hot water. Big, glossy bubbles were rapidly accumulating. She swished her hand around, testing the temp. She was wrapped in a towel, and Kaylee, still wearing her syn-leather, was perched on the edge of the tub. Lee had gone to headquarters to receive his enhancements so he'd be convincing as the superhacker. "It had to be done. Jordan wouldn't've taken less. The deal had to be substantial."

"If I tried the same thing—offering something like that to a baby hacker who probably has purple pubes—there's no way McAllister would've approved it."

"Yes, he would've." Mina dropped her towel, sighing as she stepped into the eighty-nine-degree swirling water. She lowered herself in as big, fizzy bubbles lapped at the tops of her shoulders. "I can't wait to get this alt dissolved. My scalp is literally screaming for freedom. It's been trying to broker a deal with me since the gel cap went on, and I would've taken a lot less to get this off than what I offered Jordan."

Kaylee began to pace. "Back to the thing we're arguing about. I beg to differ. McAllister would not have said yes. You just negotiated one of the biggest deals I've ever heard secured by any agent in our agency. Half a million in real currency and access to secure government information—to a *hacker*, no less. That's unheard of. And you did it in under two, like I said." She spun to face Mina, a scissor heel clacking on the marble floor. "I *need* to know. Oh, Guru of Deals, tell me how it's done." She mocked steepling her hands and bowing her head. "Please impart your graceful wisdom upon me." She broke the steeple, waving her hands in front of her, wiggling fingers in Mina's general direction like she was casting a spell.

Mina giggled, then took a breath and slid under the water, arching her head from side to side. The effervescent bubbles tingled in her ears and on her face. The purifiers and dissolvers were supposed to be nontoxic, but at this point Mina would take toxic just to get rid of the alt.

Ten seconds later, she surfaced, taking in a breath as large hanks of fake hair began to slide off her scalp, bobbing on the surface of the water like a dissected, bloodless marmot. "It's going to take a few more dunks, but I can already feel the gel cracking." She brought her fingers up to massage the top of her head. "*Oooh, yeah. That's soooo* good." Pieces of rubbery skin cement peeled off, landing in the water with tiny splashes, popping bubbles left and right.

"Here, let me get this for you." Kaylee leaned over and plucked out a big chunk of hair with two fingers, rushing it over to Mina's vanity as it dripped water all over the floor. She dumped it in the sink. "Gross. I should've put it in the grinder. I'll let you deal with that later." She clapped her hands as she walked back to the tub, then placed them on her hips, scarlet hyperglo still blinking. "I'm not letting this rest, no matter how much you dodge. Have you met me? Arranging that deal was nothing short of a miracle, and I want to know how you did it. Best friends don't keep sweet tactics like that from each other. They share so others can benefit from their knowledge."

"It wasn't a miracle." Mina sighed. "McAllister didn't have a choice, and neither did I. If Jordan hadn't come willingly, the op would've been compromised, and Tedesco would've gone free."

"Yeah, maybe. But that's a hell of a lot of currency and privileged government information to give away to bring down a shipping ring. I understand chemis were involved, and really big hive bombs could blow up at some point, maybe, but it doesn't add up. I need this to add the hell up, and I'm getting cranky while I wait."

Mina ducked under the water for another few seconds. She surfaced, feeling even better, her scalp fully free of binders, her real hair streaming down over her shoulders. "You're right, it doesn't add up. And the reason is I haven't shared all the info with you. When you arrived, we focused on Lee, and the rookie doesn't know either. I didn't want him more nervous than he already is. The truth is, Tedesco isn't only involved in shipping illegal goods. I found out, almost by accident, he's involved with Veritus."

He could *be* Veritus. But that was speculation at this point.

"Veritus?" Kaylee's mouth tumbled open. "Are you shitting me? The murderous crime ring *Veritus*? The ones responsible for the mass killing last year in the Southern Hemisphere, among countless others?" Kaylee spun around, her hair fanning out like a ballerina in midspin. This is the way Kaylee processed information. Movement. "It's been impossible to get any intel on them in forever. How in the cosmos did you find out?"

"The bad guys installed a plant among the gardeners. The low-IQ felon tried to feel me up, so I protested— physically. Then I told him I was going to test his strands. He panicked. I found him trying to communicate with Frankie, Tedesco's son, behind a couple of drones, so I took him in for questioning." Mina refrained from summarizing the entire shitshow. "I don't think he was planning on spilling, but I convinced him that Frankie was about to drop all the blame on him for what's been going down. He believed me. I guess he figured he'd be fingered for mass murder, not just the helping-out-with-the-chemi stuff. I've never heard anyone talk so fast in my life." Andy had even shed a couple of tears at the end.

It'd been pathetic, really.

"Well, then." Kaylee took in some air and held it, puffing out her cheeks. Then she exhaled. "I think that was a pretty good deal to catch a ring of serial murderers."

Not much was known about Veritus other than it was a large criminal ring known for killing for financial gain. Their signature method was noxious gas. Deaths were painful and violent. There'd been widespread panic for many years and pressure all the way from the top to track these guys down, but they'd evaded capture. Until now.

"Samesies," Mina said. "And just so you know, I didn't have prior approval to authorize the deal. But McAllister and I did bounce around a few what-ifs. I didn't go in cold. I hope that makes you feel better."

"It does. You're just so damn smooth. It's hard to compete sometimes."

"We are not in competition." Mina swished her head back and forth, luxuriating in the feeling of her own hair, clean and free. "We both do the same job."

"The hell we do." Kaylee stamped her foot. A clack exploded in the air. Those boots were perfect for accentuating points. "Great agents get primo ops. So-so agents get shitty ops. I want top-of-the-line ops."

"You have nothing to worry about, Agent Poston. You're a badass agent. You get great ops," Mina declared. "Hold that thought for a second." She slipped under the water again. It was just too delicious.

When Mina surfaced, Kaylee made a gagging noise. "*Ew.* Your nose just slid down your face. I am *not* picking that up."

"Don't you mean *your* nose?" Mina joked as she scooped up the finely crafted polymer skin creation and set it on the edge of her soaker.

"Jesus." Kaylee shied away from it. "I'm going to have a talk with Perry. No more making agents look like me. It's creepy."

"It is. Though I thoroughly enjoyed our little charade posing as the Ford twins."

"Yeah, okay, that was fun. I'll tell Perry you're the only one who gets the Kaylee treatment from now on. I'll be firm, yet gentle."

"Hah. Gentle doesn't flow through your helix strands."

"Very funny—"

Veronica intoned, "Incoming physical delivery. DNA, retinal, and voice authorization required."

Kaylee's perfectly sculpted eyebrows rose into their two perfect vees. "DNA, retinal, *and* voice. I'm pretty sure I've never had a package delivered that needed that much authentication. Don't tell me it's something involved with Veritus."

Mina scrambled out of the soaker, reaching for her wrap. "No, not Veritus. It's something else," she hedged.

"'Something else' is not an answer," Kaylee accused, following Mina down the hallway, scissor heels reverberating as they hurried along.

Mina was dripping but fully covered a minute later when she opened the door to the delivery bot. She completed the three levels of authentication and was given a small, black box. She brought it in and set it on the counter.

They both stared at it.

"Are you going to tell me what it is?" Kaylee asked. "Or are we going to keep eyeballing it like it's stuffed with priceless crater stones from Mars?"

"It's from Vince."

Kaylee made a grab for it. Mina reached out to stop her.

"Hey!" Kaylee complained. "If it's from Vince, then it might be *actual* gemstones. Let's see, shall we?"

Mina shook her head, picking up the box and turning it over. It looked bland and harmless. "It's a device encoded with Vince's current location. If anything happens to him, I'm supposed to deliver it to Chaz Burquist."

"Burquist? The head guy of the International Judicial Committee? *That* Burquist?"

"The very one."

"Well, that's...complicated." Kaylee's forehead creased. "What else did Vince the Prince have to say?"

"Not much."

"So by giving you this, he's letting you know he's up to his ass in trouble. Can the colonel-in-arms of the French

Protectorate actually be in need of outside help? I mean, the Protectorate is well connected. As far as smarts go, that group is up there. Sneaky, too. Why you? He must have important friends that can get to Chaz fairly easily." She gasped, reaching out to clutch Mina's forearm, curling her fingers and pulling. "Does he know you're an agent?" Instantly, her expression morphed to pissy. "Is he playing you? If he is, he's off the damn list. I don't care if he's an international heartthrob with glossy black hair and big, beautiful lips. He's off. The. List."

"Honestly, I can't tell if he's playing me, and that's a huge problem. I make my living off reading people. And his lips are completely normal. See for yourself." Mina ordered, "Veronica, play back the vid chat Vincent Kramer and I had last night. Include my audio. Living room screen. Sixty percent."

As the vid began to play, Mina kept her eye on her fellow agent and best friend, assessing her reaction.

At the end of the replay, Mina heard her own voice. *"You can't expect me to sit here and worry about you. I'm not asking you to divulge your secrets, Vince. I know what you do for a living. Your job is risky. But you can't ask me to wait for days, unsure if I should deliver your encoded message to Chaz or not. It can be a one-word message. Safe. Or alive. Set it to auto and punch a button. I don't care what you do, but make it happen."*

"Fine. I'll make it work. Thank you."

"You're welcome."

"I'll be in touch tomorrow at this time. I have to go."

Vince popped off the screen.

Mina turned to Kaylee. "Well?"

"Damn. Good lips aside, that man has an excellent poker face. You won't catch me gambling against him. His distress is apparent, but it was hard to read if it was genuine or not. Slight hint of something under his left eye. His insistence about getting word to Chaz rings true. Therefore, if that's authentic, he's worried. He hinted that he had somebody personal in his life before that he would've confided in instead of you. But he has to know that tasking a civilian to get in contact with the grand dom of the International Judicial Committee is a huge ask. Most people wouldn't be able to achieve such a thing on their own, even with their name on a preferred list." She bit her lip. "So basically, I'm not sure."

"Join the ranks. I'm not sure either. And it's bugging me. I pride myself on accurately analyzing human expressions, and his are throwing me."

"Yeah. You read face like a bibliophile on Jump. But you're dealing with a pro here. He's a colonel for a reason. He's an agent in the French Protectorate. He's good. So, what are you going to do?" Kaylee angled her head toward the box in Mina's hand.

Mina grinned. "Have Lee hack it."

"Excellent idea. That was on the very top of my Vince to-do list. That, and getting him to recite a sexy bedtime story. His voice should be bottled and saved for a rainy day. Or hell, all days."

Mina produced an eye roll adequate for the situation. "I can't have Lee do it until the op is over and we have the murderous Tedesco bastard locked up tight. If Vince checks in, and everything seems fine, finding out where he is will be a precaution, not an emergency."

"And if he doesn't check in? Will you go to Burquist right away?"

"That remains to be seen. The CIU will have to make that call, not me. McAllister knows everything."

"Makes sense. On another note, do you think Lee can handle the pressure of the Tedesco sting now that you know Tedesco's involved with Veritus? That's a huge op by anyone's standards. The kid is set to go in all by himself."

Mina rubbed her face, happy that it felt like her own again. "Damn, I hope so. I'm not telling him until right before. Not only does Lee need to airmeld the files, he has to try and get his hands on a physical key located in Tedesco's locked desk. Andy indicated the key will lead us to a storage unit that contains the nerve gas they're so fond of using."

"Dang. Good luck with that." Kaylee blew out a breath. "Makes me wish I could stick around and watch this unfold, but I have a date with a freaky weapons dealer tonight. The guy wears a foiled titanium helmet to keep the 'rays' out. He's set to make a drop in an hour." She brought her cuff up to check the time. "I really want to keep this syn on." She glanced down at herself longingly. "But I'm posing as a medi-worker. Not the right look. Nothing about this outfit says, 'Sedate, helpful person who cares about your well-being.' Wearing a uni stinks. Medi-workers should really think about updating their look. Syn is so much better."

"Fashion is low on a medi-worker's agenda. And thanks for coming by today to help out." Mina grinned. "We made quite an impression."

"Yeah. That purple-haired baby-faced superhacker won't be forgetting about us anytime soon."

"HERE, STICK THIS in your ear." Mina handed Lee an ear node similar to the one Grigg had given her, but bigger. "It's sticky. Make sure you set it deep inside your canal so there's no visual from the outside. We'll test it in a second. It's made of an elastomer compound with conductive-plastic circuitry. Tedesco, likely with the help of Frankie and his goons, are going to scan you. If they don't, they aren't worth their weight in currency. This won't trigger a read. Neither will the cam, but it has to go in your mouth first."

"My mouth?"

Lee and Mina were flying inside a nondescript government craft heading toward Jordan's residence. McAllister, along with a crew, was already in place at The Mega. Tedesco was set to leave the production meeting in twenty. He was sending private transpo to pick up Lee as the superhacker.

Lee's enhancements were undetectable. He looked

nothing like himself. His new purple hair was slicked away from his face. The goatee was spot-on, sparse with a solid jerkoff vibe. The purple was brighter up close, but it was an exact color match, according to Jordan. Lee's eyes had been diffracted a light violet that made him look vaguely like a specter, which was the point.

"The cam is wrapped in a protective coating that keeps the metal circuitry undetectable," she told him. "In order to use it, you chew through the bubble, spit it out when no one's looking, and snap it into this buttonhole." She tapped his shirt. "The cam contains full audio and vis. It's very high-tech, your favorite. It just came out of R&D a few months ago."

Lee was dressed in shiny head-to-toe black. The snug long-sleeved shirt had three buttons running parallel along a curved neckline. The black peg pants were accompanied by tall lace-up boots. This, according to Jordan, was what he wore on "outside jobs." The superhacker had gotten cooperative once the currency had been transferred into his account. At this very moment, he was probably imbibing a heaping plate of printed sweets while spying on official government data. Not bad for not doing any work.

"Okay." Lee took the cam and stuck it in a pocket. "I'll put it in my mouth once I land."

"Lee, I can sense your jitters, and I'm here to tell you there's no need to be worried. You can complete this op in your sleep. Your instincts are good. You have to learn to trust them—and yourself. All this job requires is for you to sit at a desk and pretend to blast files.

The government satellite is hovering over our heads right now. That means you'll have a clean, undetectable interface in which to transfer those files. Easy."

Lee nodded, seeming more confident. "I've decided to make a hard copy, too. Just in case."

A hard copy wasn't in the plans. But it could be. "Tedesco might notice a data drive sticking out of his superunit."

Lee reached into a pocket and pulled out a rust-colored pebble. He squished it between his fingers, and it mashed into a baby pancake. Then he began to roll it back into a ball. "This is moldable electron plastique that can be adapted to any port. It's a hacker's secret weapon. Most people use this for quick file sharing."

Mina had used it before, but not since elementary programming. It wasn't very powerful.

"It's usually good for simple data memorization and a quick transfer, nothing more. But a hacker god by the name of Ernest Forsyth invented a powerful reader for this stuff. It allows you to download large files of super-complex data, and the reader deciphers it, no problem. It set me back a ton of currency—actual *physical* currency—to get one of those readers."

Mina nodded. She understood the value of physical currency. She'd graduated from elementary programming, after all.

"It was worth every single coin I spent. It was lucky I got some when I did, because they don't make them anymore."

Mina didn't question who *they* were, but assumed they were sneaky hackers with access to laboratories.

"Forsyth died six years ago, and you can't find any today." Lee's face took on a dreamy expression. Mina figured he was recalling an excellent memory involving sneaky tech. "I'll insert the plastique when Tedesco isn't looking. Then download his entire superunit onto it. If they ask, I'll just tell them it's a tool I'm using to help with the purge. They won't know the difference, and they can't check because they don't have a reader." He produced a triumphant smile.

Mina grinned back. "That's good thinking. Having a backup will help ensure Tedesco goes down and this op is a success." She nodded toward the rust-colored ball he was still spinning between his fingers. "That reader sounds like a valuable tool you might want to share with the tech department at headquarters. Maybe they can adapt or copy it?" Government agents were even better at their jobs when they had better tech.

Lee dropped his triumphant expression, looking aghast. His mouth dropped at the corners, and his violet eyes sparked with actual anger. "That would go against everything Ernest Forsyth stood for." He was genuinely offended. "He was a genius hacker. Not to mention, if I did that, I'd shatter the oath I took. No way."

Instead of arguing and pointing out that the rookie now worked for a *different* team and had sworn to uphold and protect the *public,* not hackers, Mina muttered something about squirrels, nuts, and misguided oaths, before calmly stating, "Let's move on, shall we? We only have a few minutes before touchdown. I realize this is redundant, but I have to ask. Did you memorize the airmeld codes?"

The codes were complicated, with lots of numbers and symbol combinations. The meld was government-assigned and ensured that any data gathered through this particular interface was encoded without interference so it would hold up in court.

"Of course." Lee sniffed, obviously still put out by her previous suggestion.

"I had to ask. It's my job as lead agent to make sure everything's covered, so that's what I'm doing. I'm covering it." She was also mentoring. Which meant she had to make sure Lee was comfortable and ready. Mina attached a mic to the front of her shirt. "I'll test this once you're out of the craft. Otherwise, it'll give too much feedback. I don't want to blow out your eardrum. Your mic is embedded in the cam. Once you pop it out of your mouth, we'll be able to hear and see everything." She had to add this next part, because rookie. "This kind of tech is tried and true. I've used it many times before. But if something goes wrong, it's imperative for you to keep your cool. We'll be monitoring the airmeld connection from start to finish. If things fail with the cam, switch to the comp and send us an alert. Agents will be posted at all exits, and drones are already in the air, monitoring the penthouse. Do you have any questions?"

The craft was setting down a block from Jordan's apartment on a public landing pad. "No questions. I understand." His expression was eager.

That's the spirit, Lee. "There's one more thing." They bounced once, and the passenger door began to rise. Mina took a deep breath. She had to get this out.

The rookie deserved to know what he was getting into. "Tedesco is involved in more than shipping illegal goods. We found out, by way of Andy the Stooge, he's linked to Veritus." Mina didn't know if Lee knew what Veritus was until his eyes went owly, which only enhanced the weird specterness of the violet color.

"Veritus?" Lee's response came out in a whoosh. "*The* Veritus? The murderers who went after the Juniper Group?"

"Yes. That Veritus." Mina hadn't heard specifically about the Juniper Group, but she was certain there was only one Veritus. "This doesn't change the parameters of the op in any way. Physical danger to you is very low." Her voice stayed firm. "Keep your head down, stick to the mission. Hack the system and airmeld the data. That's it. You said a job like this would take four to five hours. Jordan confirmed. You'll be done and out by midnight."

Mina didn't add that she might have a little side job for him once he was finished—hacking the tech Vince had sent. She'd have to wait to see how the rookie came out of his first solo op.

Lee continued to look stunned by the Veritus news, so Mina added, "This doesn't change our tactics."

Yes, Tedesco's links to Veritus were big, but that group's modus operandi was to attack large groups for major financial gain, not kill superhackers they invited into their homes in cold blood. Mina hadn't lied—the threat to Lee was very low. She would've aborted the mission otherwise.

She continued, "They have no reason to suspect you're

anyone but Jordan Maybach, and they have no reason to hurt him. They reached out to him. You can do this." She settled a hand on his shoulder, gripping it firmly. Lee was pale. And sort of listless. Mina shook him. "Lee." He was hunched in his seat. She bent down to look into his eyes. Passersby were starting to notice them. "Do you want me to enter Jordan's residence with you?" He wouldn't meet her gaze. "I can. Tedesco's transpo is not due for another ten."

Lee physically shuddered. After a good ten seconds, he looked up. His expression had morphed into resignation, his chin tilting upward. "I don't need an escort. I can do this alone. You're right. Knowing Tedesco is with Veritus doesn't change the op. It just makes it more important. *Much* more."

He exited the craft.

Wondering if she should've held him back, Mina called after his retreating back, "We'll be monitoring you the entire time. Good luck!"

She slumped back in her seat as the door began to close. The female sim announced, "Next destination is The Mega, hub level twenty. Do you wish to make any changes, Agent Kane?"

"No. Proceed."

"Travel time three minutes, seventeen seconds."

Mina's cuff beeped. She ordered the sim, "Link incoming call from Director McAllister to in-craft system."

"Linking call."

A soft beep sounded, affirming the connection. "This is Agent Kane."

"I just received an alert that Agent Adams is on the

ground," McAllister said, his voice surrounding her. "Confirming everything is a go."

"It's a go." Mina sighed, bringing her fingers up to her temples. She wasn't on screen, so McAllister couldn't see her. She had to be honest with him. "I told Lee about Veritus, as planned."

"Is there a problem?"

Mina hesitated. "I'm really not sure. He brought up the Juniper Group. It seemed personal. I offered to accompany him inside, which wouldn't have compromised the op. He refused. I let him go, but I think maybe I should've held him back and quizzed him more."

"Agent Adams can complete this op to a high standard. Do you still believe this to be true, Agent Kane? If not, we abort now. It's too late to put another stand-in for Jordan this evening, but we can have the hacker try to reschedule. It may buy us another day."

"Or it might be enough to spook them to purge the evidence without a superhacker in residence. Hackers don't quit when there's that much currency dropping from the clouds. It's too risky to reschedule." Mina blew out a breath. "I believe in Lee." There, she'd said it. She believed in the rookie. "He's still green, but he has solid instincts." Which was what she'd just told him. It mattered. Bad instincts got you killed. "He's a phenomenal hacker. Even if we could get another Jordan look-alike, they wouldn't match Lee's talent. He can do this." Her voice was firm.

"I trust your opinion," McAllister said. "Once you arrive at The Mega, Agent Darian will be there to escort you up. She has a uni waiting for you. I'll see you shortly, Agent Kane. We have a lot riding on this op. We'll be sharing the space with three different agencies. Assume regulation backstory. We're posing as Street Crime." That was CIU's standard when dealing with other federal agencies. It wasn't easy being a secret agency.

"Understood. Signing off." Mina immediately ordered the sim, "Conduct an internal data search on the Juniper Group as it pertains to Veritus. Audio playback only."

"Conducting search," the sim replied. Not thirty seconds later, it recited, "In the fall of 2086, Juniper Group was the target of an attack purported but not proven to be the work of Veritus. Noxious gas trace elements were found in the filtration system where Juniper leased offices, as well as in the bloodstream of all victims. Due to similarities to other major events and the basic atomic structure of the molecules in the lethal gases, the attack was linked to Veritus. Seven of the fifteen victims died on location. Three more died during medical care. The remaining five suffered serious, lasting effects. No arrests were made. The case is still open."

That attack had taken place nineteen years ago. Mina had been seven years old. No wonder she hadn't recalled it.

"What line of work was the Juniper Group in?" Mina asked.

"The Juniper Group specialized in tax accounting."

"Why was it targeted by Veritus?"

"Juniper Group filed a lawsuit against a former client called Dandelion, citing fraudulent filings. A federal investigation found that Dandelion was a shell company, and all traces of its origins had been destroyed only days after the attack. No links to any person or corporation were ever recovered."

"List names of the deceased," Mina ordered.

"Carmen Ackerman, Langley Adams, Bobby Conroy, Sylvie Edwards—"

"Stop. Personal data on Langley Adams." Mina's heart began to beat irregularly.

She shut her eyes as the sim continued, "Langley Adams, age thirty-three. Son of Percy and Renata Adams. Survived by partner Jillian Adams and son Langley Jr.—"

"Stop. Personal data on Langley Jr."

"Langley Adams Jr. Current age twenty-two. Identity-chipped Lee Adams at the age of ten. Early programming included—"

"Stop."

Mina placed her head in her hands as the craft made its landing at The Mega. She had just sent the rookie off to a face-to-face with a man who might be directly responsible for the brutal killing of his father and nine others.

What in the hell was she going to do?

For that matter, what was Lee going to do?

Chapter 20

THERE WAS NO doubt Lee knew every detail of the Juniper Group attack, down to the tiniest particle. The same was true about Veritus. The hacker had probably burrowed deeply into government reports over the years, trying to piece together the events that had killed his father. Lee's sense of moral duty, his sense of right and wrong had likely been shaped by this huge, emotional event. Now he was going to confront it head-on.

Mina entered the transpo hub at The Mega and acknowledged Agent Darian, who stood across the room. She followed the agent, keeping her distance, noting that her CIU coworker, a compact blonde with an athletic build, had already donned the simple black and gold uni The Mega staff wore. Agent Darian indicated a nondescript box sitting on a table. Mina tucked it under an arm as she passed.

Agent Darian exited the hub, pushing through a public waste room door. Mina followed. The first two compartments were open, the rest closed. Agent Darian entered the first, Mina the second.

Once Mina finished changing into the same uni, she emerged, her original clothing boxed up under her arm. Mina found her fellow agent outside, standing next to a large cart filled with covered platters on the top, packages stacked three high on the bottom. Operating the cart required two individuals or one bot. Mina grabbed the handle, and they began to walk.

After a few meters, Agent Darian directed them down a long, narrow hallway. At the end sat a bank of tubes. She didn't speak until they were inside with the tube door closed.

"It's a madhouse up there," she whispered.

Mina nodded, assuming as much. Bringing down a murderous crime ring didn't happen every day, not to mention they were in crossover territory. DGS and the Serial Crimes Unit would want their guy as well. Mina felt a little easier knowing that Tedesco thought he was safe, tucked away in his fortress in the sky. The man had gone undetected for so long, he had no reason to think that it would all come crashing down around him tonight.

The tube whisked them nearly to the top of the four-hundred-story mega in five seconds. They steered the cart out together. The hallway was clear. Agent Darian made her way to a door at the end, pressing her thumb against a smudger above the handle.

The door clicked open immediately.

The unit was packed with personnel. Three different workstations had been set up, with a cluster of three to five agents around each. Despite how crowded the space was, it was eerily quiet.

Agent Darian shut the door as they rolled the cart to the side. Then both headed to where McAllister and two other agents sat in front of a large, portable screen made of a large sheet of crystalline. Data scrolled down one side, and still images occupied the other. Instead of canal phones, each person wore large headsets that covered both ears.

McAllister acknowledged Mina and Agent Darian by lofting a single finger in the air. Then he removed his headset and stood. "Lee is in transit. Frankie Four just returned to the penthouse. The DGS placed a small listening device outside a large bank of windows. The range is minimal, but we're getting useful intel when they wander close enough. Keith Brown, the man included in your report, has been inside the inner offices all day. Apparently, he hasn't gotten far enough in whatever he's doing, and Frankie is angry. They're waiting for the elder Tedesco to arrive, as well as Jordan. Things are tense."

Mina indicated with a nod that she'd like a moment alone with her director. She had no intention of airing the rookie's private life to the entire room. McAllister understood, ushering her down a hallway to a utility closet, shutting the door.

"Thanks," Mina started. It was best to get it out quickly. Mina's boss was big on being direct. She ran her fingers through her new long black hair, a simple enhancement from her closet so she wouldn't resemble the woman who'd been out with Vincent Kramer, at least from a distance. "We might have a problem." She held up a hand. "Just to preface, I'm hoping there won't be a problem, but we'll need to prepare for the possibility. I conducted some research on the Juniper Group on the ride over. Lee's father died in the attack. The rookie didn't disclose this information to me. He looked shaken, as I reported, but then he appeared determined. He's clearly unfamiliar with our rules of full disclosure, which I'll remedy as soon as possible. It was wrong of him not to tell me."

If an agent had personal history that could affect an op they were assigned, they had to fully disclose that information before reporting for duty. It was almost a law. Not quite, but close enough. The risk of compromising an operation was too great without full disclosure.

"In hindsight, I should've pressed him when I noticed his reaction." Mina sighed. "But, to be honest, he looks like that a lot. Or close. Wide-eyed and a little overwhelmed. I don't know much about his past." Practically nothing. "There's a strong possibility Lee altered his personal data years ago. It's not uncommon for hackers to erase aspects of their lives they don't want anyone to see."

Mina wasn't telling her director anything he didn't know. The government had certainly performed a thorough background check on Lee before hiring him. A notation about how his father had died nineteen years ago would be there, but what those details said would be another story. Lee could have wiped the specifics of his father's death from his file, but wiping them from crime scene documentation would be harder—not impossible. But he hadn't.

"If I'd known about his personal connection to Veritus, I would've aborted the mission."

McAllister looked thoughtful for a moment, his eyes focusing somewhere over Mina's shoulder. "Agent Adams is already in transit. We can't communicate directly with him until he inserts the cam or accesses the airmeld. What are your feelings on this new information, Agent Kane? Do we abort immediately, once we establish communication, because of fears that Agent Adams will expose himself in some way, or do we proceed as planned?"

Mina bit her lip. "I think we should proceed. Lee may be an inexperienced agent, but he's a master hacker. To get to that level, one has to be extremely intelligent. He knows how much is riding on this op. Justice for his father is within his sights for the first, and likely, only time in his life. Based on that, I feel like he'll stay on task—or at least try his best to. If something goes wrong, and they start questioning him, I'm not sure how he'll hold up. But we should give him a chance to do his thing."

A rap sounded on the door. "Sorry to interrupt," Agent Darian called. "Agent Adams has landed on the roof, along with Tedesco."

McAllister wore a determined expression. "I have teams monitoring every exit and entry to this building. We have two agents stationed in the main tubes, authorized by a warrant from the US government to bypass to penthouse level on our orders. I'll keep them on high alert. I want you as the primary liaison between us and Agent Adams for the duration of this operation. I'm counting on you to keep him steady, Agent Kane. I hope you're up to the task."

Mina nodded. "I'll do my best." So much rode on this op that it was hard not to feel the pressure. But Mina had been involved in tricky cases before. They could do this. She tried to forget that they were counting on the rookie rather than her inside Tedesco's residence. She would be there, just not in person.

They exited the utility closet.

Every agent in the room had gathered around the CIU station.

Mina locked eyes with Grigg. He gave her a small nod, but otherwise kept his mouth closed. McAllister ushered her into the chair he'd been sitting in, handing her a headset, putting on his own so he could listen in. Mina activated the mic on her lapel as she secured the sleek black fiber around her ears. Everything was tense and quiet for the next minute.

Static erupted at the same time a visual snapped onto the screen.

Lee was straightening from a bent position. He stood inside a grand entryway that Mina hadn't glimpsed during her run-through of the penthouse the day before.

Four men were gathered in a semicircle around him. Mina readily identified three from the intel, facilitated by the stills on the screen in front of her. Tedesco, Frankie Four, and Keith Brown. Facial rec was already running on the fourth man, a tall, skinny blond who held a high-tech scanner at his side. They must've just finished processing Lee.

Mina was impressed that the rookie had gotten his camera adhered right in front of these guys.

Very quietly, so as not to startle him, Mina whispered, "We have eyes and ears, Lee."

Frankie Four, a burly man with shaggy dark hair, stepped forward, aggressively wagging a finger in front of Lee's face. "You'd better be as good as they say you are. We're not paying you that much currency to mess around. We want everything zapped *immediately*."

"Calm down, Frankie." Tedesco laid a hand on his son's arm. The son jerked back like he'd been seared by a hot laser.

The father was shorter than Frankie by at least a head, with close-cropped jet-black hair and enhancements that made him look at least fifteen to twenty years younger than he actually was. These types of enhancements were typical of older men who desperately wanted to hold on to their youth. He wore what looked to be a very expensive suit, designed in the European style, with a curved collar and skinny lapels. The other two men— Keith and the skinny blond guy—were nondescript, each looking as though they had to work hard to earn their borrow credits. The henchmen.

"Let's invite our esteemed guest in." Tedesco swept his arm forward.

Lee followed the group as they moved into the residence, passing through a few formal rooms Mina hadn't seen and into the large living space with the grandiose furniture.

"Lee, try to angle your body as you walk. We want a good look around," Mina whispered, adding, "You're doing great."

The rookie moved as she'd asked. He hadn't said a word. Jordan had assured them that he'd never had any vocal contact with the man who'd hired him. All their business dealings had been done through secure written communication, the ult-encrypted type that hackers preferred. Jordan hadn't known if he'd been in contact with Tedesco himself under a false alias or one of his lackeys.

The group stopped. "Can we offer you anything before we start?" Tedesco asked. "We enjoy real drinks here, not printed. We have various fruit juices, alcoholic beverages, anything you desire."

"No, I'm good." Lee's voice cracked. He was nervous. *Come on, Lee. You can do this.* "I'd rather get on with the job. We have a long night ahead of us." Less quake. Better.

Mina examined each of the men as Lee spoke. The two henchmen seemed indifferent. Frankie had his balled fists at his sides, clearly on edge. Tedesco seemed relaxed, like this was the kind of casual business transaction he was used to performing. Mina supposed a cold-blooded murderer would have to keep his cool at all times, or he would've cracked by now.

Mina seethed at what Tedesco had done, the countless lives he'd taken. The bastard was going to pay for it if she had anything to say.

"In that case, follow me through here." Tedesco led the way into his inner sanctum. The outer room looked exactly as Mina remembered, cluttered and full of knickknacks and vid memorabilia. The secret wall was already open, the private office illuminated. "I've provided everything you've asked for." An array of tech littered the massive desk, including Tedesco's superunit nestled inside a leather compucase. The case was likely the real thing and not printed. That poor animal.

This was the computer that held all things incriminating.

Lee took a seat at the desk. The men filled in around him. Frankie spoke first. "You're not leaving until you get it done."

Tedesco chuckled, a sound that seemed intended to diffuse his son's anxiety. "Calm down, Frankie. This man is not our prisoner."

Mina caught a look that passed between the two henchmen.

If she'd seen it, Lee might've, too. She leaned closer to the screen, assessing. "Don't panic, Lee," she murmured. "We have the penthouse surrounded and a federal warrant to enter the premises. Keep your head down and finish the job." She clipped off her mic and slid her headset off of one ear to address the integrated screen in front of her. "Computer, rewind vid ten seconds, display right, enlarge still, facial zoom to eighty." While Lee's live video continued to play on the left, the computer enhanced the video she'd requested on the right. Mina focused on Keith Brown and the man the computer had identified as Lawrence Base, a felon with a long rap sheet.

Mina used her fingers to tug the image of the men to the center, enlarging it further. "Computer, play back vid from here." Frankie began to speak. "Freeze." She addressed the agents behind her and her boss. "To me, this look says it all. They're not planning to let Lee leave while he's still breathing." She shifted her hand, moving to Tedesco, enhancing him. Tedesco's face was serene. "The elder doesn't know. This is a business transaction to him. He's clueless about what his son has in store for the superhacker. Frankie is not planning to leave any loose ends."

Lee's voice sounded in Mina's ear. She pulled the headset back on.

"I'm going to need some privacy," the rookie asserted. "I can't work with people standing over me." His voice held some Jordan-style arrogance.

Good play, Lee.

Frankie Four, predictably, took umbrage. "You're not in charge here." He swiped the air in front of him. He was a swiper. "We are." His hand thumped his chest. Also a thumper. "If I want to look over your shoulder the entire time, I will."

Lee stood. The camera tracked upward. "Fine. Then you can continue on your own. Good luck. The only way encrypted data can be destroyed is by knowing the tangine code. Hope you're well versed in it."

Mina's pulse sped up.

Tread carefully, Lee. These are very bad men.

 CHAPTER 21

"EASY," MINA WHISPERED into her partner's ear. "I see what you're trying to do, but the son is highly unpredictable." Judging by what they were witnessing, Frankie was also likely behind lots of the murder stuff. "Ease out from behind the desk slowly. Give the elder a chance to repair the damage." Lee was trying to establish a working hierarchy. It was the right move, but doing it in an environment this charged was risky. Without a working order, Frankie would continue to run amok.

The men in the room erupted in anger.

Except Tedesco. He barely broke a sweat.

"There's been a misunderstanding," the father reassured Lee, moving closer, face calm. "My son and his men will leave immediately. Is it all right if I take a seat here? I'd like to be present, but I won't be in the way." He gestured toward one of the gilded chairs on the other side of the desk.

If looks could manifest hot lasers, Frankie Four's

pupils would've sliced his father in two. It seemed Frankie had stayed out of trouble, but trouble hadn't stayed out of Frankie.

As Mina got a better feel for the family dynamic, theories began formulating in her brain like lightning bugs popping up in zero gravity.

Frankie Four snapped, "I'm not going anywhere."

"Lee, if you try to leave, things could get ugly," Mina warned. "The henchmen are probably moving in behind you. Stay where you are and let Tedesco smooth it over. He'll win." It was his home. He controlled the currency. Therefore, he won.

McAllister grunted his agreement as they waited for Lee to react.

"You are indeed leaving the room," Tedesco told his son, voice tight. "I'll summon you if there's an issue. You're not talking to some low-borrow hacker here. I hired the best. Jordan is in charge of this operation, not you. It would be nice if you remembered that." His voice held a threat so thinly veiled that everyone in the room heard it.

Frankie crossed his arms and seemed like he might hold his ground, then abruptly dropped them. "We'll be in the next room," Frankie growled. "But I have my eyes on you, kid. Don't forget it." He moved out of Lee's direct line of sight.

Tedesco gestured. "Please. Sit. I'm anxious for you to get started." He certainly was. His livelihood was at stake.

Lee moved behind the desk. "Sorry about that," Lee said, his tone suitably humble. *Good choice, Lee.* "You're paying me top currency to complete this job. If you want it done correctly, you have to follow my rules. Distraction can cripple a process this intricate." Lee was channeling Jordan, including the superhacker's cadence when speaking. Apparently, Lee had acting skills no one had known about.

Mina allowed for a teeny sigh of relief.

"Please transfer voice access to me for the duration of six hours," Lee instructed, getting down to business.

Once Tedesco ordered his system to allow him access, Lee began to type.

"What's he doing?" Agent Darian whispered, leaning closer. "Those aren't airmeld sequences."

Indeed, they weren't.

Lee was typing furiously, but he wasn't using letters, numbers, or known symbols. Instead, the page began to fill with black and white pixels. Mina sat forward. "Lee, is that what I think it is?" she asked, hoping Lee would type an answer like *hell no* across the screen, even though she knew there was zero chance that would happen. "What you're doing isn't authorized."

Lee kept going, unfazed. The kid was on a mission.

"I don't get it. What's going on?" Agent Darian asked.

McAllister murmured behind Mina, "He's sequencing a pixel mirror to expose what's on that computer. He's essentially creating an open channel to the outside world, and by doing so, he can successfully evade security encryptions on Tedesco's computer. A pixel mirror won't send up any flags or alarms. But not many hackers know how to code them correctly."

Except Level XIII Lee.

Mina shut down her mic. She didn't want to panic the rookie, even though he'd panicked her. "What are my orders?"

Every agent in the room had an opinion, and they shared it at once.

Exposing an op of this scale without approval would not only get Lee fired, but put in a box. Agents weren't allowed to just do whatever they wanted. There were rules and laws in place. Mina wouldn't let Lee be incarcerated if she could help it. She knew she could get the rookie to listen to her before he activated the mirror, but she wanted a direct order first.

McAllister didn't speak for several seconds, then said, "Agent Adams has my approval to proceed." His voice held complete authority. Most of the agents in the room quieted down. "If for some reason, Tedesco satellites interfere with our airmeld, we lose, and these murderers go free. We won't get another chance. Agent Adams is making sure this operation is a success by amplifying what's on that computer to the public. Once the mirror is in place and the data is exposed to the world, there will be no way to delete it."

Mina didn't mention Lee had special plastique and a reader invented by a geek god. Apparently, Lee had decided to go with a barrel laser approach.

"You can't be serious," one of the senior agents argued.

You could always tell the senior agents by the way they dressed. This one wasn't in uni, and although he wasn't wearing a suit like Mina's boss, he radiated similar authority with his crisp white shirt and neatly pressed pants.

"We have no idea what's on that computer!" the senior agent complained. "What he's doing is insubordination, plain and simple. A field agent does not have the authority to make these kinds of decisions. Especially not on his own without proper guidance."

"This operation has evolved significantly in the last few hours," McAllister stated calmly. "Veritus is a group of killers who have evaded capture and penalty for over twenty-five years. They're at the top of the Planet's Most Wanted list and have been for a very long time. It's within my authority to approve any and all exposure that leads to capture. What my agent is doing is ensuring this mission will be a success."

Mina had never felt more proud to work under McAllister. He knew what Lee was up against emotionally and physically, and he was backing his agent despite that agent performing a risky, unapproved tactic.

The man who'd been arguing shook his head. "A success or a circus. You have no idea what's on that computer. You're Street Crime, for chrissake! Why are you in charge? I'm contacting my superior immediately." He stormed off, shouting something into his cuff.

"Tell Lee he may proceed," McAllister said. "But focus the mirror to media outlets, not civilian comps."

"Once it's activated, we're going to have to get him out of there quickly," Mina said. "A frenzy will break out once the media gets hold of this, which, according to my limited knowledge of mirrors, will be immediate once the pixelization is complete. It will be screencast to the masses within moments. This story is too big to keep under wraps." Mina flipped her mic back on. "Lee, focus the sequence to media only. Once it's complete, we're getting you out. Make an excuse to use the waste room. We'll have agents at the door, ready to make arrests." Mina had never used a mirror herself and wasn't anywhere near talented enough to pull off something like that, but she was familiar enough to know Lee could focus it based on the specific configuration he built. The tech world was made up of sectors, each defined by specific data quadrants. Media was easy. This type of mirror would blink across any screen coded to receive uploads. Since media relied on uploads from civilians to get story tips, that quadrant would be primed and ready.

The camera jerked up suddenly.

Tedesco was walking toward Lee. Apparently, the man had been trying to get his attention, but Lee had been too entrenched in his work. There was a chance Tedesco might recognize what Lee was doing if he caught a glimpse of the screen.

"Placate him," Mina murmured quietly. "Let him know everything is going fine."

Instead of placating, Lee chose to sound angry. "Can't you see I'm busy? I can't work with constant interruptions. Please sit down and let me do my job!"

Tedesco stopped. He maintained a fixed, serene expression, but Mina saw something change in his gaze.

Tedesco wasn't used to insubordination from his lackeys. Having him suspicious would not do the rookie any favors.

"I simply asked what technique you are using," Tedesco said. "We talked about you downloading one of your famous viruses. I'm interested to know how you're going to approach the purge. I'm paying for it, after all." The last was said lightly, but firmly.

Mina flipped off her mic. "Somebody get Jordan on screen." The superhacker was on close standby. "He never said anything to us about a virus. This might be a test. Frankie Four's unease might be rubbing off on Tedesco." While she waited for intel, she flipped the mic back on and murmured, "Finesse him. We're getting Jordan on the line to ask him about the virus thing. Don't forget this man is lethal. He's playing Mr. Nice Guy now, but if he gets a look at what you're doing, or you don't have the right answers, things could turn quickly. Bring on the charm. You can do this, Lee."

Lee cleared his throat. "Of course you can ask what I'm doing. As far as viruses go—"

"Don't say anything specific," Mina ordered.

Another agent from her department, Agent Caldwell, moved forward with a handheld. "Jordan said he spoke about the Gemini virus, but dismissed it as not being powerful enough."

"Did you get that, Lee?" Mina asked. "Jordan talked about Gemini, but ultimately dismissed it."

In her headset, Mina heard Lee say, "I know we discussed Gemini, but it's not strong enough to destroy encrypted nanobites. Since we talked, however, I've been working on a brand-new virus. I call it Venus. Its strength is military grade, and it has the power to wipe away encrypted nanos without a trace. Almost like it was never there in the first place."

"*Lee,*" Mina hissed. "Tread carefully." If she was picking up on Lee's hints, Frankie could, too. "We know your father died in the Juniper Group attack. I'm so sorry. You have the right to be angry. Keep your cool. Once you complete this mission, you win. Your family will get their long-awaited justice. If not, Tedesco wins. Stay the course." She refrained from begging. "Assure Tedesco everything is fine. Finish the mirror, and we'll get you out."

"The Venus?" Tedesco was saying. "You were pretty specific when you said a virus couldn't wipe everything out, as there are too many counterviruses that could undo the work. Short of launching this into an industrial-size grinder, and even then, fragments could be retrieved, you said you must hand-code to be certain everything is gone."

"I did say that," Lee agreed, still pecking out pixels on the screen at a rapid pace. He'd better be careful. If he didn't get the mirror exactly right, it wouldn't work. "But that was before I figured out Venus' charm." He stopped typing and glanced at Tedesco, who hadn't moved any closer. "It produces a reflection, and anyone looking in will see only what we want them to see. Here, take a look."

To Mina's horror, Lee slid the supercomputer toward Tedesco, and Tedesco peered at the screen. Mina scoured his face, searching for any telltale signs Tedesco knew what he was looking at. It appeared he didn't. But Mina wasn't ready to breathe just yet.

"Is that the virus code?" Tedesco asked, gesturing to the black and white pixels covering three-fourths of the screen.

Lee slid the computer back into place so he could continue to work. "It is. But, of course, the virus won't stand alone. Once it's enacted, I will also hand-code specific data-sensitive deletions, at your discretion. Once I'm done, anyone searching this computer will see only a reflection of the programs we want them to see. It's pretty genius. It ensures nothing can be found, no matter how hard anyone looks." Lee held up the small ball of plastique.

What are you doing now, Lee?

"I'm adding this to the data port." Lee proceeded to mold it into a port before Tedesco could object.

"Isn't that—"

"Yes. But it's a very special plastique. It's been precoded to blow up specific language." Lee was coming off as cocky and confident. Mina sent a prayer into the ether that it would be enough. Before Tedesco could speak, Lee continued, "Why don't you take a seat? When I get to the next phase, I'll let you know, and you can watch."

To Mina's surprise, Tedesco went back to his seat. His face was inscrutable. Mina had no idea if he knew anything about cyberhacking. Though if he was well versed, he wouldn't need the help of a superhacker. But he might know enough to suspect Lee was working against him.

That would put a blaster hole in things. "Lee, please remember Tedesco was suspicious earlier today that his inner sanctum was breached. We don't know what's going through his mind."

The senior agent who had disagreed with McAllister came up behind Mina. She clicked off her mic. She didn't want to distract Lee with the bureaucratic ins and outs behind the scenes.

"What's the timetable for data release?" the agent asked. His voice held a hint of anger, but he'd calmed down, likely because of a command from his superior. Mina had no idea how many of the higher-ups knew McAllister's actual rank. But she did know that when an agent was told to obey an order, for the most part they did.

"We need to mitigate the explosion of information the best way we can," he went on. "Agents have been deployed to several media hubs around the city. They will be monitoring, downloading, and authenticating the data as it comes in. Is he planning to mirror everything on the computer? That may overload what media computers can handle."

"My guess is he's triggering key words first, the rest to follow," Mina said. "But I can't very well ask him. He knows what media comps can handle. He's a Level XIII. We're going to have to trust him." The agent huffed, but remained quiet. "As for the timetable, I'd say it'll be less than ten."

Their current view on the monitor was the screen in front of Lee. There was movement in the corner as Tedesco stood. The man was restless. Or he'd figured out what Lee was doing. Mina clicked on her mic as Frankie Four suddenly appeared next to his father. He whispered something in his ear. By the way the camera jogged up and down, she figured Lee had heard it and didn't like it.

"Lee, if you think Frankie is up to something dangerous, you have to get out."

The camera shifted, showing Lee's focus was back on the supercomputer. The screen was almost fully pixelated. That kind of computer language was lost on Mina, completely indecipherable, like a system of ancient telegraph, but in dot form. Lee was executing it speedily, which proved he was proficient. But there was a chance he would run out of time.

Tedesco and Frankie were arguing.

Mina wanted Lee to look that way, but he was too focused. It was important that he finish, but also important to know where he stood with these guys.

Frankie stormed forward. Mina saw something in his hand as Lee looked up. It was the scanner that Lawrence Base had been holding.

Frankie jerked his thumb upward. "It's time for another check. I don't trust you. Stand the hell up!"

 Chapter 22

DAMMIT. THEY WERE going to search Lee again for contraband tech. Frankie knew there were ways to smuggle things in. He'd probably invented a few of them. Mina hadn't anticipated this much paranoia.

"Lee, excuse yourself to go to the waste room. Say it's an emergency."

The room full of agents held their breath as they watched Lee rise from behind the desk. Lee's fingers became large as he reached for the buttonhole with the camera.

"Don't..." Mina's voice trailed off. What other choice did he have? Honestly, getting rid of the camera was the best thing he could do.

The tech inside the camera would trigger a beep on a close scan. The circuitry was small, but not small enough to evade detection. If these guys found the camera, Mina wasn't sure agents could get to Lee in time. Frankie was volatile.

As Lee coughed, patting his chest as he bent over, he removed the camera. "I'm happy to be scanned. I've got nothing to hide."

The camera dropped to the floor, bouncing twice before going dark, probably because it landed facedown. It was so small, Mina knew it hadn't made a noise when it hit the ground.

Someone behind Mina said, "If he could kick it out from under the desk, we might be able to see something."

"Lee," Mina said. "If the camera stays in range, you'll still be able to hear me. The scanner won't pick up on the ear node. As long as we know you're okay, we'll let you finish. We think the camera landed under the desk. Once you get back to the desk, try to toe it forward so we can see what's going on."

Frankie's scanner wouldn't detect the cam on the ground, unless he got creative and started scanning the entire area. That could happen, but Mina didn't think so. Frankie was running on anger, not smarts. Because the mic source was now under the desk, low murmurs filtered through instead of clear voices. She assumed Lee was getting scanned.

"He's clear." Tedesco's voice came out authoritatively above the murmurs. "Now head back to the other room and wait."

"I want to see what he's doing," argued Frankie. "I don't trust him. He could be hiding something."

Some shuffling sounds and the squeak of a chair sounded, like Lee had taken his seat again.

Over Mina's shoulder, an agent said, "Look, the camera's moving."

Sure enough, spots of light and flashes of undetectable shapes came up on screen as the camera spun in circles.

"It's lucky he got a hold of it," another agent commented. "It's so small, he could've easily crushed it or missed it altogether." Mina heard grudging respect.

Every agent in the room knew this was a tense, complicated op that none of them could complete, since they weren't even close to a Level XIII hacker. She also knew most of them didn't have big enough asteroid belts to do what Lee was doing. He was blowing this case wide open, risking both his career and his life.

Mina knew that Lee's sense of justice was guiding him. But she couldn't ignore that the deep emotional scars the rookie had carried for so long had to be right there at the surface. She desperately hoped that the justice part would prevail and keep Lee steady. If not, it was anyone's guess how this would end.

"Once you get back to work on the supercomputer," Mina instructed, "establish the meld so we can communicate. I want to know you're okay." A shot of overprotective mother filtered through her. Strange.

"The camera stopped moving," Agent Darian said, pointing at the screen. A small cheer erupted behind Mina. It was facing straight into Tedesco's and Frankie's faces. Frankie held a wand at his side and had a scowl on his face. Tedesco had his arms crossed, frustration with his overzealous son clear in his body language.

They were arguing, which came in clearer now that the mic was closer.

"He's already shared what he's doing," Tedesco said. "He's configuring a virus and has already stated he can't work with people peering over his shoulder. I will alert you if I need anything."

"What kind of virus?" Frankie questioned.

"What do you mean what kind of virus?" Tedesco asked, throwing his arms wide in exasperation. "He's a superhacker. He's configuring a virus that will decimate the files. Then he will hand-code to make sure they're gone."

"I want to see the coding," Frankie insisted.

All the agents collectively held their breath.

No one had eyes on Lee. No communication had come through the airmeld.

Mina clicked off her mic. "Any confirmation of the pixel mirror from media outlets?" she asked the room in general.

The lead agent who had had an issue with McAllister spoke. "Nothing has come through yet. The agents under my command have all arrived at their destinations. They have orders not to say anything until files start appearing, in case your agent changes his mind. They will contact me immediately."

"He's not going to change his mind," Mina quipped, but that was all she was willing to share.

Tedesco was arguing with Frankie, telling him to mind his own business and that he could see the code later.

"What's that there?" Agent Darian squeaked from

behind Mina, gesturing frantically at the screen. Everyone was on edge.

"Looks like Lee opened the airmeld sequence." There was no personal message, but files were pouring in, hundreds per second. Mina clicked on her mic. "Lee, files are coming through. The airmeld is a success."

Several agents rushed to their workstations. Each of them had the sequence open on their own units. They would start to analyze the data, making sure the files coming through were the ones needed to make the arrests. The quicker they figured it out, the quicker they could get Lee out of there.

She clicked off her mic again. "He's backing things up in case the mirror fails."

"No need to be overly worried yet, Agent Kane," McAllister said. "Agent Adams realizes he's running out of time. Having the airmeld to authenticate increases success. I don't think the mirror will fail. We'll get him out. Agents are awaiting my command."

Mina nodded, clicking her mic back on just in time to watch Frankie storm forward, then blink out of view of the cam on the floor. He had moved in the direction of the desk.

"What the hell?" he bellowed. There was more shouting, and something clattered to the ground, bouncing once on the floor in front of the camera.

"What's happening, Lee?" Mina said. "Communicate through the airmeld if you can. We need to know you're all right." She turned her head. "Did anybody see what bounced off the desk?"

"It looked like a key to me," Agent Darian replied. "Shiny and small. But only part of it was in view."

A key? Was it *the* key?

"Where did you get that?" Frankie shouted.

Tedesco's legs rushed by. "I must've left it on the desk by mistake," the elder said. "Get a hold of yourself, Frankie."

"Stop telling me to get a hold myself!" Frankie yelled. Nothing was visible through the camera, but their voices were loud enough to come through clearly. "This morning, you thought there was a breach. I didn't think so. But then one of my men went missing. Everything feels off. Then this guy shows up, and because things are happening, I decide to check him out. But I sit down in that room over there, and I can't find out anything about him because all the boards are shut down."

The hacker boards were down?

If Jordan had sent out an alert, he'd broken the rules of their agreement and would forfeit his gains.

Jordan wasn't going to give that up lightly. Mina clicked off her mic. "Get me intel on the boards. Somebody get Jordan's face on my screen. I want to talk to him."

"I don't know why you're so worried." Lee's voice came through snarky, like he thought Frankie's outbursts were a joke. "I'm handling this for you. Isn't that what you want?"

"What I want is to see the code, you little asshelmet. I want to make sure you're not messing with me. This is sensitive information. It has to be done right."

"Yeah, I know," Lee replied. "That's why your father hired me. Remember?"

"If it's not done perfect, you're not leaving here on your own two feet. Just remember that."

"Is that a threat?" Lee asked.

Jordan's face blinked on the right side of Mina's screen, taking her attention away from Lee.

The superhacker was wearing a feckless expression. "What?"

"Why are the boards down?"

"I don't know what you're talking about."

"Don't mess with me, Jordan. I don't have time, and I shouldn't have to remind you that if you interfered in any way with this op, you get nothing. Did you or did you not shut down the boards?" Mina saw the moment he put together that she was the same agent he'd spoken to earlier, even though she looked nothing like her syn-leather alter ego.

In Mina's ear, Lee was arguing with Frankie, and Tedesco was trying to insert himself, trying to convince his stubborn son everything was fine.

"I didn't issue an order," Jordan hedged.

Geek-speak for *yes, I did.* "I'm a federal agent, in case you forgot. All you had to do was move a curtain in your window, and it would trigger a shutdown for you and all your little hacker pals. If you want to keep your currency and your spying rights, open everything up in the next five seconds. Then send out an alert that you're on an important job and are not to be bothered." He began to protest. "Do it *now.*" She muted him and said, "Get someone in there to put some pressure on him and drain half the currency from his account. That should make it real enough."

She heard Lee say, "Fine. If you want to see what I'm doing, take a look."

Oh no.

There was a good chance Frankie would know what a pixel mirror was.

"All I see is the hold screen." A hold screen should be solid black. Lee knew Frankie would figure it out. "What have you been doing this entire time?" Frankie's voice was heated. "Are you flaring us?"

"What do you mean you only see the hold screen?" Tedesco said, moving forward. "When I saw it, it was full of black and white dots."

Oh no.

"Black and white dots?" Frankie's confusion came through loud and clear.

"Yes, he said he was building a virus called...Venus."

Lee's voice was smooth. "Yes, it's an enhanced version of the Gemini virus. It obliterates nanobites in seconds."

"I want to see the code." Frankie's voice was as hard as titanium. "Produce it for me now, you assgrinder. Or I'll make you hurt."

"Certainly." Lee was too chipper. "Here it is."

Garbled shouting followed.

Mina clipped off her mic.

"The mirror just came through!" an agent shouted enthusiastically.

"The airmelds are authenticated," another agent called.

With relief, Mina turned her mic back on. She was getting ready to tell Lee they were on their way in when she heard another shout from Frankie, and he was incredibly angry.

"You're gonna die for this, you little jettiehead."

It was the last thing Mina heard before she ripped off her headphones and raced for the door.

CHAPTER 22

THE TUBE RIDE up felt like an eternity. Mina was jammed in the small space with five agents, four of them in full SWAT, weapons out, and her director.

"He's going to be okay," McAllister assured her as he handed her a carbon fiber vest, donning one himself. "Another team is ahead of us. They're probably already inside."

The doors slid open soundlessly a millisecond later. Not so much of an eternity.

Mina rushed into the hallway, fastening the last clip of her vest, pulling up short. "Why isn't that door open?"

The lead SWAT gave her a pained look. "When we arrived, a different door was in place. It's six-centimeter-thick graphene. We can't break it unless we blow it up or barrel laser through. It wasn't spec'd on anything I saw. We don't have the tools to take it down."

Before she could speak, McAllister ordered, "Then get

a barrel laser up here. Now! I have an agent inside, and I'm not losing him."

Mina eyed the door, trying to figure out a solution. "Tedesco has sensicams all over. He has full audio and vid. By now, he knows we're out here. We've lost the element of surprise." The idea had been to get in quickly and swarm the penthouse while everyone was still in the inner sanctum.

That clearly wasn't happening.

Mina turned in a circle, frustrated and scared. She couldn't lose the rookie now. He had so much to learn. She had so much to teach him. Somewhere along the way, she'd developed a genuine bond with Lee. It was surprising, but not unwelcome.

"Wait a minute." She slid a hand inside her pocket. She'd brought her tools, just in case. Every good agent came prepared. She pulled out the lock disengager and looked at it quizzically. "Lee was sending me a message." She rushed to the door. "He said the new virus he was concocting for Tedesco was a Venus, and it was military grade. I thought he was messing with Frankie, baiting him about his altered tech, but he must have noticed this door on his way in. This one looks just like the one we broke through on the other side of the residence. He was telling me how to get through." Smartly. Mina indicated with a sweep of her hand that the agents in front should step back. The dial on her disengager was already set to MM. "If there isn't a bastion lock, and it's not coded, this should do the trick."

She depressed the button, waving the gadget in circles, making sure she covered the entire area.

With relief, she heard a small beep, and the door began to slide into the wall housing, exposing a regular door.

Mina shoved the disengager back into her pocket and moved back.

The lead SWAT shouted instructions. "Get the sonic ram up and at the ready! On my signal, we go. One and done. And get me military techs on-site, stat!" He gave the signal.

Two agents rushed forward and battered the ram against it.

The door exploded open with a loud, booming echo.

Sonic rams were made of a hollow titanium tube with supersonic wave generators inside. Alarms sounded immediately. The two agents who took down the door veered out of the way as Mina, McAllister, and two SWAT agents went in.

It was clear. Not even a security bot was waiting for them.

Mina's only thought was getting to Lee. She was more familiar with the layout and raced ahead, McAllister close behind.

She reached the inner sanctum to find the huge ornate door was firmly closed. With frustration, she kicked it. She knew the men inside weren't stupid, but she'd been hoping for a little chaos and forgetfulness. This door wouldn't pop with a disengager. It was coded. Lee had had to crack it last time.

"He lives, or you don't!" she shouted, knowing Tedesco could hear her. He would be listening and watching at this point. "He's the only bartering currency you have, Tedesco. You're a smart man. This is it. We have everything we need to convict. All you have to do is turn on a screen to find out what the whole world now knows. You're going down. The penthouse is surrounded, the airspace frozen. The only way you're getting out alive is if you let the hacker go and surrender."

Instead of Tedesco's voice coming through the aural system, it was Frankie's. He was pure fury. "You provide us with a shuttle out of here, or I spill his blood all over the floor! That's it, end of discussion!"

Two military agents dressed in fatigues rushed in with compucases. One nodded to the other. Then the other spoke, addressing McAllister. "Sir, all cameras are dead. We just killed them. Eyes are blind. We can do ears next if need be."

"Keep communication open for now," McAllister ordered.

"We can cut power with the push of a button," one tech said. "We are well versed in Venus technology." He grinned. "These guys think they are so smart altering our tech, but the military has emergency canceling tech, and it always works."

"What I need is for you to open this door." Mina indicated the monstrosity in front of her. "The hacker who's being held hostage cracked it yesterday in about two minutes."

The other tech had been tapping things into his

compucase. He cleared his throat and glanced up. "So far I haven't been successful. I'm still working on it."

"Hurry up."

The military tech's brow furrowed. "It's…complicated coding. I haven't seen anything like it before. It's going to take some time."

Frankie's voice boomed around them. "You're not getting in here. I've enacted a safe-room protocol. Try all you want, but the system is jammed. Agree to what I want, or this asshole dies."

Agent Darian entered the hallway, carrying a crystalline board. She brought it to Mina without speaking. The cameras were off on Tedesco's side, so they didn't have a vis on the team outside their door, but Mina knew Tedesco and Frankie were listening closely.

Mina took the board. It was live vid of the camera still shooting from the floor where Lee had kicked it. It showed Frankie and Tedesco standing within range. Lee sat in the chair Tedesco had vacated. The side of his face was bloody, but he was alive.

Agent Darian handed Mina a canal insert. Mina slid it into her ear.

Now she had eyes and ears inside.

"What are we going to do?" Frankie raged as he paced back and forth in and out of range of the cam. "I knew this was a setup. I *knew* it. You never listen to me!"

"We have options." The elder was eerily calm.

"What *options?*" Frankie gestured widely toward the interior of the house. "We're surrounded. You heard her. There's no way out. The only leverage we have is this kid right here who just exposed us. You should've listened to me! We could've been on an island in the middle of the Caribbean. Instead, we're about to be boxed up for life! Either that or dead."

Tedesco ignored his son's tantrum and turned his attention on Lee. "You're not a hacker at all, are you?" Tedesco's voice was still, no emotion rang through. He was like a zombie. The man was morphing into something else right before Mina's eyes.

"I *am* a hacker," Lee answered petulantly.

Careful, Lee.

"Ah," Tedesco said. "But not Jordan Maybach. You're a government agent."

Frankie stormed back into the frame. "This little piss bucket is an agent? Can't be. He's all of about eighteen or nineteen. I don't believe it! He's just a lackey cut-rate hacker the feds hired to do their dirty work for them."

"If that were the case, they wouldn't care so much about saving his life. Why not be rid of a hacker who gets in their way? No." He looked thoughtful. "This is one of their own." Tedesco turned and walked toward a cabinet, placing his palm on the front. It popped open immediately.

The entire thing was packed with weapons. Various guns mounted on the wall, knives lined up on a red cloth like glittering jewels, swords hanging in the back on special hooks.

Agent Darian made a startled sound, and Mina shot her a look, shaking her head, bringing her finger up to her lips. As of right now, Tedesco didn't know they were watching. She wanted to keep it that way.

A sim voice addressed Tedesco. "Sir, would you like me to unlock the drawers?"

"That won't be necessary, Victor. I have what I need." From the cabinet, Tedesco had taken a large, gleaming, serrated knife the length of Mina's forearm. Very calmly, he paced back to Lee, settling it, not against his neck like Mina had assumed he might, but at the top of his ear. "Tell me where the camera is, or I will cut off your ear. And while this knife is very sharp, and it will do the job quickly and precisely, it will hurt a great deal and bleed a lot more."

Tedesco had ice for blood. He wouldn't think twice about dicing Lee up. This showed who the true head of Veritus was. As much as Frankie squawked, Tedesco was the malignancy. The head of the beast. The leader. Mina was certain he was a psychopath after seeing the way his face had drained of any real emotion, like it had been a chore for him to keep up the charade before.

Mina strode over to the military technician who was in charge of breaking the code for the door. "I need in there now," she growled. "Make it happen."

Lee's voice drew her back to the board. His head was at an angle, his jaw clenched. "I don't know what you're talking about," Lee bit out under the force of the knife at his ear, blood beginning to dribble down his neck. "There's no camera."

"No," Mina murmured very quietly, willing Lee to take heed. "Tell him. Distract him. Don't refuse him."

Tedesco chuckled. It was a hollow sound. "I'm not as stupid as you think. The agents knew when to kick my door in. They've been watching all along. Tell me what I want to know, boy, or you lose one ear and then the other. Then I'll start on your fingers. We have time to kill, and killing is a particularly favorite pastime of mine, so let's start with the basics. Where is the camera?"

"You scanned me," Lee gritted. "You know I didn't bring any tech with me."

"Oh, the federal government has its ways." Tedesco began to move his hand in a sawing motion, and Mina had to stop herself from screaming. "Tell me, or it's gone." Blood gushed down Lee's neck, and he squeezed his eyes shut.

Lee was going to lose an ear because he was unwilling to break.

Another sound came from inside the room. Mina watched as a large screen emerged from the floor. Frankie commanded it on. Thankfully, that distracted Tedesco, who looked up and froze.

The screencast was already in progress.

Melissa Socorro was eagerly delivering the sordid information to her viewers, decked out in a sparkling red top. "More files are being exposed as I speak. The contents of the files have been mirrored to almost every media outlet in the city. This might be the biggest story we've had since the murderous Cannibal Creep was captured twenty-five years ago. The evidence is undeniable." Her voice bubbled and popped with unbridled enthusiasm. "It seems Franco Tedesco the Third, known for his movie investments and shipping enterprise, is the leader of Veritus. I repeat, this influential man—a gigantic supernova of an icon in the building industry who co-owns The Mega, the first megascraper in the city—is *head* of a group known for the vicious killings of dozens and dozens of citizens with lethal gas over the past twenty-five years. He's been living right under our noses the whole time. Or actually, right above our noses, in a penthouse in the sky. He's been masquerading in broad daylight—"

A keening tone emanated out of Frankie as he marched up to his father and grabbed the knife out of his hand. "You mirrored the files on our computer!" he screamed at Lee. "You exposed us to the world! I'm going to end you now, you double-crossing motherfu—"

"Put the knife down!" Mina shouted, knowing they were listening, her anger and fear for the rookie pouring out. Her own voice echoed in her ear as she heard it reverberate inside Tedesco's inner sanctum through his aural system. "Put it down! Or I will personally see that you're placed in a deprivation tank for the next fifty years. You'll be begging for a box. You'll be nothing more than a shadow begging for mercy." Her voice was feral enough to garner attention.

Mina watched Frankie lower the knife.

The elder Tedesco chuckled. "It seems you've hit a nerve, Frankie. We can work with a nerve."

McAllister's hand landed on Mina's shoulder, steadying her, giving her a single nod.

"What are you talking about?" Frankie raged at his father. "We've got nothing to work with!" He tossed a hand at the screen, where Melissa Socorro was gleefully flashing pages and pages of incriminating documents for all to see. "It's all out there. You allowed this hacker to *mirror* your computer. There is no getting rid of the evidence, ever. We're totally screwed, and you're just standing here like a moron with a rod up his ass like always—"

As Frankie continued his tirade, Tedesco walked quietly back to his weapons cache. He calmly turned toward Frankie, another knife in his hand. This one was some kind of carving knife.

It was skinny, thin, and had a double-edged blade.

Instead of resuming his intention to sever Lee's ear, Tedesco plunged the blade straight into the neck of his only son.

He hadn't even paused to think it over. A crowd of agents had gathered around Mina. Everyone had been riveted on how this would play out. Several agents swore under their breath, a few others gagged.

Frankie's jugular had been completely obliterated, blood erupting out of the gash like a geyser. He gurgled as he fell to his knees, clutching the wound, his hands dripping with his own blood.

"Holy shit," one agent murmured.

"His own kid," another whispered.

"That's cold-blooded, man."

Tedesco clasped his hands together, the knife, now covered in blood, still in his grasp. "You'll forgive me if I don't know which way to face so that I'm on camera. Send the woman in. She comes alone, or this agent suffers the same fate as my son. You have ten seconds. Victor, disengage safe-room protocol and open main door. If more than one person crosses the threshold, activate lethal gas." His eyes were eerily devoid of anything. Nothing lurked there.

"Did you think I would do any less?" he asked as if someone had asked him why he'd outfitted his own home with gas. "The entire residence is piped for it. Gas has always been my preferred method of killing. Do come in, won't you?"

Chapter 24

THERE WAS NO time to talk through a plan of any kind, not that they could, as Tedesco was listening. Mina had no choice but to do as she was told. She, along with every agent here, knew that if she didn't, Lee was as good as dead.

She walked toward the door as it began to slide open, McAllister accompanying her. He didn't bother to tell her not to go in.

Instead, he leaned in, close to her ear, and whispered one word, "Ballpark," as he handed her a tiny object.

She placed it in her pocket.

Mina had no idea if Tedesco would scan her for tech, but he wouldn't be foolish enough to think an agent would come in with nothing. He still thought he was invincible with his threat of releasing the gas, even though his empire was crumbling around him.

Mina was educated in psychopaths, as was every agent. Training in mental illnesses was mandatory, as many of their quarries presented with these traits. Psychopaths had a disjointed view of the world, were usually extremely intelligent, were incapable of feeling empathy or remorse, and were well versed in manipulation. They felt most rules didn't apply to them. Knowing how they operated worked in Mina's favor.

As she crossed into the first room, the door slid shut behind her.

It was hard to believe she'd been sneaking around here a little more than twenty-four hours ago.

The doors to the inner office were wide open. Two strides later, she stood in front of Tedesco and Lee. With shock and a bit of confusion, she saw that both Keith and Lawrence were out cold on the floor. They hadn't been in camera range, but Mina had figured they were skulking around someplace.

Tedesco noticed her reaction to the men. "I needed them out of the way. My son barely noticed. If he had, maybe he'd still be alive. He's never been very astute."

Mina moved forward cautiously. "He wasn't as smart as you."

"Not many people are. It's a shame, really. But he was useful. Until now." He held up his free hand, which was red with blood. "That's far enough."

Mina had barely entered the office. She gave Lee only a cursory glance. She didn't want to focus on him and give Tedesco any indication she was partial to the rookie or that she wasn't planning on leaving the residence without him.

Lee was in rough shape. There was a lot of blood.

"There is no way out of here," Mina told Tedesco. "You're smart enough to know that." Start with brutal honesty, go from there.

"Of course there's a way out. There's always a way out. That's why you're here. You and I will banter for a bit." He twirled a finger in the air for context. "Then after the pleasantries, we will craft a reasonable solution. It will end up being my life in exchange for all of yours, because as I pointed out already, the entire residence is piped with gas that will kill on contact. Once the negotiation is finished, I will depart in a shuttle and head to an island very far away from here, where I will voluntarily exile myself, and business will go back to normal."

He had it all figured out.

"You're forgetting that you've committed gross atrocities for which people will demand you be held accountable."

"That's the very reason I killed my only son." He barley gave Frankie, sprawled in a pool of his own gore, a glance. "He will go down as the head of Veritus. You can claim you brought him down any way you'd like. I will concur. Then I will give the media my statement, complete with heartfelt emotion, claiming my innocence and ignorance of his criminal activities. It will all blow over in a week or two."

He was a psychopath *and* a madman.

As Melissa had already stated, this was the story of the century. There was no way it was gusting anywhere anytime soon. But Tedesco genuinely believed the scenario he was presenting could be a possibility.

"That's one option," Mina countered. "Another is you come in willingly, tell us everything we need to know about who you've killed over the last twenty-some-odd years, beyond what we already know, and in return, we give you some leeway"—fat chance—"for cooperating."

A spark of anger ignited. "You are mistaken. You cannot force me to leave this residence against my will. Either I go free, or we all die. It's as simple as that."

"Why did you plant the key?" Mina changed tactics. "I followed everything you did"—most everything—"until Frankie found the key, which was planted in front of the hacker."

Tedesco shrugged almost imperceptibly. "This young man thought I was stupid." Rage flitted across his face. "He showed me the workings of a pixel mirror and thought I wouldn't know what it was. Once I saw it, I knew instantly who he was and who he was working for and that you were watching and listening. I needed Frankie unhinged." He shrugged again. "Well, more unhinged than he already was. So I dropped the key on the desk where it bounced to the floor. If this agent had to die, I wanted my son to do it. It also had the benefit of being a distraction so I could put an end to Frankie's henchmen, as they would've likely tried to stop my actions. He knew how to pick loyal supporters."

Not always. Placido aka Andy, for one.

Mina glanced at the two men on the floor. She'd originally thought they were unconscious. Now she noticed they weren't breathing. She looked back at Tedesco, who flashed her a morbid grin. He reached his blood-free hand into his pocket and pulled out what looked to be a standard medical airpen.

"An injection? That's fairly mundane for a big-time killer like you." Mina's voice stayed evenly modulated, bordering on bored. "I bet you were bummed you didn't get to use your beloved gas."

"Oh, but I did." He waggled the pen. "A single dose of oxygen to the bloodstream. Done right, it blows up the heart." He beamed as he glanced down at his handy tool. "I've had a number of these made to get the dosage exactly right. The correct medical term is *air embolism*, and it's not nearly as rewarding as watching them squirm and tear out their throats, fighting for their last breath."

Lee stiffened next to him. He was trying to keep it together. Tedesco was describing what he had done to Lee's father. Mina appreciated him keeping calm. It seemed his ear had stopped gushing blood. That was a relief. The wound had to be painful.

"But it's quiet and efficient," Tedesco went on. "As I said, my son didn't even notice. He was too focused on the key."

"I'm assuming the key will lead to physical evidence designed to pin all of your nefarious activities on Frankie."

"Of course. You're catching on now." He taunted her. "Everything in the storage unit is linked to Frankie. It had to be that way, I'm afraid."

"Because you knew this day would come eventually."

"Yes. I knew this day would come. Although, I expected it would arrive sooner. But I've found government officials are easily distracted by large sums of currency, so I was able to prolong my independence. It's a great shame chemis were found aboard my ship, which is why we're standing here at this very moment. Frankie forgot to, shall we say, grease the wheels in Greece. Another reason he had to die. We both knew it would lead to our downfall. We just expected to have a few more days to get things in proper order." He glanced around his office. "I will miss it here. No one had ever managed to breach my sanctuary until yesterday. Was it you? Or another?"

"It was me."

His eyebrows rose.

Tedesco thought he'd picked a messenger. A female agent who had a tender heart toward the hacker he was trying to saw into pieces. He'd wanted someone malleable. Someone he could manipulate.

Instead, he'd gotten Mina.

"You couldn't have accomplished it alone." His tone was matter-of-fact.

"Oh, I was alone, and it wasn't really that hard. You should've entrusted a professional instead of your son. Your security was cheaply done and easy to breach." She'd hit a nerve. Tedesco's eyelid began to twitch. "Frankie barely hid the fact he'd altered military tech— and badly at that, I might add." Mina faked a yawn, patting her mouth briefly. "I could've done it in my sleep."

She didn't dare look at Lee, who was probably flashing a *yeah, right* look. The rookie never kept his face clean. It's a good thing Tedesco stood behind him.

"If my system had recognized an intruder, you would've died a very painful death," Tedesco spat.

Mina feigned more boredom. She hoped it was convincing. "Yeah, at the time we were just trying to figure out where your shipping records were located. Thought maybe you were manufacturing chemis. We didn't know about the Veritus stuff. You can blame Frankie for that, too. He put a plant in your garden. Literally. Once caught, that guy sang like he was auditioning for *Screen Voice Sensation*. We ended up giving him a pretty sweet deal." Tedesco was predictably hating everything she was saying, as none of it benefited him. "It all worked out in our favor in the end."

"I'm tired of this banter." He took a step closer to Lee, placing the knife against the rookie's neck. "It's time to make *our* deal."

Mina mocked concern, glancing around. "I'm not sure you want to do this on camera, you know, in case I have to promise you things *off the record*." She whispered the last three words, indicating she had the ability to propose something good. "So far, everything you've said has been recorded, including your love of killing and your admission to ending three people in this very room. You've actually given us everything we need to convict without a trial, even without all that pesky pixelated mirror stuff floating in the ether. That means you're a proud member of the small but very notorious group of lawbreakers imprisoned by the Unequivocal Evidence Act of 2073." She gave a half-hearted laugh. "But having our deal on record before we agree on terms would not be advantageous, which I'm sure you're well aware of with your degree of intelligence—"

"Where's the camera?" Tedesco asked stiffly as he moved the blade away from Lee's neck, like she'd wanted him to.

"I'm not sure, actually. Maybe we should ask the hacker, since he's the one who brought it in."

"I'm not going to ask twice. Produce it or die." Tedesco shoved Lee out of his seat.

Lee, taking his cue from Mina, fell to his knees and began to search the fiber covering of the floor *away* from the desk. *Good job, Lee.* Mina hadn't been sure the rookie had been following her as closely as he'd needed to.

"I tossed it over this way when Frankie came to scan me the second time." Lee stroked the area in front of him back and forth with his hands. "I'm sure I can find it."

Tedesco curled his top lip, looking feral. "You have thirty seconds."

"How about if I help? It'll go faster," Mina suggested.

He pierced her with a cold, calculating gaze. "Stay right where you are."

Mina whipped her hands up in mock surrender. "No problem. I'll stay right here."

"Found it!" Lee exclaimed, scrambling up from the floor. Tedesco held out his hand, and Lee placed the tiny tech into his open palm.

Tedesco brought it close. "This is an old model. The video you have will be crude at best. But it's bigger than I thought you could get in under our nose. I'll give you that." Tedesco tapped the minuscule button on the top to stop it from recording and dropped it into his pocket.

Then, unfortunately, he ordered Lee back into the

chair and brought the knife back up to his neck. "Now, where were we?"

"I believe we were in the process of negotiating your freedom. I have to be very upfront with you," Mina admitted in a tone that rang with mock apology. "There's a slim-to-none chance you'll get anything you ask for because, you know, you killed a ton of people, and you have very little bartering power, and we have all the evidence we need to put you away until your last dying breath."

Tedesco's face clouded. "I have plenty to barter with! I have this agent in front of me who ruined my life." He slid the blade up Lee's cheek, thankfully not hard enough to draw blood. "Then I have you." He waved the knife in front of him. "And the other agents crowded into my residence like hyenas waiting for the kill." He gestured toward the hallway. "All who will die a very painful death if I don't get—"

Mina swished a hand, cutting him off. "Yeah, yeah. I get it about the gas. I'm not sorry to tell you the other agents are long gone. We subbed with SWAT-bots as soon as I entered your office. Ask your sim to do a human scan. He'll tell you. It's just us. And, not sorry again, the two of us are considered disposable." She gestured between her and Lee. "The hacker, who you think is an agent, isn't one. Frankie was right. He's only nineteen."

A small squeak came from the rookie. *Don't ruin it now, Lee.*

"We hired him because Jordan wouldn't cooperate.

This young hacker signed a waiver, though. So it's not our fault if anything bad happens to him."

Another squeak.

"I came in here against my superior's wishes. I hoped you'd see reason, because you're smart." She gave him a sunny smile. "And smart people tend to see what's right in front of them." No way was Tedesco going to see reason.

"You're toying with me. I don't like it when people play games." Without hesitation, he inserted the tip of the blade into Lee's neck. Blood began to trickle at a steady pace, but at least it wasn't pouring out like a major artery had been nicked.

Shit.

Lee closed his eyes, gritting his teeth. He trusted Mina to get them out of this. And she would. She just had to shimmy a few steps closer, and they'd be there.

Mina cleared her throat. "The best I can do is put in a provision that you get some of your favorite meals once in a while and maybe keep a few plants in your box. We know you're a big fan of plants. But that's only if you surrender to us right now."

"Absolutely not. I want full immunity for the atrocities my son committed. I will accept exile, as I realized my son was a vicious murderer, and I did nothing to stop him." *So generous.* "Anything less is unacceptable."

"I haven't seen the documents Melissa Socorro is talking about..." Mina gestured at the screencast, which was muted but still flashing document after document. "But I'm pretty sure they implicate *you* and not your son."

"That's neither here nor there." He waved his knifeless hand around. "My litigators will plead my case to the public. All you need to do is arrange a shuttle, and everything will work itself out. You best do it soon. He's losing a lot of blood, and I'm feeling the urge to sever his jugular."

Mina tried to will Lee to open his eyes. He was too close to Tedesco for her to initiate the protocol McAllister was waiting for.

"You're not going to kill him," Mina said evenly. "That would severely diminish your chances of leaving this place alive, and I know you're a practical man. Do you remember the Juniper Group?"

Lee's eyes flew open.

"They were tax accountants. Nineteen years ago, they noticed something wrong with the books of one of their clients, a shell corporation by the name of Dandelion, and reported them to the federal government. The next day, they were gassed while they worked. Fifteen people died in that attack, all of them innocent of any wrongdoing. One was a man named Langley Adams."

Tedesco looked as though Mina had slapped him. He hadn't expected her to bring up a particular instance of his evil. He found his rage soon enough. "Of course I don't remember!" he bellowed. "Those attacks were *never* personal. It was a necessary means to meet an end. If they had exposed Dandelion, we would have lost several million in world currency." In his distraction, the blade Tedesco held slipped away from Lee's neck. "I couldn't allow that to happen. I had several ships in production and two vids I was championing. Losing that money would've been *detrimental* to my business."

Mina took a step forward. "The reason you don't remember Juniper Group is because you can't *feel* anything. You're nothing more than a husk of sagging, enhanced skin. No soul lurks inside of you. No human emotion. Everything is an act. You have to pretend your way through life because everything is flat and gray to you. If you didn't play the part, people would see your true self, and they would run away screaming."

Tedesco dropped the hand that held the knife and took a step toward Mina, his voice quaking. "You want to die, don't you? That's why you're baiting me. You can't wait for death."

"I can promise you I don't want to die." Mina angled her head a fraction to the right. Lee slipped out of his seat, scooting that way. Tedesco was oblivious. "But you don't know that, because you're having trouble reading the situation. You don't know what I'm up to. I'm confusing you. This wasn't the holo dance we were supposed to do. Where did the banter go?"

"You're going to die a slow, painful death, and I'm going to watch." Spittle dribbled out of his mouth. "You will give me what I want, or I will kill you right here." He lifted the knife.

"I don't think so. That's not in the *ballpark* today."

Mina sprang to the right.

Chapter 26

THE BOMB WAS small, but concentrated. Instantaneously, Mina was back on her feet calling, "Lee, are you okay?" She ran toward Tedesco. She couldn't give the man time to speak, or they all would die from inhaling noxious gas.

Mina reached him quickly, clamping her hand over his mouth. She didn't want to look at the damage, but she had to.

The "camera" he'd placed in his pocket had actually been a mini hydro-bomb that had blown a hole in his abdomen and damaged the top of his leg.

Lee scrambled toward them, clutching his neck, blood dripping between his fingers. "Is he dead?"

"Unconscious." Mina glanced around. Agents weren't swarming the room yet. "Lee, I need you to open the door. Apparently, the military needs a Level XIII course in breaching a coded door. But do it very carefully. As you heard, this place is piped for gas. One wrong move, and we're all dead."

"Oh, I shut that down."

"What?" Mina peered at him, momentarily confused. "There's no gas?"

Lee shook his head, then grimaced in pain. "Once I was inside his computer, I found the controls to the main residence and deactivated the deadly security protocols. Since they were marked 'deadly,' I figured I should probably shut them down."

Mina sat back on her heels. "Okay. Yeah. That was good."

Before Lee could move to open the door, agents burst in. Several medi-workers rushed in behind them. Tiredly, Mina rose to her feet. Adrenaline had kicked in throughout her interaction with Tedesco and had peaked during the explosion. Now she felt a little off-balance.

McAllister entered next, decked out in full SWAT gear, including a gas mask dangling around his neck. He was talking to another agent, who was nodding. "Then get me Chance Landers. We want a full press setup in fifteen outside the building. We need to move fast. News will leak about the status of father and son quickly. It's imperative we control the narrative. Commander Jenkins from DGS will take lead, followed by Agent Groening from the FBI High Crimes Unit."

The agent excused himself to rush off to complete the tasks.

McAllister stopped in front of Mina and Lee, giving them each a thorough appraisal. "Well done, Agents. We achieved our goal. You two have brought down Veritus and done the CIU proud."

It hadn't sunk in yet that this had morphed quickly into the biggest op Mina had ever been involved in. It'd happened so fast it was hard to keep up.

"Your seventy-two hours of leave begins immediately. Agent Adams, there's a medi-drone waiting for you on the roof. Get that ear and neck taken care of. We'll debrief tomorrow after you've had a chance to rest."

"Sir," Mina started, "I don't need that much time off—"

"That's an order." McAllister lifted a brow, giving her a hawkish stare that rivaled Cots' any day of the week. "Use this downtime to do some *research*. There are two more events that need, shall we say, revisiting."

McAllister was giving Mina permission to address the issues with the French Protectorate and Vince, as well as the Plush incident with Quinn's acquaintance Daphne. Mina appreciated that.

"Permission to accompany Agent Adams to the Medi Center first."

"Granted. And when he's well enough, clue him in on what's going on outside this unit."

"Will do."

"Good. Because I'm pairing you two together for the foreseeable future." He grinned. "It seems Agent Adams will have no better partner in the field than you, Agent Kane. You've proven yourself to be loyal and *uniquely* dedicated in your mentorship." His chuckle had an evil-genius ring to it.

He was right. Or right-*ish*.

Mina had a hard time believing it herself, but there it was.

She'd raced toward possible death without thought, all to protect the rookie. She accepted her burden with a long, tumbling sigh, while reaching out to propel a confused Lee toward the door.

"We'll be in touch," she called over her shoulder.

As they walked through the crowd of agents who'd assembled, most looking at them with respect, a few looking agitated, she nodded to Grigg, who gave them a small salute. She turned up a marble staircase with a banister carved with ornate lion heads that led to the roof. Typical mass murderer décor.

Once on the landing pad, two medi-workers rushed forward, leading Lee into the drone. She entered and took a seat out of the way, settling her head in her hands. She and Lee had just taken on Veritus and won. What a strange day. Agents could go their whole careers without executing an op this massively consequential. It would take time to sink in.

Mina had at least seventy-two hours.

⸻

"He's going to be fine," Kaylee commented for the seventh time as Mina paced the white, sanitary hallway. Why was it so white? Colors could be clean, too. "It's just an ear. Well, the top of an ear. It didn't even come all the way off. It just kind of flopped over." Kaylee plucked absently at her own ear. "He'll be good as new." Her gaze tracked Mina. "Sit down. You're making me nauseous. Or maybe those are the oysters I bought from the kiosk in the lobby. The trace was on point, but I'm not sure if my stomach can handle them after all. Why they have an oyster kiosk in a medical facility is another thing entirely." Kaylee rubbed a hand over her stomach. She looked oddly at home in this environment since she was still wearing her medi-uni from the op she'd just completed. The Sunny Ford syn suit was long gone.

It was almost two in the morning. They were both beat. Mina was glad Kaylee had come, insisting that Mina needed company and a calm-inducing presence. A misnomer to a great degree, but Mina was glad for the company.

"I'm not pacing because of his injuries," Mina said. Well, mostly not. The doctors had told her the same thing. That he'd be fine. He'd been stitched up and was taking a turn in a medi-pod, which would knit the tissue mostly back together in a matter of hours. "His mom lives halfway around the world."

"Yeah. You said that."

"She was aloof when I called her. Told me she couldn't make it home."

"Not very motherly."

"I told her that her son took down Veritus. She didn't seem to know what I was talking about."

"Maybe she's had a head injury."

"Lee's been on his own since he was sixteen."

"And?"

Mina took a seat next to her pal, scrubbing her hands over her face. She'd been alone for a few hours, thinking about it. Lee had been dealt a rough hand. "His father was murdered by Veritus when Lee was only three years old.

His mom left him when he was sixteen. He hasn't had any real guidance or anybody to look after him since then."

"You can't know that. He could have a quirky Aunt Mickey or a cousin named Beau who's his number one bestie. You don't know anything about him."

Kaylee was right. But that was, oddly, going to change. Mina was going to get to know the rookie—cousins, aunts, and everything in between.

"I mean," Kaylee went on, "it totally sucks that his father was murdered so horrifically. But how many people get to say they avenged their father's death and took down his killer? That's pretty damn spec."

It was.

"Mickey and Beau?"

Kaylee shrugged. "Sounds believable to me. Listen..." She shifted so she was facing Mina. "I'm not letting you take Lee under your wing like he's some broken chick that crashed out of the nest and rolled down a hill. I know you. You like to fix things. Lee's going to be fine. He's a good agent. He's an adult now. He'll figure this out. Not too long ago, he was The Wrong Lee. Now he's The Right Lee—or the Second to Right Lee—and that's fine, but he's not a child. After all, I was pretty much on my own at thirteen, and I turned out just fine."

Right then, a door opened, and Lee entered the hallway wearing medi-scrubs that looked two sizes too big. His head was wrapped in gauze that dipped low over his forehead, running behind his neck. His hair was a riot of violet unkemptness flopping all over, and his owl eyes were even more owly.

"Okay, well…" Kaylee cleared her throat as they both stood. "My mistake. He does resemble a baby bird that has tumbled out of a tree and rolled down a hill. You win. He needs a wingwoman, and you're it." She patted Mina's shoulder as they both moved toward the rookie. Kaylee leaned over and whispered, "Just try not to get too attached. I don't want to have to formulate adoption papers anytime soon."

"Very funny," Mina muttered. To Lee, she said, "How do you feel?"

"Um, good?"

"Is your ear still attached?" Kaylee asked.

"I think so." His owl eyes blinked.

"They must have him hopped up on painkillers," Kaylee said to Mina. "How many fingers am I holding up?" She lofted two in the air.

Mina tugged her pal's hand down and gave Kaylee a *be quiet* look as she guided Lee toward the transpo hub, which happened to be on this floor. A government craft was waiting.

"You'll be home in no time," Mina assured him.

Once outside, Kaylee waved goodbye. "My ride's over here. I'll talk to you two tomorrow. Congratulations, Lee. You're pretty solid for a rookie. It's not every day you can claim you took down a Planet's Most Wanted. This will go down in agency history for sure."

"Um, thanks."

Mina narrowed her gaze. Lee could, in fact, be hopped up on painkillers.

"This is us," Mina said as she propelled Lee into the craft.

They both gave their customary DNA sample, and the female sim intoned, "Welcome, Agent Kane and Agent Adams. What is your destination?"

"The Spire, public hub, level twenty," Mina asserted before Lee could order up anything else. To a confused and possibly high Lee, she said, "The doctor said you require a twenty-four monitor. So I'm it." She didn't mention she'd spoken to his mother. "My lounger is not very big, but it'll do." Nowhere did she add, *You have to stay with me because you're alone in the world, and you just brought down your father's killer, and you might need to process that with a friend.*

Lee didn't argue. Instead, he leaned his bandaged head back against the gel-rest. "Thank you." He closed his eyes. After a moment, when they were in the sky, he said, "I should have told you about my dad and my connection to Veritus. I just...I just couldn't get the words out. It was a mistake. It won't happen again."

So, not high after all. Actually fairly coherent.

"Damn right it won't happen again. If it does, you can kiss your badge goodbye." Mina's voice was calm and measured. She wanted to give him the facts, not chastise him. Well, maybe chastise a little. "By not telling me, you placed the op in jeopardy." Then she added a little comfort. "But it all worked out. You should be proud of your actions. You brought down a serial-killing ring. That's no small feat."

"I was prepared to die. Or I thought I was." Lee's eyes were still closed. "About halfway through, I kind of realized I didn't want to die. My dad wouldn't have been too happy with me. My mother always said I was the light of his life. He was an accountant, but also a hacker. Then you came in, and I really didn't want you to die." Lee opened eyes filled with fatigue and a hint of sadness. "I made a mess out of everything."

Mina shook her head. "No, you didn't." It was a miracle he hadn't. "Honestly, that op had the potential to be an epic fail, crashing and burning in a massive heap all around us. But the reason it didn't is because you made good choices under immense stress. I've learned in my six years as an agent that you either have what it takes in this profession, or you don't. Some agents who don't have a sense for the job try to learn, but they never really get it right. Their instincts are off. Other agents, such as rookies like yourself, might make strategic errors from time to time, but their instincts are on point. You were made for this job. You just need a little guidance." *That I will now dole out to you at every opportunity.*

"You're just saying that. McAllister is probably going to fire me."

"I'm not, and he would've fired you back at the penthouse in full view of everyone. He doesn't play favorites, and he doesn't shield failures. You didn't do everything right"—especially not the go-on-your-own-rogue stuff—"but you did a lot correct. If your father could see you now, he'd be proud."

Lee pressed his fingers into his eyes and rubbed. "I was too cocky. I showed Tedesco the pixel mirror. I assumed he wouldn't know what it was, but he did. We all could've died."

"Are you forgetting that you had the wherewithal to disable the gas? All these choices go hand in hand, Lee. The reason you showed Tedesco the mirror was because you were too close to this op. It was emotional for you. Your dad and all the other victims were on your mind. That compromised you, and that's exactly why we don't allow agents to go in when they're emotionally connected to a case. If you had told me about your connection to Veritus, we would've figured out another way. A safer way. You would've still been involved, but at a distance, where no emotion could affect the outcome."

The sim voice announced, "Destination imminent. Landing in ten seconds." The craft descended straight down, bouncing once, the doors opening.

They exited the craft and took a tube up to the three hundred and twentieth floor. Once they were inside, Veronica announced, "Welcome home. Ultras at forty percent. Do you wish to listen to any music or have me fill the soaker?" Two things Mina often asked for on her arrival home.

"Not now. Engage level five security. Messages?"

"Security engaged. One message from Quinn Kane. Would you like to hear it?"

"No." Nothing from Vince. She'd given him a six-hour window. She glanced at her cuff. He was two hours overdue.

"What's this?" Lee asked as they walked to the meal counter, where the delivery from Vince sat unopened. "Looks like it's made of black Midas. Nothing gets through this stuff." He picked up the small, black box and opened it. "Is this a Cupid's Bow?" He reached in and plucked out two tiny chips in the shapes of a tiny bow and arrow.

Mina moved closer. "I'm not sure." She hadn't investigated it yet. "I believe it's an encrypted locater."

"It is. Once you insert the arrow tip into the bow, a connection downloads from a remote location. They're really cool—and pretty rare."

"Are they hard to hack?"

Lee glanced up, startled. Then his eyes narrowed back on the chips. He was beginning to look more Lee-like. Mina was relieved. "For some people, maybe." He shrugged. "I've watched a few vids of hackers dissecting these. Didn't look too hard."

"Glad to hear it. First thing in the morning, you're going to hack it."

"Who's it from?"

"Vincent Kramer."

Lee's eyebrows rose to the edge of the gauze wrapped around his head, but he said nothing.

Mina was too tired to go into the whole story right now. Even though Vince was a few hours late checking in, she had to believe he was okay. He was the colonel-in-arms of the French Protectorate, after all. The man was cunning and smart and worked for a powerful organization. He could wait until morning.

Lord knew he would dominate her sleep tonight.

She felt the blush rising up her cheeks, so she busied herself getting a blanket and pillow for Lee and making up the lounger for him. Once it was ready, she asked, "Are you hungry? Eggie makes a mean cheeseburger."

Lee yawned. "Nah, they filled me up with fluid nutrients. Just tired."

"If you need anything, alert Veronica. She'll wake me up."

"Got it." Lee settled on the lounger and pulled up the blanket. Mina began to walk to her room. "Agent Kane?"

Mina stopped, turning around. "Yeah?"

"You're turning out to be the best agent mentor I've ever had."

"I'm the *only* agent mentor you've ever had. Get some sleep. It's going to be a long day tomorrow tracking down foreign leaders who've mysteriously vanished. That's not even counting on figuring out what's going on with Bliss Corp and their illegal experimentation with Plush."

McAllister had put them on leave, not holiday.

"Plush?" Lee asked tiredly. "You mean...um...the sex enhancement drug?"

"The very one. I'll fill you in tomorrow. You heard what Director McAllister said. We're going to be working together for the foreseeable future."

This should have been more of a shocker. Only a few days ago, Mina had vowed never to be assigned to work with the rookie again. Now he was sleeping on her lounger. Baby chick, indeed.

Kaylee was right. She did like to fix things.

"Good night, Lee."

"Good night. And thanks."

"You're welcome."

CUPID'S BOW

A MINA KANE NOVEL: BOOK THREE

AMANDA CARLSON

Chapter 1

Mina woke to the smell of bacon. *Odd.* She opened her eyes and realized she could actually hear it sizzling. She slipped out of her platform by rolling to the edge and climbing out, because she hadn't gotten the settings just right, and it was still too soft.

Once on solid ground, she grabbed a modest wrap to put on around her gown, belting it as she walked, and padded into her living area to see what was up with the bacon.

The scene took her a moment to comprehend, as her synapses weren't fully firing. She rubbed her eyes.

Lee, the unseasoned rookie who'd been irritating the hell out of her only a short time ago and who'd helped her take down a serial killer the night before, stood at her island, frying bacon on what looked to be a molecular induction skillet she'd had no idea she owned.

His head was still wrapped with thick gauze because said killer had tried to saw off his ear. Shockingly violet hair stuck out all over like some kind of ridiculous enhancement gone all kinds of wrong. A fake goatee, dyed the same deranged purple, was peeling off his chin. He looked like he'd gotten into a fight with an old-fashioned potato peeler and lost.

He smiled. The goatee flapped. "Good morning." He poked at the bacon with a long contraption she also hadn't known she owned. Or maybe he'd printed some specialized bacon-flipping tool? Once fully awake, she'd find out. Or not.

The rookie looked nothing like the baby chick who'd fallen out of a tree last night. This morning, he was more like a lunatic escaped from a bad-hair asylum hell-bent on eating perfectly crisp bacon.

"What are you doing?" It was the only thing she could think of to ask. A cup of coffee sat on the counter, slightly creamed. "Is this for me?"

He nodded.

She picked it up and took a sip. "*Ahhh.*"

"One of my only memories of my father is of eating bacon together," he said. "I woke up thinking about him, so I asked your Magnito to print me some. But everyone knows printers don't ever get the crispy part right, even a top-of-the-line unit like yours." He shrugged. "So I looked around and found this skillet. I'm making breakfast partly as a thanks to you for taking me in last night and partly because I'm feeling nostalgic. I appreciate you letting me stay here. You didn't have to."

Well, jeez.

Hard to argue with dad bacon.

Mina pulled out a stool and sat, clutching the warm mug between both hands. Lee asked Eggie, her now-cooperative meal printer that had created this excellent cup of coffee, to make two orders of scrambled eggs and two orange juices. Eggie complied.

Once the printer had provided the eggs and juice, Lee deemed the bacon ready and added it to their plates. Then he took the seat next to her.

Mina raised an eyebrow as she picked up a slice of the bacon. She brought it to her nose. Smelled like bacon. Was greasy like bacon. She took a bite.

"*Mmm.* That's really good." She took a moment to savor, chewing slowly. "I haven't tasted decent bacon in, I think, forever." Who took the time to cook something twice? Mina barely had time to eat the meals Eggie gave her. "Thanks, Lee. Greasy goodness is a really great way to start the day."

Neither of them mentioned it was almost noon.

Lee picked up a piece of his bacon. He closed his eyes.

Mina gave him a moment. Lots of big things had happened last night. Veritus, a serial-killing crime ring, had been brought down after being on the Planet's Most Wanted list for over twenty-five years. The kingpin, Franco Tedesco the Third, who was also a full-blown psychopath, had been responsible for the death of Langley Adams, Lee's father. None of this information had been helpfully imparted to Mina ahead of time, so Lee had been forced to face his father's killer on his own, with almost no warning whatsoever.

Intense for a seasoned agent, unthinkable for a rookie.

He'd made mistakes—like creating a pixel mirror to expose sensitive data to the world without prior approval—but in the end he'd gotten the job done and had helped bring a nefarious and previously out-of-reach criminal to justice.

As far as Mina knew, Tedesco was still alive, even though he'd taken a hit to the abdomen from a mini hydro-bomb. Neither she nor Lee had been debriefed by their director yet. They were technically on leave for the next sixty-something hours. Mostly to recuperate from an emotional op, but also to conduct some necessary off-duty research.

Lee opened his eyes. "Are you sure I'm not getting fired?"

"Not that I know of," Mina answered, shoveling in a forkful of eggs. Eggie had nailed them as well. The consistency was A-grade fluff.

"That's good." Lee was fairly low-key. It seemed he needed some cheering.

Mina across the counter and grabbed the black armored Midas box he'd looked over last night and slid it toward him. "This encrypted locator is going to need your attention as soon as breakfast is over, but *after* you take a turn in my soaker with some dissolvers. That horrid violet needs to go, and I can't even discuss that goatee for fear of ruining this delicious breakfast."

Last night, Lee had posed as superhacker Jordan Maybach, who went around looking like that on purpose. Some people couldn't be trained. Mina appraised Lee and added, "That is, if your ear and neck are all healed.

The medi-specialist said you could take off the bandages this morning. I don't see any blood. That's good. Does anything hurt?"

"Not really, just kind of a lingering ache." Lee popped the last of the crisped perfection into his mouth, then wiped his hands on a cloth. The kid had thought of everything. He picked up the Midas box, opening the lid. "Why did Vincent Kramer send you a Cupid's Bow?"

"Why in the *hell* is it called that?" The words tumbled out with more fervor than anyone anywhere would have deemed necessary for the situation. They just kept coming. "It's an encrypted locator. It has nothing to do with love." Why had she immediately jumped to the L word? Maybe she didn't want to think about her childhood pal, who'd turned out to be quite the international heartthrob, sending her cutesy little love symbols? It was a reasonable assumption.

Judging by the look on Lee's face, Mina had overreacted to a stratospheric degree. She shoveled in another forkful of eggs.

"Um, because it's small and cute?" Lee plucked out two data chips that were nestled inside some serious gel-cush. A tiny bow and a tiny arrow. No hearts anywhere, thank goodness. "I don't think…um…love was on the mind of whoever created this. I think Cupid is considered sneaky. This device is actually pretty rare, very costly, and really well-made. I've only known of a few hackers who can crack them." He demonstrated placing the arrow in the little niche of the bow without actually doing it. "The arrow fits into this groove. If you place them together, a signal is generated, and the encryption is downloaded from the remote database where it's cloaked and waiting. To receive the location without a hack, you have to have a Cupid reader that inserts right here." He tapped the end of the bow where Mina noticed a pinhole connector. "The trick to hacking this cleanly is to figure out where the database is located without actually connecting them. Once you have the coordinates, it's fairly easy. You just siphon the information, while trying not to alert the sender of what you're doing."

He was sounding more Lee-like by the second. Nothing like a good geek-out to get a techie back on track.

"I never thought I'd get to play around with one of these. It's pretty spec."

Mina finished her eggs and took a swig of juice. "Well, today's your lucky borrow credit day." Her voice was jolly, verging on singsongy, which she normally abhorred, but everyone forgetting about the angry-love stuff was a high priority. "The reason the colonel-in-arms of the French Protectorate sent me that is so he can be located if he goes missing. He was supposed to contact me last night between eighteen hundred and midnight, but didn't. So technically, by the parameters I made him agree to, he's missing. He asked me to deliver that"—she bobbed her head toward the tech—"to Chaz Burquist, the head of the International Judicial Committee so they can start an inquisition into his whereabouts." She glanced at Lee to find him studying her with a quizzical expression.

"If he's missing, shouldn't you deliver it now?"

"Technically, yes. But there are questions with his vid

chat that don't add up and are making me think twice. I've been going over it in my mind a kiloton. Originally, he didn't want any set check-in times, which was odd. Why not give me a specific timeframe if a real threat was breathing down his curved eurocollar? If I waited too long, it might be too late to help." Mina listed the other issues, which helped organize them in her mind. "He had a possible black eye, he was uneasy and fidgety, he was quiet and appeared vaguely unsure. He presented a stark contrast to the confident guy who took me to dinner." Lee nodded along. "I mean, why ask me, of all people, to go to Chaz, when picking a colleague in France would've made more sense? Chaz is located in Italy, which is much closer to France. Vince and I only reconnected like a week ago. We hardly know each other. I'm ill-suited as the trilinguist he believes me to be, to provide any real help or even to carry out the request, even with my name on a list." She took her empty dishes to the grinder. "Even though there's a lot of issues, I do plan to take his request seriously. If you can't break the encryption, and we can't locate him fairly quickly, I'll go to Chaz." That was definite. She didn't want anything to happen to Vince. "But all these discrepancies are making me cautious. We'll have to get an okay from our esteemed director to hack, of course."

"Of course." Lee looked thoughtful. "I trust your take on this. You're good at spotting all the details. It seems like we should try to hack it." He shrugged. "There's a possibility Vince wants you to. I mean, there could be a message hidden in the device because he thought he was being monitored and felt he couldn't tell you something secret over a regular channel."

Mina's eyebrows rose as she considered. "That didn't occur to me and it should've. Lee, you're brilliant." The rookie blushed and looked away. "A hidden message is a possibility. Once we check in with McAllister, I'm sure he'll make the hack a priority."

Veronica, Mina's home sim, announced in her light, plucky British accent, "A vid chat request from Kaylee Poston is coming through. Do you wish to accept?"

"Yes, screen at fifty."

An image of Mina's best pal and fellow federal agent popped on the wall a second later. Kaylee was dressed for work in functional charcoal tuck pants and an orange flow shirt, her black blunt-cut bob perfectly styled, not a strand out of place.

Unlike Mina, who was still in her sleep clothes, hair uncombed and tumbling around her shoulders, and Lee, who still wore the ruffled green two-sizes-too-big medi-patient scrubs from last night.

"It's nice to see you two are finally up and at 'em," Kaylee announced. "While you were snoozing the day away, I was off doing my patriotic duty chasing an ID-smuggling thug through a city park. Good times. After I brought that creep in, I went to headquarters to do a deep dive on a currency bandit. Apparently, some punk thinks it's funny to gather up other people's solid currency and toss it out of megas. Not only is it utterly stupid to waste coin like that, but falling hunks of silver from four hundred stories up can actually *kill* someone.

Thank the great cosmos above nobody's died yet. I think I've narrowed down his position. He's either a kilometer away or somewhere in Nebraska."

Chucking, Mina said, "Seems like you've had a busy morning, but you didn't bring down one of the Planet's Most Wanted last night by almost blowing him in half. We did such a stellar job that McAllister ordered us on leave. We're off for another sixty."

Mina left out all of Lee's emotional dad stuff, as Kaylee already knew lots of it from last night. Also his emotional mom stuff, since she had basically left him when the rookie had been just sixteen and was refusing to return now, which was why Mina had taken him in, all of which Kaylee also knew.

And they weren't technically *off* off. They were going to hack stuff—like the Cupid's Bow—and hopefully start investigating the Plush issue that had come up when Mina's brother's new friend had had a bad reaction.

"Last night was child's play." Kaylee swished her hand. Then she leaned forward, squinting. "What's wrong with your face, Lee? You look like you're molting."

Mina was waiting for the rookie to add his dishes to the mix before she initiated the grinder. Having another person in her home was weird. "Lee has a date with some dissolvers very soon. Then we're going to deal with the Cupid's Bow."

"Cupid's Bow?"

"Apparently, that thing Vince sent me when you were here yesterday is called a Cupid's Bow. And it's not what you think. It has *nothing* to do with love. Lee thinks there might be a message coded inside. He's going to hack it once we get the okay from McAllister."

Kaylee tossed her head back and chortled so loudly that, Dag, her big, lovable dog, barked along in tandem. Once Kaylee recovered, she squealed again, slapping her thigh. "He sent you something called a *Cupid's* Bow. That's completely adorbs. See? I was right! This is even better than gemstones. He's declaring his love after one date. I'm sure there's a supersecret message inside. Afterall, I watched that vid chat with you. Something was off." She held a single finger in the air that looked as big as a toddler because Kaylee's image took up half her wall. "One date. That's all it took."

"It wasn't a date. It was an impromptu dinner. There's a difference." A dinner where Mina had stupidly allowed the media to capture her image. Since then, she'd been forced to wear annoying disguises so civilians wouldn't recognize her. "And he's *not* declaring anything. There's nothing adorbs about it. He could be in trouble, we're just not sure yet. Lee said the bow"—she refused to say the Cupid part—"is *super* rare and *super* complex. It's going to take him time to hack." Since Lee was a Level XIII hacker, that was saying something. She waggled her finger at her friend. "I know that look. Don't you dare go there."

"Go where? To Love Town?" Kaylee hooted. "Can't stop me, the mag-lev has already left the station. I'm shooting fric-free straight to *Looove* Town." She started humming a beat from a popular song and snapping her fingers. "He shot an arrow through my *so-oul*. He doesn't know where this is going to *go-oh*. It might take an awful *to-oll*, but in the end he'll score a *go-oal*."

"Those aren't even the right words," Mina groused.

"They are now," Kaylee countered, still giggling. Dag wagged his tail, ears perked, ready to play.

Lee glanced between the two of them like they'd lost their minds. They probably had.

"The man is not in love with me. We've seen each other *one* time in seven years. We hardly know each other."

"He could've sent you a regular encrypted locator that's not associated with the cherub of love," Kaylee offered.

"Too easy to hack," Mina replied. "Obviously, it has to be secure, because if it was intercepted, then everyone would know his business."

"He could've sent you a coded quantum drive."

"Yes, but he didn't."

"He could've sent you an obelisk," Lee offered helpfully. "Those are sealed up *tight*. It would take me a week to hack one of those."

Mina shot him a look. "That's not helpful." Kaylee hooted some more while Lee resumed his confused face, which in his lunatic state made him look manic. "Never mind," she told him. To Kaylee, she said, "We have pressing matters to attend to, like getting Lee into the soaker before his goatee sheds all over my floor. Is there anything else you need before you go?"

Kaylee hiccup-laughed as Dag bounded to her, dropping his ball in her lap. "No. I'm good. I'm going to take this big lug out. I just wanted to check on you and make sure you're both up and functioning after your huge Planet's Most Wanted night. I can see you are. After that, I'm heading back to the grind, because, you know, someone has to deal with the bad guys in while you two are off relaxing."

Mina snorted. "The last time I relaxed was 2086. I was seven."

"Good luck with the *Cupid's* Bow. I bet once it cracks, the message points straight to Love Town." Kaylee held up her hand, cackling. "Fine. *Fine.* I'm going. Lee, take care of that issue with your face and hair." She swirled a palm in Lee's general direction. "Tag me back later. Kevin, end vid." She popped off the wall.

Not even two seconds later, Veronica announced, "Quinn Kane and guest are requesting entrance from the transpo hub on level twenty. What would you like to do?"

Nothing is completed without a great team.

My many thanks to:

Awesome Cover design: Damonza
Digital and print formatting: Author E.M.S
Copyedits/proofs: Joyce Lamb
Final proof: Marlene Roberts

Head to my website to sign-up for my Book Alert newsletter to receive new release info in your inbox so you don't miss a thing!

About the Author

Amanda Carlson is a graduate of the University of Minnesota, with a BA in both Speech and Hearing Science & Child Development. She went on to get an A.A.S in Sign Language Interpreting and worked as an interpreter until her first child was born. She's the author of the high-octane **Jessica McClain** urban fantasy series published by Orbit, the **Sin City Collectors** PNR series, the contemporary fantasy **Phoebe Meadows** series, the dystopian **Holly Danger** series, and the futuristic thriller **Mina Kane** series. Look for these books in stores everywhere. She lives in Minneapolis.

FIND HER ALL OVER SOCIAL MEDIA

Patreon: Patreon.com/authoramandacarlson
(Get my books early & for less than retail)

Website: amandacarlson.com

Facebook: facebook.com/authoramandacarlson

Twitter: @amandaccarlson

Instagram: @author_amanda